PERCEPTION AS REALITY

The Life and Times of Tedy Merrill

Paul Howard

Perception as Reality: The Life and Times of Tedy Merrill is entirely a work of fiction written by Paul Howard. The storyline, plot and characters were all created in the mind of the author and do not reflect any real human beings or any actual Russian Mafia members. Tedy Merrill, M.D., the protagonist of the novel, is not meant to represent a real plastic surgeon, at least I hope not.

Cover artwork and design by
Donna Peters
donnapeters.com

ISBN-10: 099642430X
ISBN-13: 9780996424301
Library of Congress Control Number: 2015945355
Dba Paul S Howard MD, Birmingham AL

Dedicated to the beautiful women in my life, Pamela and Alexandra.

INTRODUCTION

There are myths, fantasies and aphorisms with little basis in fact proposing that people who become plastic surgeons are similar in personality, that these similarities represent flaws and are the result of unfulfilled emotional needs. Thirty years of plastic surgical experience tells me that nothing could be further from the truth. Our flaws have little or nothing to do with emotional needs and everything to do with the hubris of an individual who thinks he or she has limitless power over the scalpel. This is the misinterpretation of great notions; the results of the creative mind are easily and often misinterpreted by the less creative as self-absorption and arrogance. The pashas of organized medicine are usually the latter misinterpreters. They sit in judgement of others, usually ill-equipped to do so and frequently do more harm than good while handing out reprimands for perceived wrongdoing. The life of Tedy Merrill, from his earliest experiences in the South, his evolution as a student and scholar, and finally his development as a doctor, a surgeon and a plastic surgeon of immense creative energy and skill, shows there are many pathways to fulfill one's destiny. Having an uncanny memory for details augments his personal scholarship in medicine and surgery but his diverse human experiences from an early age are what truly mold his reactions with other humans and literally drives his need to carve out of clay an altered appearance; a sculptor whose medium is flesh and blood. When a man such as Tedy Merrill looks into the cheval glass mirror he doesn't see a single image, he doesn't see what others see. He sees the reflection of the man he has become: images of both good and evil. Tedy sees it all in his reflection; others just see the subtle difference in his eyes.

PART 1
"EARLY ON"

CHAPTER ONE

"We checked coke bottle bottoms to see how far was far...we loved our dogs like brothers, our bikes like rocket ships."

FROM *BOY'S LIFE* BY ROBERT R. McCAMMON

There is nothing more important to a young boy than the quality of their bicycle. Mine was a red Schwinn with three gears. The bike had been my Christmas but the weather since had been too cold for a bike trip. Waiting for summer break started at the end of Spring Break when we started to count the days until school was out. From March until June seemed like an eternity. The days got longer but not long enough for me and my best friend Brian to take our usual bike trip after school. Major league baseball season was in full swing so we rode our bikes up to the shopping center pharmacy where we bought our baseball cards with a hard piece of bubble gum and three cards per ten cent pack. We would sit at the counter, get a cherry coke and open our cards wishing for a Mickey Mantle or a Willie Mays. We even chewed the hard dried out gum like it was important in getting good cards we could trade. We asked the pharmacist if we could have his used cigar boxes to house our growing collection. Most of us had four or five full cigar boxes of cards but we kept our best cards in one box and had other boxes for the extras and cards we were trying to trade. Cataloguing and organizing our cards was time consuming and trading cards with other boys at the shopping center was a big part of every afternoon. Baseball cards were so important that one day walking home from school I found a "Roberto Clemente" on the road, run over at least once, but still in good shape. I thought I was the luckiest boy in town. Years later when dad uprooted the family, mom probably discarded the boxes because they stank of old cigars not realizing the treasures the old boxes contained.

When summer finally came Brian and I planned our first of what we hoped would be many summer bike trips. It was about three miles to the very end of our road. From there it was a short ride down to the creek and railroad trestle that crossed it. Once there, we would park our bikes out of the sun down near the creek where we would hunt for crawfish and other critters that lived in the muddy waters all the while hoping a train would cross the trestle. Those long, hot, humid summer days were full of adventure. If no trains passed, we left pennies on the track planning to find them flattened on our next trip.

After several hours of exploring we would find some big creek rocks to sit on and eat our sack lunches. Next we would listen carefully to the tracks like we had seen the Indians on television do to detect the presence of a train long out of sight. After listening for a while we would decide if we were going to try to make the walk across the rather long trestle. We had calculated that if we were caught by a passing train on the trestle we could climb off the side of the track and hold on without being hit by the train or falling. At its tallest, the trestle was at least a hundred feet above the creek bed making each crossing not only an adventure but dangerous. We rode home in the late afternoon so that we were always home before our parental curfew at dark.

During the summer we rode our bikes everywhere without a care in the world until the day that Brian's younger brother Carl was hit by a car riding down our driveway into the street. Neither Brian nor

I saw the accident but we heard the impact and were the first to see Carl in the street, unconscious, with his clothes torn and bloody and his leg twisted the wrong way. The man that hit Carl was crying as he held his head in his hands saying over and over that he never saw him. Everyone just let Carl lie there in the middle of the street until the ambulance arrived. Minutes before the ambulance arrived, announcing its presence with sirens blaring and red lights flashing, Carl's mother jumped out of her car screaming for Carl to wake up yet afraid to touch him as he appeared so small, vulnerable and fragile lying there in the street- broken. I always thought it was somehow odd that she still had on her nurse's uniform and pristine white cap and white hosiery that nurses wore at that time. I knew Carl's father because he was the surgeon who had taken out my tonsils several years before; he must have been in surgery as he didn't see Carl in the street. Weeks later I overheard my parents talking under their breath about Carl's dad who was being accused of being with his nurse in the throes of a licentious relationship the day Carl was hurt and that was why no one could find him. They didn't have beepers back then.

My younger brother Johnny was playing with Carl that day and no one knows why he wasn't in the street with Carl. Carl remained in a coma for three weeks before he woke up in a body cast that stayed on for six months. Today Carl would have a titanium plate and a bunch of screws without the body cast. Carl was never "right" after the accident. He suffered some kind of brain damage and always walked with a limp. My brother remained Carl's best friend after the accident and eventually became his protector when one day some rowdy neighborhood boys decided to have some fun teasing Carl, accusing him of being a "retard." I was outside in our yard across the street when I heard a commotion in Carl's back yard. I ran over to see what the matter was. My younger brother, five years old at that time, was taking murderous swings with a baseball bat at the three older boys who were teasing Carl. I think he had every intention of decapitating those bigger boys who ran from Carl's yard never to be seen again. I didn't know how to tell my brother that I was always proud of him the way he stayed Carl's friend and protector until Carl's parents divorced and they moved away.

After Carl woke up in the hospital mom and dad took Johnny and me to see him. I don't remember much about my first hospital visit except that I knew you didn't come here unless something was terribly wrong (like having your tonsils taken out) and I couldn't get past the smell of antisepsis which at the time didn't smell particularly clean and actually made me want to throw up. Carl had his head shaved, covered with clean white bandages and from his chest down was encased in that full body cast that seemed to stay on forever. Carl was awake but did not acknowledge either me or Johnny. It was months later when Carl came home and was finally able to communicate with us. The beauty and magic of riding our bicycles was never the same after Carl was hurt. We still rode but always with the nagging thoughts of what was possible with cars on the road. Brian and I never again went on a riding trip; actually I don't remember Brian riding his bike ever again. Many years later when I was a general surgery resident the smell that almost made me sick the day we visited Carl in the hospital now smelled the same; but now as a doctor it had the fragrance of money.

The next summer my bike was traded in for a baseball glove and a Louisville Slugger bat. As young boys we were all pretty much equals on our bikes but as our growth plates expanded our bones grew as our genetic makeup was revealed; some of us grew inches each summer and some did not. As it turned out, I grew, could hit a baseball a mile and most of my friends couldn't. My father taught me how to win and I learned on my own that the girls liked the boys who played sports. It was a lesson that lasted a lifetime.

I started school when I was five years old. State law at that time required that one be six years old to enter public school but my father was adamant that I start early rather than go to kindergarten which he considered glorified babysitting. Even though my parents both worked and had trouble with money, they paid the extra tuition to start me in private school even though it would cause me to remain a year younger than my classmates. I remember my first two years in private school more than any of the other grades. My mother kept those report cards and I still have them today. Those early reports seemed to indicate I was a perfectionist tending to want to please my teachers and tended to color carefully between the lines. These traits evolved into a "fear of failure" or "failure to please" mentality that still accompanies me today.

As the years passed there always seemed to be some task, some sort of competition that occupied my attention. Anything that required effort where there was competition involved caused my fear of failure to serve me well. But even more important as motivation was the fact I didn't want to disappoint my mother and father. I can recall today very few instances where I failed to achieve a goal that I set out to accomplish. That was true except for girls. It wasn't until sports took over my life that I became more successful with girls. They tended to like me and I liked them throughout my athletic career. I learned if I applied myself to achieve goals and worked hard there was almost nothing I couldn't achieve through high school and even college.

"The truth of living, of getting older, is that with each year, each new person who enters our life, with each new romance, each career move, we find ourselves farther and farther removed from our true selves and the unadulterated magic of youth."

ROBERT R. McCAMMON

By the time I was in high school my father had been promoted into important state jobs that could be considered political. He became well known for his skills which made him someone other states coveted. As a result we moved from state capital to state capital throughout the South. In fact, we tended to move every several years and I attended three different high schools in three different states. It seemed I was never anywhere long enough to cultivate a peer group. Most children who moved around bemoaned their lack of friends and a peer group. In my case our family peregrinations probably made me a stronger individual as I made good friends at each move especially the last one where I graduated from high school. That doesn't mean that constant moving wasn't a challenge to the whole family. I think it probably made us closer as we had only each other to depend on for long periods surrounding each move. Our moving made my relationship with my father stronger than it otherwise might have been. Father became more than a parent, he was a coach and a fan that lived vicariously through my football exploits and eventually became my best friend and the best friend to some of my less fortunate classmates.

As much as I loved and respected my parents they both had a blind spot as far as my personal talents were concerned. As a junior in high school I started to get a trickle of offers from colleges to play football. As a senior the trickle became a flood and I went to college on a full scholarship with only mediocre grades. After I started college my parents thought I was out of my depth when it came to academics. As a result they had very little to say about my course work. As I became less interested in sports, my fear of failure wouldn't let me fail academically. I eventually sustained an injury causing my focus to change completely to academics; I changed my major to chemistry and made straight "A's" for the rest of college. It was my mother who advised me to try medical school which set the tone for the rest of my life. I wish I had asked them before they died, "What did you think I was going to do in college if I couldn't play ball anymore?" I suppose I'm glad it never dawned on me to ask probably not really wanting to know the answer.

CHAPTER TWO

"To see what is in front of one's nose requires a constant struggle."

GEORGE ORWELL

"What's the damn problem son?" We've had this discussion dozens of times and the answer always remains the same; you pretty much have to figure things out for yourself and things are not ever going to get easier. You know how I was raised, no father, no guidance, no money but a healthy dose of common sense. I've tried my best to give you the things that I never had but you have to use what you've got to take the next step, regardless of how difficult

it may seem. I trust your judgment so it is time for you to start trusting yourself."

My father has been dead for several years and I still have these conversations with him to this day. I sometimes wish he was still around even though I know exactly what he would tell me and how he would say it. The seminal event during our parent's lifetime was World War II. Those Americans born during the aftermath of the Great Wall Street Crash of 1919 grew up mired in the Great Depression during the twenties and thirties. All over the South there was an epidemic of fatherless homes as the stress of no jobs, no money and the embarrassment of not being able to provide for your family caused a generation of fathers to abdicate their duties, leave their families, crawl into a bottle and in some cases to ride the still functioning rail system creating a new class of the disenfranchised called hobos, who were migrant workers or tramps who didn't work at all. To the best of my knowledge my father's father, the grandfather who I never met and who my father never spoke of, ended up riding the rails through the rural countryside and was never heard from again. With no man in the house, even the children, as young as five or six years old, were required to bring in money; my father and his twin brother sold bananas on the street corner in rural Griffin, Georgia.

One of the most uplifting and accurate depictions of life during the Depression was found in a movie with the famous actor Russell Crowe who played the Heavyweight Champion J.J. Braddock. Braddock fought while his family was eating at the local New York soup kitchens and borrowing money to survive. He became the Heavyweight Champion of the World after beating the current champion, Max Bair, in what was called the upset of the Century. James J. Braddock would become a symbol to millions of disenfranchised men during the depression and would forever be known as "The Cinderella Man."

These generations of men were for the most part graduating from high school as the conflict in Europe was just beginning. After we were drawn into the war when the Japanese Empire bombed Pearl Harbor, millions of young men who would otherwise have few prospects for employment now joined the military. This gave millions of America's youth not only a job, but a job in which they could be proud as their calling was to save their country from the tyranny of the Germans, Japanese and Italians, known as the Axis powers, who had so cowardly attacked us. These generations of potentially dispossessed men and women, many starving, jobless, with no prospects for the future, were to become Tom Brokow's *The Greatest Generation.*

At the same age my father and his twin brother were fighting overseas, placing their lives in danger, I was the beneficiary of my parent's commitment that I never have it as hard as they did during and after the war. Before life became so difficult for me, years before, I was a typical college student with the usual hopes and dreams. Working for spending money, studying only when necessary, no business sense, talking politics as if our opinion really mattered and drinking a lot of beer thinking that this is what normal people do every day. I was dumb-as-a-post and did not even know it. The fact that any of my generation was able to make important decisions about the future was amazing. It's hard to contemplate the future when the sum total of one's knowledge of it comes from a book called *Future Shock* by Alvin Toffler. The only constant through the lectures, papers, reports, exams and labs was the constant undercurrent of activity directed toward female companionship.

My college roommate was a good Italian guy from a big city who also happened to be the President of the Student Council which came with all of the trappings of college life at the top. There were no Chemistry major groupies but plenty of political groupies, including scores of girls with long blonde hair, cut- off jeans, braless in tank tops with Birkenstock sandals. It was unthinkable that during the bacchanalia that was college life, important decisions had to be made that would affect life forever. In what could be considered a lucid interval, I opined that college was not a career; I took the Medical College Admission Test (MCAT) on the advice of a classmate who said it was a breeze, did well, got accepted and was suddenly off to medical school. I don't know if actually knowing a practicing doctor would have made a difference, it really didn't seem to matter at the time that I had no idea what I was doing. At least there were no Vietcong shooting at me due to a student deferment obtained because my University football coach thought I would be a better suited to help his team win games as a linebacker than as a soldier killing the enemy. I thoroughly agreed with his assessment.

Medical school was overall an interesting phenomenon, a bit more intense than college and similar to the challenges of playing Division I college football after excelling at football on the high school level. After a short acclimation period, all was well again, and we all settled into our own routines that usually included a lot of coffee and all night study sessions in the anatomy lab followed by breakfast in a restaurant. For months we had no idea why the other patrons in the restaurant tended to either leave or move as far away from us as possible. Our waitress finally told us we were stinking of the formaldehyde we had become nasally blind to in the gross anatomy lab. The main problem most of my colleagues had with medical school as it related to having been an undergraduate was the lack of self-directed or independent study offered as an undergraduate but not in medical school. In medical school everyone does exactly the same thing with the only differences being the order of the course work for four years. Maybe this is a reason that doctors are easy to stereotype intellectually; this type of education definitely does not encourage independent thinking.

There were several rites of passage during the four years of medical school. The first was the first day of gross anatomy when we were split into groups of four and formally introduced to our cadavers. Taking in the ambiance of the entire room bordered on the comical as there were one hundred and sixty bright, shiny new and wide-eyed medical students, just out of their college experiences, trying to seem nonchalant as we gazed upon our first dead human being. We were lectured extensively about the gift we were given by the individuals on the table and our collective behavior should reflect our respect for the person our cadaver had been. The reverence lasted about thirty minutes, the exact period of time it takes to recover from the intense smell of form-aldehyde and the overwhelming realization that we were really in medical school. To relieve the tension we proceeded to name our cadaver "Lucy" and divided up the "readers" who directed the activities of the remainder of the group who were henceforth known as the "cutters" who were considered as future surgeons. It turned out that the most aggressive "cutters" were the first to declare in the third year that they wanted to be internists. Nicknames were assigned during the first clinical rotations in the third year to delineate (read: denigrate) the future surgeons (cutters) from those leaning toward general medicine (fleas) because they flitted around and were annoying. The first insult we were taught by the surgery residents was: "Why are internal medicine rounds and ascites (a collection of fluid in the abdominal cavity) alike? They are both a shifting dullness."

A recurring theme seemed to be emerging according to my mother, it had been four more years, so it must be time to graduate from something and move on yet again. (Four years of high school, four years of college, four years of medical school and looking forward to five years of general surgery). She probably never even considered that I was capable of delaying the start of my medical career for another seven or eight years to become a Plastic Surgeon. Life changing decisions were made that would determine the type of medicine we would practice for the remainder of our lives. These decisions were made without a scintilla of information on which to base a career altering plan.

The future of medicine and the American economy in general became rather easy to predict once we elected a progressive President and once socialized medicine was passed without a single Republican vote leading to a complete disintegration of the private practice of medicine. Millions of people choose to remain uninsured, after a temporary reprieve the cost of insurance continued to spiral out of control, and the best healthcare system in the world was destroyed for what we know now was no good reason. If I had foreseen this event, I never would have taken the MCAT and probably would be an engineer with a future. No one was clairvoyant enough to envision medicine as a trade rather than an art steeped in science. It was entirely luck that led me to plastic surgery which became the last bastion of the private practice of medicine. As it turned out a majority of the practice of plastic surgery fell outside of insurance coverage and the government control of medicine. In other words, plastic surgeons were the last doctors with the ability to charge a reasonable fee and actually be paid that fee- usually in cash.

Indeed, I was able to maintain a private practice (a small business) for several years after The Affordable Care Act went into effect. As with all government entitlements, the cost was miserably underestimated, it was run poorly by bureaucrats and there were not nearly enough doctors willing to work for next to no pay. At one time "the best and brightest "of our college students were applying to medical school but this is no more as the number of top applicants to medical school decreases every year. As the population aged and the cost of medical care continued to spiral out of control the benefits promised were too expensive to pay for. The politicians elected by promising what people thought would be free medical care, lost the will to ration the available care but retained the willingness to search for new and ever more creative ways to increase revenue in the only possible way the government has at its disposal- raise taxes and create new taxes which are now euphemistically called mandates. The outcome was historically predictable; there were not enough businesses or individuals working to tax the amounts promised in entitlements. Trying to keep their jobs, politicians borrowed massive amounts of money and printed trillions of dollars of worthless money exploding the national debt, devaluing the dollar and causing the first real depression in a hundred years. All of the expendable income was sucked out of the economy, the middle class ceased to exist and there was no money to buy plastic surgery. The last profitable part of medicine disappeared almost overnight.

Making money was demonized and success became a cause for guilt rather than celebration.

The sum total of the intelligent decisions I made over the years became a dead end business model and ultimately bankruptcy. There had to be a way out of this mess. We needed another "Greatest Generation" to emerge, or at least a growing economy.

━━◁┼▷━━

I was born Edward (Tedy) Mark Merrill, a son of the South, polite, hardworking, athletic, well spoken with a hint of a Southern accent noticeable only to my friends who don't live in the South. Where I come from, my people were all small town poor Southern folk, not farmers but only one small step from the hardscrabble okies John Steinbeck describes in **The Grapes of Wrath.** I have always considered myself a typical Southern male in my upbringing. In my stories I tend to think that I am talking for all Southern guys, nothing special, the mainstream, but I don't speak for the fringes of the South, North, East or West. The fringes are populated with what we called "outliers" in high school; those are the ones who never really engage in the normal juvenile activities of the teenager. Their taste in music is usually off-putting; I truly do not know what happens to these souls but I do think they probably grow up hating people like me. The country music star Toby Keith had a hit song titled "What Do You Think of Me Now?" that seems to address the fate of an outcast teenager who becomes a country music star and dreams in the song of singing to the high school girl who rejected him in her room through the radio. The video that was released with the song was interesting in that the singer finally meets her years after high school on the football field and she realizes who he is and she *still* doesn't like him-not the ending I would have written. It only makes sense if you know that Toby Keith was a star football player as well as a great singer-songwriter. It seems he was getting back at the high school girls who didn't like him "then" as he sings "How do you like me now, now that I'm on my way, singing in your radio…" In a song he seems to relate to the teenage angst we all felt with girls and that never really leaves us; it becomes part of the fabric of adult angst when we finally realize some of the missed opportunities of youth. I've actually wanted to sing that song to a few girls I knew in high school but instead we all aged together and I came to represent their attempts to recapture our high school days by rejuvenating their faces as a plastic surgeon.

There has been much made of fatherless families in the last twenty or so years. I had a great father who was my best friend until the day he died but I knew a bunch of kids who were raised by their mothers. In a lot of circumstances the family was better off without the father who was generally an uneducated, downtrodden, heavy drinking waste of humanity yet uniformly proud to a fault of his Southern heritage. A proud drinking man was the worst and the most likely to beat the children and wife or even do worse. That singular entity known as "Southern Pride" is probably the cause of more broken families than any other reason including the drug scourge of today. The combination of pride, drinking and no jobs has run ramped through the South since the demise of America's manufacturing jobs in the sixties. The only factor that made a positive difference in the results of the loss of the middle class was the Southern woman. When I speak of Southern women I'm talking about mothers and grandmothers. I was never quite sure the role of father until I was about twelve years old and sports became a big part of life. Up until that point in time mother ran the show with backup from grandmother. Everybody's mother worked outside the home so everyone either had a grandparent available or spent the afternoons after school unsupervised as not many people could afford domestic help. Regardless, there was not a soul out after dark as the evenings were dinner, homework and answering for any of the afternoons indiscretions.

As far back as I can remember there was grandmother who came to live with us after her no good husband (my other grandfather who I never met) treated her poorly. The details were kept from me but it did draw my father's ire so he went to grandmother's house and punched old Frank, her husband, right in the kisser. Father proceeded to help Georgia (grandmother) pack and take her home with him. I think this happened when I was an infant because I have no recollection of life without her. Of course no good deed goes unpunished and old Frank had father arrested the very next day for assault and battery. Not wanting a lawyer, father stayed in jail until his hearing in front of the judge. The judge allowed him to represent himself with Frank and his broken nose sitting in the gallery. Father simply told the story (he was a good orator) of Frank and his despicable sister using grandmother as their personal maid service. This became intolerable to Father when Georgia had a hysterectomy but Frank continued to insist that Georgia keep working after the operation. In the end father had the judge shedding tears leading to a not guilty verdict. Georgia Echols Lee lived with us until the day she died at eighty-three years of age.

We lived in what was considered a big city at that time, but there was no hanging out after dark until one had a driver's license and a car. There always seemed to be destinations rather than aimless driving like you see today unless you had a muscle car, then you were considered rich. The local hamburger joints were popular drive-throughs as well as Drive-in theaters but only on the weekends. Hanging out on foot without purpose was frowned on and considered "low class." I don't recall a police presence but it really wasn't necessary as we all had a curfew and a mother willing to grab the car keys and not return them quickly. In the South, fear of father was expected but fear of disappointing mother was visceral and kept most of us out of jail until the day we walked out of the house to begin our own lives. Thanks to a lot of luck, family and tolerance, the vast majority of us began life with a clean slate and very little baggage and usually no criminal record to speak of.

Everyone in the South loves to play ball. Long before desegregation in the South we may not have gone to school with the black kids but we played them in football. There was and still is nothing like Friday night in the South; high school football under the lights with cheerleaders cheering for our guys to beat their guys. Back then every county had a high school and a football team that was their pride and joy. Most cities were not big enough for a team of their own so every team we played was a "county high" drawing from a larger population with some of the most rural counties fielding the best teams year in and year out. Since there wasn't much else to do, cheering and playing for your school's football team was the highlight of the school year.

In the late sixties there was racial turmoil across the South after the integration of the public high schools several years before. The story of the integration of my "county high," while not typical in some ways, still stands as an example of how it happened in one high school in the deep South in the late sixties; a story to my knowledge that has never been fully reported. Many people across the country view our ways as "simple or backwards" and cannot understand why Southerners are so ridiculously fanatical about our football teams. Many "sons of the South" have stories similar to mine that mean much more to us than the simplicity of sport. In many cases athletics was our first step into manhood and the first time we had our own experiences different from that of our parents which required us to develop our own personal responses to the situations we faced. In most cases these were the first things we believed or did without thought of parental approval. I believe my parents became more tolerant people as they watched my responses to high school during what were racially charged times. The core development of my theories on race relations happened solely on the gridiron. The beauty of learning about your contemporaries on the football field was that football life paralleled real life and the playing field was supposed to be level for all participants; a much different scenario than the real world. Yet if forty-four guys can learn to treat each other equally then others seeing that success could also try the same thing and in our school I believe that experience of the 1969 football team made our "county high" one of the more progressive in the South for years into the future and even today.

We were no different than the other schools in our conference which had all been recently integrated. We had issues of race that made us a stronger team rather than a weaker one, a more unified team rather than a team of individual players and a coaching staff that held us together by challenging us as players and more importantly as young men. As a prelude to 1967 there was racial turmoil, rioting and violence of the streets of America. It would have been easy to parrot our parent's position on the issues as presented on the nightly news for both black and white kids. The difference was that we were owned by the coaches four hours a day where shear survival was much more important than the news. Our race relations were practiced during tackling drills, Oklahoma drills and in first vs. second team live contact scrimmages. Disagreements were handled mano vs. mano, black vs. white when necessary. Exhaustion usually leads to détente and détente leads to mutual respect. But as the coaches found out the process takes some time as there are still hard- headed players of both races trying to game the system. We had no need for the police; we had to govern our behavior by following the coach's leads. As a rule it always came down to the baddest of the bad, black vs. white for playing time and more importantly mutual respect.

Indulge me a few words of social reportage from the years 1967-1969, a seminal time for black and white relationships in small southern towns. The assassinations of Bobby Kennedy and Martin Luther King galvanized the black community which began to see the beginnings of support of college students whose anger over the Vietnam War made for strange bedfellows as they coalesced with the radical black groups to become one large youth movement that changed the country. Luckily the movement stayed away from high school campuses in their recruiting activity, generally waiting until we entered college for the full court press usually carried out in local pubs and announced meetings which were allowed to occur on campus and generally sponsored by a contingent of liberal-leaning faculty advisors in collusion with the older, more radical students. The high school student was left to his own devices on how to respond to the racial issues of the day with many taking the path laid out by their older brothers and sisters not making up their own minds.

After our almost great season in 1967, everyone was expecting a championship the next year. The '68 season we were preseason number one in the state. Summer practice was going well until the issues of that time intruded on the gridiron. Black receivers thought our All- American white quarterback was throwing more to the white guys than the black players. The statistics that are kept on such things proved it to be untrue; I always thought that outside racial influences played a big part in the black players walking out on their teammates. They missed the entire summer campaign and when the black players eventually came to their senses the team was set and coach would not let them return that year. They sat out what was supposed to be our championship year where we went a respectable 7-3.

We were all called back for the summer camp of '69. There were no hard feelings in the group and we pushed on trying to become the team we knew we could be. We practiced two, sometimes three times per day in the wicked heat of July and August in the South. Survival was much more important than any petty racial issues held over from the previous year.

The coaches worked us so hard there was little time to be concerned about the news or who was getting the most catches. It was clear from the first day that the best players would play, no matter what. The result was that we were a complete football team, completely integrated with no weaknesses and with a singular desire to win all of our games. We started the season of '69 unranked in the state; evidently the sports reporters didn't think much of our chances due to our previous racial turmoil. As a team we had a lot to prove after the debacle of the previous year.

Our first game was against the number five team in the state. We were playing at home and were at least a touchdown underdog. The visiting team had an All-State running back that was to go on after high school to a great career at an SEC school. But the Friday night we played them he broke his leg during a vicious tackle and we went on to a three touchdown shellacking of that team. That year we won and we won big, every game, and entered the playoffs 10-0. There wasn't a single player that played for individual accolades; we played as a team- a very integrated team. The first playoff game we were down for the first time at halftime 12-7. On the last play of the half a white player from the other team committed an intentional foul on one of our black defensive linemen. During the half time we were, as a team, mad as hell at the other player and mad as a team that we were letting our season slip away. We won the second half 28-0 and the game 34-12 as the black guy on our defense dominated the remainder of the game with the help of a few of his white friends on the defensive line. The championship game was several weeks later. In the interim we played a powerful team from the central Florida coast in the first high school playoff game ever played in the Florida panhandle, a once in a lifetime opportunity. Our coach and their coach had some sort of disagreement having to do with our lack of common opponents and other team's unwillingness to share their game films with us. Our week of practice was particularly intense as our coach seemed to want to prove the point that we didn't need films to beat this team. The slight reached the local paper making the run up to the game very intense.

At the start of the game, since we knew nothing of the team, we came out with a huge chip on our collective shoulders stimulated by one angry coaching staff. We were ahead 35-0 at the half. By the middle of the fourth quarter we were up 59-6. We pulled the offensive and defensive starters by the final quarter but at the 2:00 point of the game we got the ball back for one more drive. The second string offense had played the entire fourth quarter to this point. We were all surprised when coach called for the first team offense. Over the final two minutes we drove eighty yards and scored one final touchdown completing the worst defeat for a team in Florida high school playoff history, 66-6. The next week was the championship game, again, the first championship game to be played in the panhandle in Florida history. We were down at half time, this time by seven points 14-7. I remember thinking at half time, "Who will it be that steps up to help us win this thing?" It was very tense but to a man no one thought we could be beat; partially because of the team we had become and partially because of what we had been through the previous season. There was very little rah-rah stuff but the coaches realized we needed to change up our schemes a little bit to cover for the weakness we had with a few of the slower white guys who had been beaten deep on a play in the first quarter. As a team we knew they were certain to go back to that play when they needed it. We had more blacks on our team than any of the schools we were playing and the stereotype was true for us; we were faster as a team because of it.

The second half was a dynamic struggle but a struggle that we won with a blocked punt and a goal line stand leading to a 24-14 win. There were no identifiable heroes; every player in our band of 44 brothers played a part in the win. Our season of 1969 was one for the ages and a testimony to the possibilities that exist due to integration of our county high school. We were a perfect 13-0 for the first time in school history(a school in existence since 1910), and yes, we elected a black cheerleader that year who went to the senior prom with starting linebacker, Doug Sileo, an Italian-American from Naples, Italy via Miami, FL who became one of my best friends and worked for father for years.

One of the beautiful things about the South, different from other geographic areas of the country, is that in the face of all of the terrible things that have happened in the South, we are a people who live in a way that offers the possibility for redemption. My father was also brought up in the South, a much different South than I know, but a version of the South just the same. The seminal period of his life was the nineteen thirties which was a horrific time in America regardless of the part of the country you lived in. Father had two brothers and a younger sister- he was a fraternal twin. Evidently there were very few men in our family at that time except as sperm donors. I can recall a few distant uncles but the nucleus of the family was the women, and strong women they were. Times were bad for both blacks and whites such that it required much too much energy to hate anyone for any reason unless they got in the way of your next meal. Poverty and despair were the new normal, there was no middle class just the "haves" and the "have nots." The financial benefits of WWI were soon evaporated and America fell back into lethargy, isolationism and a chronic unemployment rate in excess of twenty per cent. Franklin Delano Roosevelt followed Herbert Hoover as the 32nd President of the United States of America and is credited with helping America out if the first Great Depression through governmental policies called "The New Deal." Since governmental policies generally do not create wealth nor jobs, the depression continued until the dawn of WWII when military spending and young men joining the military effectively dropped the unemployment rate to zero turning the economy around almost overnight. The final impetus for economic recovery was the bombing of Pearl Harbor on Dec 7th, 1941.

The chance to fight for one's country was a Southern boy's dream, especially in light of a failing economy and little or no prospects for a job. Father did what many young boys did and lied about his age and joined the military prior to graduating from high school at age seventeen. Coming from a family so poor that he couldn't even afford dental care to replace two front teeth knocked out when he was ten years old, the Navy sounded like a dream job to a generation of poor Southern boys. Father couldn't understand why a lot of the guys would cry themselves to sleep at night missing home. By the time he was eighteen he had his teeth fixed, gained thirty pounds eating three square meals a day, was learning a trade, got to see most of the Pacific Ocean and became proficient with a handgun and a rifle. The war was a godsend for thousands of Southern boys who were basically starving to death. The patriotism fueled by the Japanese and the Germans was a much more fulfilling hatred than any racial tendencies that Southern boys may have had. In fact, father thought that being in close proximity to so many other guys of diverse backgrounds in dangerous situations made it less likely that soldiers would later be racists.

My father and most Southern men of his era were brought up by their mothers and grandmothers-Southern women. That is why most Southern men, including myself, will always be somewhat intimidated and therefore submissive in important relationships with Southern women. I have taken this attribute to the next level by always being attracted to the smartest and strongest among our Southern women; enter Jessica who is all of that and more.

Plastic surgery became my thing and I fell into the trap laid by a smart, pretty, small town Southern woman. As Southern women tend to do, Jessica became fully involved in my plastic surgery practice and became invaluable in our transition out of everyday plastic surgery into the post- Affordable Care Act medical environment in the U.S. She alone created our internet business and has always acted like a mother hen for me, our employees and our businesses. Among her many attributes is what she calls her "female antennae," known to others as women's intuition. Sometimes she is wrong about people but she is right just enough and has spotted unforeseen danger when it presents itself just often enough to save us on occasion from danger that I was blind to. Her antennae, at times, make her appear hypervigilent or paranoid. She makes me look aloof or out-of-touch but the combination of the two averages out to an extremely productive partnership; Southern boy who likes a good fight and momma bear with the instincts to protect what is hers.

Jessica never thought of being married, not really. Life seemed complete and on course, she intended to be self-sufficient. She was and still is both a dreamer and a doer simultaneously. This seems confusing to most people but was perfectly normal in Jessica's world. Reflection was her way to work through an impetuous nature yet even through reflection she found it hard to be self- critical. Jess could be hard-headed and always believed in the ultimate "correctness" of her actions and decisions. These attributes among others made it hard to develop relationships with men as she had little time or patience for people trying to understand her or trying to determine ulterior motives because she had none. "I am what I am, no explanation necessary" was her mantra.

All of that changed when Jess met Edward Mark Merrill, MD, Plastic Surgeon. He was the first man in her life who thought that a woman could be beautiful both inside and out. He said he always had a way with women that he learned by being raised by strong Southern women. They had the same goals and aspirations and a similar lust for life without the need for children. More importantly, he was every bit as smart as Jessica making them intellectually compatible; his thing being plastic surgery, hers being computers and the internet. It's amazing how far a large dose of mutual respect can go in a relationship. Jessica's life experiences have left her with a wide streak of skepticism whereas Tedy believed in the goodness in everyone- until proven otherwise. This made for a good balance in everyday business dealings. During difficult economic times it was important for both of them to contribute to the bottom line. The goal was to use the individual skills developed over the years without either one having to morph into something they were not. The collapse of the U.S. system of health care after the full implementation of socialized medicine turned into an opportunity to do something positive which ultimately became very lucrative. It's hard to change horses in mid-career but they were psychologically and intellectually able to do it.

PART 2
"THE PARIS YEARS"

CHAPTER THREE

*"America is the most grandiose experiment
the world has ever seen, but, I am afraid it
is not going to be a success."*

SIGMUND FREUD

We took the Air France red-eye, business class, from Atlanta to Paris-Orly arriving at 9:30 a.m. local time. I have always had a problem sleeping on an airplane and this flight was no different. It's always a mistake to use alcohol as a transatlantic sedative, but it's hard not to try.

This flight had an entirely different mindset as Jessica and I were traveling one way on an open ended ticket. There's an element of the unknown when you're actually staying and not returning a week later as I had done at least a dozen times since living in Paris as a Plastic Surgical Trainee twenty years ago.

Jessica, my wife and partner, and I booked a room at the *Hotel Meurice* right on the *rue de Rivoli* across from the Tuilleries Garden in the epicenter of the tourist area of Paris. We availed ourselves of the Mercedes S600 and driver so graciously provided by the hotel as we had become regular customers. After checking in, checking out the room and changing a few worthless dollars into Euros, we set out to find one of my favorite Paris haunts, *Angelina's*. It was early afternoon, the early spring tourist crowd had thinned out so that we could get a table in the main room with its murals, mirrored walls and green marble- topped tables. We were not disappointed with the notoriously snobbish, inattentive waiter. The prices are high but worth it for the main reason we chose *Angelina's*- the *Africana,* which is pure African chocolate, melted and served in demi-tasse cups. There is no better treatment for the combination jet lag, fatigue and champagne hangover than a sub-lethal dose of caffeine in the form of chocolate. I offer a strong admonition based on previous experience. Do not leave the café until you are absolutely sure that the colonic spasm that occurs with large quantities of caffeine has passed. If you miscalculate as I once did, you will find that there are few if any

toilettes available on the street and those public toilettes that do exist require exact change or are otherwise occupied.

After a few weeks of dealing with American and
Japanese tourists we abandoned the luxury of the
Meurice for a rental apartment on the left bank near
the Latin Quarter. Addresses in Paris are usually designated by the closest metro station; we chose a one
bedroom flat at *Cardinal-Lemoine* near the Pantheon.
We spent the next couple of months living like college students, visiting every important church including *St Chappelle, Sacre-Coeur, St Sulpice and Notre
Dame* on Easter Sunday. We spent what seemed like a
week in the Louvre, the d'Orsey, the Picasso and the
Rodin Museums.

As our French language skills improved we began the process of locating a suitable home in the
city. We finally settled on a two story home in a one
hundred and fifty year old building in a relatively
quiet area of the city in the 8th *arrondissement* on the
rue de Courcelles. The space had been owned by the
same older couple since after the war and had fallen
into a state of disrepair. Finding a reputable builder
was harder than finding the property. Craftsmen in
Paris are relatively hard to deal with and charge a
lot, take a lot of breaks, smoke a lot of cigarettes and
work a challenging thirty hour work week with no
concept of deadlines. We were more than willing to

accept certain foibles in exchange for quality work and discretion. Remy, our builder had done some work through the American embassy and came highly recommended. The upgrades to the three bedrooms and a complete restoration of the kitchen and bathrooms to American standards was fairly straight forward as the French appliances were all available locally. The fourth bedroom or office was a different story. This final bedroom/office was smaller than the others and was an odd shaped space as if it was left over after the remainder of the apartment had been designed. It could have been a large walk-in closet or a hidden office space. It was easy to design a hidden door entering from the master bedroom. It seemed almost a cliché yet we used a floor to ceiling bookcase as the entrance point. The floor joists had to be reinforced to accommodate the extra weight of the walk-in safe and the entire room wrapped in insulation for both temperature control and sound proofing. The room had its own environment control separate from the rest of the apartment with a backup generator in case of power outages. The computer mainframe was also backed up separately and ventilated to the outside to help dissipate heat. Since the apartment was on the top floor there was almost direct access to the roof where our high- tech satellite dishes looked no different from the dozens of standard satellite dishes providing television reception to the remainder of the building. The ventilation was complicated due to the heat generated by the computer mainframe and processors. We finally decided on a high output fan and ventilation system similar to the ones used in surgical operating suites. In fact, we consulted with the main engineer for the operating suites at *Hopital Necker* where many operations are performed on infants where temperature control is paramount. As a final touch a state-of-the-art security system was installed with high definition cameras for the entire apartment accessed via the internet and our smart phones and ipads and fingerprint biometrics at the entrance from the garage. The garage was located on the street level with access directly to the street and the main residence via a small but functioning forty year old elevator with manual sliding door and a lever for going up and down. The elevator was loud and tended to break down but it was still one of my favorite things in the house. The garage was sumptuous by Paris standards with room for two cars as well as a work area and a generous storage area. Knowing Paris drivers and the lack of parking as I do, a slightly used 2012 convertible Smartcar, two matching Vespa motor scooters and two sturdy mountain bikes were chosen as city transportation. For traveling outside the city and for road trips, Jessica and I went to Stuttgart, Germany and picked up a European model Porsche

911 turbo cabriolet, black on burgundy, which we rarely uncovered or drove in the city. The scooters and bikes were outfitted with riding baskets for the obligatory frou-frou dog outfitted with doggy GPS units in case they went missing. Each bike and the scooters had a basket for the daily purchase of groceries and the ever present baguette. Within a short distance is *Fauchon* where there is an exquisite delicatessen where prepared dishes are available as well as an extensive selection of fine French wines and cognacs. Just around the corner from *Fauchon* is *La Ferme Saint-Hubert* a small compact store with probably the best cheese selections in Paris. For special occasions there is *La Maison de le Truffe* where one can sample French black truffles, foie gras and a variety of *charcuterie.*

Our decision to divest ourselves of dollars was easy as the financial events unfolded in the States. The Federal Reserve was short sighted in their attempt to save the faltering economy by printing money at a phenomenal rate and keeping interest rates artificially low. The dollar was rapidly becoming worthless as the world was now less likely to invest in American bonds and consideration was being given to changing the primary oil currency to something other than the dollar. The U.S. debt was downgraded for the third time in three years; OPEC continued to adjust the price of their oil to reflect the devalued dollar finally reaching $200 per barrel. Economic growth, the only possible way to decrease the crushing debt created by deficit spending, remained less than 1% with no signs of growth policies by the government. Our congress was increasingly elected by the majority of the country on entitlement programs and could not muster the backbone to slow entitlement spending for fear of losing their jobs. The economic trends seemed clear; divest the dollars and acquire gold and other precious metals, invest in real estate and work the futures market for commodities.

Simultaneous to my realization that my career in plastic surgery was rushing toward a disastrous end, there suddenly appeared a number of possible pathways. There were still billions of dollars in The Affordable Care Act that could only be accessed by those NOT practicing medicine. The government seemed to be slowly coming to the ultimate conclusion that the lack of physician reimbursement was going to wreck the system and needed to be addressed. I knew from my training days in Europe that when faced with similar circumstances upon the implementation of their version of nationalized health insurance, the Germans and to some extent the French encouraged their physicians to enter the new "beauty" business by offering liposuction, fillers and Botox for cash. In America the idea was already in practice informally as doctors of all kind, surgeon and non-surgeon, were already dabbling in cosmetic surgery without proper training. The full implementation The Affordable Healthcare Act further reduced incomes leaving regular doctors with no options except to dabble in procedures they had no idea how to perform. A paradigm shift in government thinking occurred when they finally realized the massive nature of the problem and patients were being hurt by untrained "beauty" physicians. It was time to acknowledge the problems within The Affordable Healthcare Act and the doctor's dilemma that they cannot work for free and shouldn't be asked to do so. There simply is not enough funding in The Affordable Healthcare Act to pay the doctors a reasonable fee for service. The first and hardest step was to acknowledge that The Affordable Healthcare Act was a flawed system. The second step was to find a way to augment doctor's incomes so that they can continue to see government patients and feed their families. Jess and I offered the government a contract to provide an internet based training program for physicians who needed to augment their incomes in the cosmetic surgery industry. The basis of the contract was to provide training in the intricacies of the beauty business so that these doctors could practice safely and yet help those willing to forge on in medicine a way to survive. A generic business plan was offered to help with allocation of funds and marketing in the beauty business arena. From our point of view the project was a no-brainer and could be managed from any computer with an internet connection anywhere in the world. The Dept. of Health and Human Services saw the necessity for our training to be delivered on line and the necessity for patient result reviews through cases submitted on line and a system to identify those physicians whose practices may not be up to what are now federal standards for the practice of cosmetic services; a standard that we had a hand in creating. Free training online was offered those doctors not up to snuff. The entirety of our business plan created a lucrative on- line business based in our home in Paris.

There is no doubt that having spent time in Paris as a young man has now led full circle back to the "City of Light." The spring and summer were particularly pleasant drawing one outdoors to walk the city and enjoy a *café-au-lait* at any of a thousand street cafes. The flower market at *place du Ternes* and my favorite walk through the largely unknown *Parc Monseau* provide daily exercise and a chance to think. Occasionally Jess and I would take the Metro to *Hopital Necker* or *Clinique Belvedere* at the lower edge of the *Bois de Boulogne* where my plastic surgery training got its French nuances under the guidance of great French surgeons, all now deceased. It was during one of my therapeutic walks in Monceau that I met Alex. For companionship I was walking Rosie, our female, vocal, hyperactive white Pomeranian. Alex was equally out of place walking a feisty male Maltese called Scout. We probably noticed each other because of the manliness of our canine companions who were more suited to an elderly French couple than two masculine middle-aged men.

"*Bonjour monsieur*", I offered.

"*Bonjour, comment ca va?*" Alex replied.

"*Ca va bien*", I replied in my barely passable French.

"Maybe we should speak English, what do you think?" Alex asked.

"Thank god, I didn't know how long my French would last. My name's Tedy.

"Alex", as he offered his hand. "How long you been in Paris?"

"Several weeks on this trip but we intend on staying awhile this time. How about you Alex?"

"My wife and I have been here for a while. I work through the American Embassy for the Foreign Service. How about yourself?"

"I'm a recently retired plastic surgeon and now an expatriate choosing to live abroad. My practice was a victim of the American recession." Alex seemed surprised to find out that even plastic surgery had become a dead- end profession.

"Don't those people in Hollywood still get nipped and tucked?" Alex asked.

"Absolutely", I said. "The very rich are about the only ones who can still afford plastic surgery. Even they are buying fewer facelifts and fewer Ferraris." As we departed he and I agreed to continue our conversation the next morning, meeting at the entrance of *Parc Monceau* at nine.

Our meetings at Monceau continued for the next several weeks. Each morning we convened at the parc entrance on *Boulevard Courcelles* with our canine companions and briskly walked the picturesque grounds enjoying the old columns, pyramids and Monsieur Ledoux's ancient rotunda. The parc was planted in 1783 and was in full bloom at this time of the year. After our walks we frequently found a nearby café and enjoyed a fresh croissant and a *café-au-lait*. Our discussions became livelier over time revealing more about each other. Alex was the son of a former career diplomat, brought up in his father's embassy postings around the world. Alex's last posting was in Luxembourg, Luxembourg City to be precise, which seemed like a fairly vanilla embassy posting. It was only after several weeks of cajoling that Alex revealed the nature of American interests in this land-locked, mid-European country. Unknown to me, Luxembourg was one of the most popular tax havens in the world due to its secret and well-guarded system of favorable banking regulations and agreeable tax policies. Luxembourg City was a cross between the Cayman Islands, Cypress and Switzerland. Few people know that many multinational companies including Apple Computers parked billions of dollars in this tiny country and had been doing so for years to circumvent the onerous corporate tax rates in the U.S. Alex followed his father into diplomatic service after the requisite Ivy League education at Princeton.

Alex Sosinski was a little over six feet tall, thin at the hips, small wrists, hands with long thin fingers and manicured nails; the type of physique that looked good in a tuxedo and terrible in a swim suit on the beach. Alex is a reasonably masculine guy, strong with a thin but naturally hard physique and no body fat to speak of; he obviously didn't spend his free time in the narcissistic environment of a weight room. He had a bit of the dark brooding look of his ancestors, a full head of hair offset by a touch of gray at the temples and almost colorless eyes. Out of place were his long, thin, manicured hands: soft, almost feminine, like the hands of a surgeon without the necessary strength.

The history of Alex's father was always a little vague to his family. He died of a massive heart attack shortly after retiring early to the Gulf coast. He was not the kind of father to spend a great deal of time at home doing even the simplest things with his family. Anthony Sosinski was a diplomat in the U.S. Foreign Service which means he was a high class bureaucrat with portfolio. All Alex could remember about his childhood were the embassy schools in so many countries he lost track. The education was actually pretty good and it afforded him the opportunity to learn several languages such as Russian, Spanish, French and Farsi to go along with his native English. His only friends during his family's assignments overseas were the embassy military personnel assigned to protect the ambassador and the rest of the family. Other kids had baseball and soccer practice after school but there were not enough children in the embassy to actually have teams and the children that were there were mostly nerds anyway. The younger military guys were just a few years older than Alex and were more than willing to show the Ambassador's son, who was skinny prior to a teenage growth spurt, a few tricks for personal protection that could come in handy as some of their postings were in the most dangerous parts of the world. Alex's best friends throughout the high school years were a bunch of hyper-vigilant Marines with seriously dangerous aggression issues. There were no football games on Friday night or cheerleaders for entertainment so Friday nights were spent at the nearest military firing range learning to field strip an AK-47 or learning to handle both the M16A2 and its shorter cousin the M4 carbine. Most teenagers shoot hoops, Alex shot life-sized targets dressed as Islamic terrorists. After high school he had an appointment to the Naval Academy but decided on Princeton University and a future career in government service, following in the footsteps of his father.

Alex's mom never remarried after his Dad died. He knew very little about her past until after his Father's funeral. She seemed to open up more and wanted her family to know more about her side of the family. She was also brought up in a diplomatic family. Her father, Alex's grandfather, made his money in Cuba during the late forties and fifties. He was well trained as an engineer in the U.S. before returning to Havana and starting a company that received a contract from the government of Cuba to build railroads throughout the island. The industrial revolution had finally reached Cuba. Men of vision realized that railroads would be necessary to open the entire island to tourism especially the island's interior and to move Cuba's agriculture to the markets to be shipped abroad, mostly to America. The primary exports were sugar cane, tobacco, cigars, citrus fruits and Cuban rum. Most of these products were moved to market on grandfather's trains and sold to American businessmen making her family one of the wealthiest in Cuba. Once Alex read ***Atlas***

Shrugged by Ayn Rand he fanaticized that grandfather was Nat Taggert and his railroad was like
Taggert Transcontinental in the book. Mother spent
her youth as the privileged daughter of an industri-
alist who became a wealthy Cuban aristocrat. She
loved telling fascinating stories of island life including a story of being courted by a famous American
writer who gifted her with a signed copy of one of
his novels-***For Whom the Bell Tolls***. Evidently he pro-
fessed his devotion to Alex's mother in the inscription he wrote and signed for her; the author's name
was Ernest Hemingway. Hemingway had just won
the Nobel Prize in Literature for his most recent novel ***The Old Man and The Sea***. Hemingway wrote the
novel while living in Cuba on the coast near Havana.
It was published in nineteen fifty-two and was to be
the last major work of fiction written in his lifetime.
Alex actually never saw the book Hemingway had
inscribed to his mother until after her death years
later when going through her private belongings.
Evidently she kept the book a secret from her husband and family knowing its historical importance
and what it meant to her; the book with such a long,
personal inscription, one of Hemingway's longest,
was worth at least a hundred thousand dollars on
the book market. Hemingway was in his fifties at the
time yet made a long lasting impression on at least
one young Cuban debutante.

His Mother's world was upended when the Batista government was overthrown by rebels led by Fidel Castro in nineteen fifty-nine. The entire island including all of the railroads were nationalized under Castro leaving mother's family and thousands of landowners barely escaping with their lives, leaving behind their possessions and their fortunes. Mother and her family escaped to Miami, eventually relocating to Washington where she met and married Alex's father. She became a gracious hostess for embassy dinners around the world. His mother never returned to Cuba and as far as I could tell never missed anything about it, except maybe Hemingway who committed suicide in 1960 while living in Idaho.

With a Princeton education, Alex was recruited by the State Department out of college where the government believed his language skills could be a useful asset. During this period he met colleagues who would become life- long friends and confidants. He also met Sophie Carpue while visiting his friend Jeffery in London; Alex and Sophie were married and she has been his wife and partner ever since. Sophie came with her share of baggage which mainly consisted of her father Anatole.

Alex's work with the State Department was mostly communications and logistics, no real spy stuff even though almost every paper or email that crossed his desk was either highly sensitive or actually top secret. Over the years since "9-11" most of the work entailed recruitment and payment for information and the development of ground assets in the Middle East. The kind of intelligence gathered helped the CIA and the military develop targets for drone strikes and provided after- the- fact confirmation of the effectiveness of the strikes. Monitoring local communications and word-of-mouth transmissions through U.S. assets was the most accurate information available. Alex also acted as a middle-man for the transport of arms to individual "rebel" groups which were in our favor at the time. As one can imagine, an extensive network of underground contacts was developed through arms dealing throughout the Middle East, Asia, Eastern Europe and Russia. The nature of Alex's business allowed him to reside in Europe, Paris to be exact, and still travel between embassies in the Middle East and remain in contact with assets through the internet.

The cover story Alex used in Paris was that of a retired businessman, an expatriate living in the city. All the while Alex was actually working through the American embassy in Paris maintaining contacts through the large Middle Eastern population in Paris. Sophie and Alex were married back in the states in a small ceremony before their move to Paris. Actually, Alex had not yet met Sophie's parents who are Russian but now living in Luxembourg. She offered many things about her past but only a few sketchy details about her father who was known as a very successful Russian businessman. Alex figured Anatole must do quite well as Sophie never seemed to be short of cash and in fact she made the couple financially secure without having a job. In the old days it was called a dowry and Sophie had a generous one. There was no reason for Sophie to work a real job so she spent most of her time volunteering at *Hopital Necker* and doing a variety of modeling jobs for a Paris-based photographer she enjoyed working with. Even in Paris where beautiful women were common, Sophie has an allure that is coveted by photographers and marketing executives alike. Natural red hair, pale blue eyes and porcelain skin are rare at the highest level of modeling, especially in women who are not immature looking and have a curvaceous figure at five feet nine inches tall. Sophie was a pleasant change from the anorectic teenager models with crooked teeth that used to be coveted as runway models. She became so popular modeling swim suits and lingerie she could be highly selective in her job choices and was becoming almost as sought after as the American Sports Illustrated model Kate Upton.

After weeks of walking, talking and showing off our frou-frou dogs, Alex and I decided to introduce the wives. Being a fairly accomplished chef myself and Alex a fully developed epicurean, we naturally disagreed over the dinner arrangements. Alex was a *Taillevent*-type guy with a large checking account and the patience for a classic French dining experience in a severe, poorly lit, wood accented atmosphere. I was in favor of the pedestrian version of French cuisine with local *fruits de mer* (seafood), but more specifically *huitres* (French oysters) served in a loud, smoky, Bistro-type environment. These tasty mollusks are a specialty of the French coast where the creatures grow unfettered in the differing coastal environments creating a multitude of sizes, shapes and tastes. Not everyone likes oysters like Jess and I do, but Alex and Sophie agreed to meet us at *Cap Vernet* on *Avenue Marceau*. I had only recently become aware of the restaurant *Cap Vernet* while out exploring one Saturday morning in the 8th *arrondissement*.

I happened upon a raucous crowd in front of a restaurant. The oystermen still attired in their wet water gear, well-worn *galoshes* and rain hats, recently off their boats at the coast were describing their oysters, the environment of the Brittany coast where they were procured and how the local environment affected their aroma, texture, salinity, size and taste. Each discussant reached into one of his croker sacks, as we call them in the South, deftly opened a cold oyster still encased in the sea grass and barnacles that occupy the same Brittany sea water where the mollusks were snagged. Each oysterman offered the others a taste of their catch. I have seen discussions of French national soccer matches or the taste of this year's Beaujolais that were less intense than this oyster brouhaha. On this day the tiny *boudense* oyster carried the day as the tastiest mollusk. The tiny *boudense* (small bite) or *pouter* is smaller than the standard *huitre* having a crinkled shell, a bright crisp taste and more than average salinity. After watching this enthusiastic exchange between the crusty oystermen, I was convinced to return and had on several Saturday mornings to taste that day's variety of sea creatures. I was becoming quite the expert on French *huitres*. After relating the story to Alex, he relented and agreed to meet Jess and me at *Cap Vernet* Saturday night for a delightful meal of *huitres, dourade* (sea perch) and perfectly smoked tuna. I think I saved us about 800 Euros by steering clear of *Taillevent*.

During our third bottle of *Pouilly Fume* the conversation finally turned to my favorite subject, plastic surgery. Upon meeting Sophie, Alex's wife, I had my suspicions that she was no stranger to the benefits of Botox and breast implants. She was a natural redhead, about 5 feet 9 inches in flats, porcelain skin with the slightest hint of facial freckling and no visible evidence of facial aging. She was dressed for the season and obviously liked to show off her stunning legs. Add strappy high heels, a rather revealing blouse and the picture is complete. Both Sophie and Jess knew how to show off "DD" cup implants and as such looked very American. According to my French plastic surgery colleagues, French women are less likely to have breast enhancement than their American counterparts.

Sophie asked, "Do you really think liposuction is a safe procedure? I've heard a lot of stories about people bleeding and even dying from lipo."

"Any surgical procedure can be dangerous in the hands of an amateur. It happens that lipo is the most commonly performed plastic surgery procedure and probably one of the safest," I responded.

"Did they put you asleep for your breast implants?" I asked.

"Yup," she said. "And it still hurt like a sonofabitch! How about you Jess?"

"Still painful, like an elephant sitting on your chest, even though my plastic surgeon took me home to care for me," Jess admitted, explaining one of the benefits of marrying a Plastic Surgeon.

I directed the conversation back to liposuction. "We do lipo without general anesthesia. In fact, liposuction is one of those procedures we are able to teach online to general practitioners so that they can safely supplement their income. We found an interesting 3-D anatomy training program that medical schools now use to teach gross anatomy when cadavers are not available. One can actually get a reasonable working knowledge of anatomy on line prior to actually performing liposuction."

"How much money can a doctor get for doing liposuction?" Alex asked.

"It's somewhere in the range of $2,000 to $3,000 per procedure. As you can imagine, that is a lot of money when normal doctors normally work for $35 per patient visit. We teach these doctors that with a little advertising they can increase their incomes by at least $100,000 per year before taxes. The government will help them get the proper training by providing our software and paying us handsomely to administer the program, check doctor credentials, update the science, provide marketing materials and follow the cases each doctor performs. That way any quality problems can be identified and corrected with further education and direct patient evaluations," I explained.

Sophie seemed overly interested in our plastic surgery discussion, maybe it was the effect of the wine. The topic eventually turned to facial plastic surgery. Although Sophie hadn't had anything more complicated than a little Botox and the obvious breast augmentation, she asked questions that made me think she had given the subject a lot of thought. Not many people have the depth of interest or the stomach for the details of bone breaking and how the facial features can be manipulated to alter the basic structure of the face. The dinner festivities didn't allow for any detail, so I agreed to talk to her and Alex about it in detail at a later date.

———✦✦———

The spring turned into summer and Paris began to gradually slow in anticipation of the month of August, when the entire city is evacuated for vacation time in the countryside and at the French coast. All of the good restaurants closed and museum hours reduced as the tourist season came to a grinding halt. Like the rest of the cities' inhabitants, we decided to make a plan and leave Paris for the month. During the last week of July, I called Alex but got Sophie instead. She told me Alex was working out of the city and wouldn't be back for a couple of days. Sophie insisted we get together so we could plan a couples retreat later in the summer. I explained, "Jess is taking some time to do a little shopping today. All of the stores put everything on sale prior to the August exodus."

"No problem," Sophie said. "Let's meet some-where for a glass of wine."

"How about *Ma Bourgogne* on *Haussman*?" I offered.

"See you there at three, *au revoir.*"

"You look nice and smell divine," I said, master-ing the understatement as I tried hard to not talk to her ample chest as we were seated at the wine bar at *Ma Bourgogne.*

"You too, but not so much with the smell," she said.

"Thanks, I wasn't planning to be sexy, charming and to smell good all at the same time. Actually I was planning on running errands until I got your call. It was to be a typical unshaven male weekend. The dog doesn't usually complain about how I smell," I said.

"I hadn't thought of you as the typical man around the house, drinking beer and sporting your soiled 'wife beater' t-shirt," she smirked.

"I hope you don't find me too offensive. I be-lieve the correct term for that male smell is musk. Some women actually find it compelling," I related tongue-in-cheek.

I finally asked, "What is it you wanted to talk about?"

"I just wanted to quiz you on plastic surgery, both in general and about me personally. I wanted to know what you thought about my implants, you seemed to notice them at dinner."

"I didn't think I was so obvious. I thought then as I think now: They are perfect from a plastic surgery point of view."

"You're sweet, it helps to know that I still have it," she said.

"Let's have another bottle of *Sancerre* so I can make a total fool of myself in front of the locals," I said.

Sophie and I regained our composure so we could actually talk about what was on her mind. "You don't know a lot about Alex or me, but we have not been totally open about ourselves," she offered with a momentary pause to gauge my interest.

"Go on, it is Sophie Sosinski, isn't it?" I wondered.

"It's not quite that nefarious. The names are correct, but the life circumstances have been altered slightly. The majority of our information is true," she related.

"Why the deception?" I asked.

"We really don't look at it as a deception; we are just not forthcoming with our personal history. The things that you know are basically true," she paused for another drink of wine as if to fortify herself.

"Alex and I met in London originally and then were reintroduced again after I moved to the U.S. He also spent some time working out of the American

Embassy in Luxembourg City. My parents had moved from their native St. Petersburg to Luxembourg around the time of the fall of the Soviet Union. My father was a bank officer in charge of new accounts, especially those originating from the former Soviet Union. His experience with the language and his expertise in the new capitalistic Russian banking system made him valuable to his bank in Luxembourg City which grew from a mid-sized institution into a very large bank with billions in new Russian investments. Father became a very rich man in a short period of time," she carefully related.

She told a good story: Anatole Carpue, her father, remained mysterious to his daughter throughout his life. She related that as he aged he began to slow a bit physically, but seemed to become more imaginative as a businessman. The unconventionality of his business impulses clashed with the conservative nature of most international bankers. He turned into a star in a world inhabited with older, more conservative men who could only protect their fortunes during the global economic recession. Anatole was willing to take big risks as he became the financial consultant for the dark side of the Russian monetary system; his clients generally worked for the mafia and made their money illegally.

Sophie finally realized she was talking nonstop, hardly taking a breath. "I'm sorry, it's just that I've never told our story to an outsider," taking a long breath to relax. "I also find it very easy to talk to you."

"Let me see if I've got this straight: You come from a recently rich Russian family, you met and married Alex Sosinski, but you're not sure why and now you want to ask something of me that makes you terribly uncomfortable. Does that about sum it up?"

"That's a good start but not quite all of it," she added. "We had been in Paris a year or so when we received a call from father who needed to talk to us urgently. After we agreed to a meeting in Paris, they jumped on Anatole's private jet so that we could talk over dinner the next night. Having a long history with the restaurant *Taillevent* in the 8th *arrondissement* on *rue de Lamennais*, we called and booked a reservation for the next night due to the good will of our friend Philippe Legendre."

Sophie related to Tedy that she talked very little about her family to her husband Alex and when she did it was only in vague terms and with no emotion. Now that meeting Anatole was imminent, it became important to Sophie to give Alex some idea why he would call now. Sophie's first thought was that one of her parents may have a medical problem. She has always been intensely private about her child-hood in Russia and particularly closed- mouth about her father. Alex opined that he had known women who refused to discuss their families and seemed agitated when talking about their fathers. In some instances abuse was involved with the injuries too deep to discuss with another man. She was not necessarily forthcoming, but she did open up a little bit for the first time. Sophie told the story of a family in St. Petersburg on the Baltic Sea in the communist Soviet Union. A family of modest means called middle class in America; her father was a banking official of some sort who provided a decent life for his family. She recalled that he was not very political, but was a Communist Party member as was required of all government bureaucrats. They lived in a small apartment in one of many identical buildings that Stalin had erected to house the working poor. She remembered her father well with his cigarette smoke and the smell of vodka on his breath. Her mother Teresa worked, Sophie went to the state school and they all survived.

For many years nothing changed until the Soviet economy started to slowly collapse under the weight of its self-created debt, inefficient government, corruption and inflation. Shortages of food, gasoline and almost every commodity led to rationing and the explosion of the "black market" where anything could be had for a price. She was just a teenager but felt the tension in the family as their future began to evaporate and Anatole was feeling the pressure to provide for his family. With little money flowing in the economy the need for bankers was becoming obsolete. Anatole spent more and more time away from home and began having "business" meetings at their apartment with groups of different men who Sophie and her mother did not know. The visitors appeared more frequently and the men did not look the same as the other bankers they had known. Although these men wore suits, their suits were frayed and ill-fitting and they looked rougher, like they spent a lot of time on the street rather than at jobs; and they always had a dizzying array of body paint. They usually smelled of vodka had bad teeth and had not shaved for several days. Their language was typical of the low class peasants that rarely came to the city. Although Teresa, Sophie's mother, never said it out loud, both she and Sophie were afraid of father's new business associates.

It was not long after the men started to visit that the Soviet Union officially collapsed and everyone's life changed for good, most for the worst, but some for the better. This was a turning point for the Carpue family as they began to see better times, much better times. Their new friends were mostly father's new business partners. Sophie was sent to England and to America for school. They never again lived together as a family and Sophie grew distant from her parents- until the phone call.

Alex, Sophie and her parents met at *Taillevent* and were seated at a table in a quiet corner of the elegant wood-accented dining room. The corner was quiet so the couples could have a confidential dinner, and not be disturbed by the ever-present yet invisible waiters. Over a bottle of *Puligny Montrachet* and a bowl of watercress soup with Sevruga Caviar, Anatole told Alex his story. He explained how his position at the bank was evaporating in front of his eyes and the only power he had was the power to determine which people got to withdraw their savings and which people did not. His transgressions started small, but as he realized the power he had over people's lives he wanted more and more to exercise that power. That's when he started to meet with the bank's clients who had the largest accounts and who paid him the most for his access to the ever shrinking money supply. His meetings with these nefarious men were not so much negotiations as they were instructions on how he was to claim their rubles. There were enormous opportunities in a shrinking economy making Anatole mistakenly think he was somehow in charge. At first the mobsters let him think he was making a conscious decision to help, but their attitude quickly changed to let him know that he was in way too deep to actually stop. They were ruthless by reputation and even more intimidating in person. Anatole told them he was making a lot of money but in the process he had endangered himself and his family with no foreseeable way out. Their son-in-law who they did not even know was the only person they could turn to; Alex and Sophie had to do what they could to get them out of Anatole's predicament. Sophie and Alex would need a little time to think so the Carpue's booked a suite at the *Hotel Ritz*.

Later they met at the Carpue's suite and Sophie continued on with her story of how Alex found out about Tedy Merrill, M.D. Alex thought he knew how to read people like Tedy.

"Surgeons are accomplished at presenting a façade of competence and trustworthiness as they truly want everyone including their patients to like and admire them," Alex opined. Tedy was a rather imposing 6 foot, 4 inch American whose French was passable and who projected a surgeon's confidence and self-assured manner. Many consider this kaleidoscope of traits to indicate arrogance. If it is arrogance, it is the kind that many in his field find a necessity as their patients look for it in a good plastic surgeon.

"If you step away from the act of surgery which is the most intrusive thing one human being can do to another, without malice, and you try to imagine what kind of person you would trust for such an invasion of your body; it is only natural to seek someone with supreme confidence who would not hesitate to plunge into you to find a bleeding artery when a lesser man might hesitate at the moment of truth. Cutting open the human body and expecting it to heal, while simultaneously controlling the pain that this act would cause, is truly a wondrous act," according to Alex. "Plastic surgery has taken the paradigm to a higher level as these individuals not only cut into one's flesh, but do it with the intent of making you look better, not to heal some awful affliction. It seems they are putting themselves in an awful predicament as even leaving what is considered a normal scar is forbidden when the final analysis is how you look- no scars accepted."

Alex and Sophie previously met a plastic surgeon in America when Sophie had her breast augmentation. Her surgeon was cut from the same cloth as Tedy, but without the physical presence and without the intensity as if years of practice had taken the edge off. It seems similar to the difference between a fighter pilot and an airline pilot; one living on the edge of insanity and the other simply flying an airplane. Tedy was a highly competitive, driven sort of man like a Marine fighter pilot who responded to physical and mental challenges and especially a challenge to his surgical skills. Talking to Tedy during a morning walk caused an epiphany regarding Anatole. It dawned on Alex that a man with Tedy's skill and personality type could be the answer for the Carpue family. The subject was slowly broached by questioning Tedy on his plastic surgery skills, and asking if he was the kind of surgeon who could perform surgery so drastic so as to change the way a person looks; a change so profound as to defeat the most sophisticated facial recognition software, a subject that I knew interested Tedy and his computer whiz of a wife. To lead a man like Tedy Merrill exactly where you want him to go one must appeal to his arrogance and challenge his surgical intellect. He was presented with a challenge that he simply could not refuse: To use his skill to do something very few plastic surgeons have ever attempted successfully.

"Once Alex found out you were a plastic surgeon he obviously had you checked out, both in America and in Europe. Your name was easy to research, mostly due to your internet footprint and the relentless marketing of your name in the plastic surgery arena. He was certainly excited to have run upon a plastic surgeon of your caliber. Then we came to know you and Jessica. You both seemed to be down-to-earth people and both with a good sense of humor. Actually, I wished you had been my plastic surgeon as I noticed how much you seemed to appreciate my plastic surgery."

"I am apparently mesmerized by your breasts," Tedy said.

"It may have been that I wanted you to notice," she offered coyly.

"You still haven't told me what you want me to do," I reminded her.

After finishing another glass of wine she mustered the courage to go on. "Alex got to know my parents and found out through Anatole that he was in serious trouble with his Russian investors. Alex is now in Luxembourg City trying to help arrange for Anatole and my mother Teresa to disappear. He asked me to stay behind and talk to you."

I was still in the dark, "You don't need money and your husband has any number of sleazy connections who could help a man disappear. What is it you need from me?"

Sophie's answer was direct, "plastic surgery."

Alex and I have asked all of our contacts, including those nefarious ones you mentioned and everyone agrees that the only way to truly disappear is to actually become someone else. You would have to be able to foil the facial recognition programs that most governments use to track people they want to find. The people who would do harm to my parents could gain access to the tracking information-money can buy almost anything. We originally thought that my parents could change superficial things: hair color and style, eye color, glasses and makeup. Our "experts" say that the latest programs cannot be fooled by these measures. It was at this point that Alex mentioned your stories about plastic surgeons being hired to hide criminals like John Dillinger from the FBI in the 1930's. With the technology as it is now we thought you may be able to change the way Anatole and Teresa look and defeat the facial recognition technology helping to effectively make them disappear. Alex also found out that Jessica had technical knowledge about the latest facial recognition software. We finally came to the conclusion that you two may be my parents' best chance to escape and survive.

"I don't know if I should be flattered or pissed off," I answered.

"Definitely flattered, I would easily trust you with my parents' life and my life if necessary," she said.

Jessica and I would have to discuss this proposition at length. Sophie was pushing all of the right buttons with me, but I'm sure Jess would require some convincing.

"Why don't we get out of here and take a walk so I can clear my head. I think I need to get to know you better to get my brain around your most unusual request," I said.

Sophie gave Tedy that luscious smile, flipped her hair seductively, paid the bill and they exited to the street. They walked, the direction didn't matter. Sophie locked her arm in his as the couple walked the beautiful and seductive streets of Paris. Tedy came to know Sophie, probably better than any woman he had met since Jessica. She was painfully attractive and very persuasive about the fate of her Russian parents. Tedy finally told her he would talk to Jessica about her proposal. She thanked him by pressing her body to his and giving him a long kiss on the cheek neutralizing whatever composure he had left. Tedy resigned himself to the fact that he would spent more time than he should recalling the details of their afternoon. Tedy was intent on learning more about the beautiful Sophie Sosinski.

Sophie's young life was spent in St. Petersburg, Russia. Her parents talked among themselves of other places but these conversations were not shared with their only child. This was not rare as most people in Russia never talked about where they have been; only speaking of where they dreamed to go. The schools were good in St Petersburg with an emphasis on languages and the fine arts. Sophie's early impression of the Soviet Union was dominated by the color black yet their home was full of light, and that light gave them hope.

She remembered clearly the 1976 Olympics, rooting for their female and male figure skaters and the powerful Soviet hockey team. Little Olga Korbut was a hero to all little girls. She caused everyone to participate in gymnastics and pretend as if they were climbing the podium to collect their very own gold medals, listening to the Soviet National Anthem in the background. All of the little girls had these dreams until they proved to have no talent or outgrew the diminutive stature necessary for world-class gymnastics. Sophie grew tall and thin, arms and legs too long, with beautiful red hair, thank goodness no freckles and a reluctant smile due to several longstanding dental issues including a gap between her two front teeth. She was a teenager before her family had the money to straighten her smile. She learned well the art of smiling without showing teeth, either using a hand to cover her mouth or articulating like a ventriloquist without moving her lips. As Sophie developed, her lips stayed full and the pout she had perfected to hide her teeth turned out to be an alluring smile. As the young girls entered their midteens, the girls started using make-up pretending to be American actresses and pop stars and everyone dressed like Madonna. That is everyone but Sophie. Even after she had her teeth straightened, she had no interest in drawing attention to her smile or to her face. Even under the influence of an attractive mother who knew all of the nuances of eye shadow, lip gloss and brow shaping, Sophie remained uninterested. For Sophie less was more; a porcelain complexion, an oval face with big blue-gray eyes inherited from my father, and finally a nice smile was plenty. Her girlfriends continued to make fun of her eye color saying that when you looked in her eyes it seemed like you could see the sky, implying there were no brains in between. Anatole had the same eyes but no one would dare imply that his head was empty. She learned from watching Anatole in his meetings how he used his eyes to convey unspoken messages, but left no doubt as to his intentions. With the same eyes Sophie tended to open her soul rather than hide it. It would be years before she learned by trial- and- error how to do what came natural to her father.

Toward the end of high school Anatole seemed to worry less and less about money even though the Soviet economy was crashing around us. It finally got so bad that Sophie was sent to England to finish high school and work on her language skills. From that point forward she never needed money nor did she see her parents for a long period of time. A monthly stipend of $10,000, all taxes paid in full, arrived by mail or through PayPal every month.

Shortly after moving to London Sophie found a job in a bookshop in the Mayfair district specializing in antiquities and Russian literature. This afforded her the opportunity to use her Russian language skills and to improve her English. The bookstore was owned by the same family that first opened its doors in a previously bombed out shell of a building during the early years when the city was being rebuilt after WWII. Old man Rabinowitz still came to work at the store every morning to read the newspaper, take a cup of Earl Grey steeped at 188 degrees, no milk, and two sugars and to open the cash register. His motto was to count the money in the morning and again each evening. His second motto was that he refused to sell novels by German authors: unless they were also Jewish. The only exceptions were novels published before WWI. Old Man Rabinowitz and his grandson who ran the shop considered themselves experts on Russian literature, which is probably why they hired Sophie. She knew Russian well enough to comment on the quality of the translation from Russian into English. Sophie's language skills and personality helped to create the bookshop atmosphere where Russian and Slavic immigrants felt comfortable just hanging out to hear their native language spoken and to reminisce about "Mother Russia." It was common to hear a cacophony of languages being spoken simultaneously: English, Russian and French were the most common.

Sophie learned quickly that the grandson, Jeffery Rabinowitz, was facile with all of the romance languages as well as some Russian and even Farsi. Part of her job was to help him improve his Russian, usually after work at local pubs. Initially, Sophie thought this part of the job might be uncomfortable for both of them as she knew he found her attractive. What she hadn't planned was how much she grew to like him. He always treated women with kindness and respect even those who worked for him. Jeffery's background was never discussed openly in the shop so any opinion generated was from watching, noticing the small things he did and the way he treated everyone.

They had the busiest bookshop in London so there were plenty of opportunities to see him react to all sorts of situations, both good and bad. Since he was not married, a widower for several years, he garnered the attention, and at times the frank admiration of a large female contingent of patrons. He seemed amused by the attention so he frequently directed their reading to some of the more risqué titles which the women insisted on discussing with him. Watching Sophie at work seemed a source of delight for Jeffery's well-developed sense of humor as if the two held an intimate secret that no one else knew. The secret his admirers didn't know was that since his wife's death, none of the ladies, regardless of how attractive, would get past the first pint of ale and most assuredly none would get him into their bed. It became a mind game for Sophie to try and figure out if he was tempted by any of the attractive female patrons and if so, what physical, mental or personality traits attracted him.

One day Sophie was using the phone in the back office and absent-mindedly opened the top drawer to find a few old photos of Jeffery's mother and his deceased wife. The photographic paper was of poor quality and the images were not very good, but it was still easy to tell one photo was of his mother in her twenties. She bore a striking resemblance to her son at the same age. The more recent photo must have been of his wife. She seemed a tall girl with petite features, strawberry blonde hair and light colored eyes. Selfishly, Sophie thought she looked a lot like the photo. Over the winter and into the spring seasons they developed a comfortable, and at times, a tingly relationship. Sophie spent a small fortune on Victoria's Secret bras and panties, shoes and pedicures. Jeffery tried not to notice, but he was a man with an abundance of testosterone coursing through his system. I think the old man knew what was going on but kept his council.

The first Saturday in June the bookshop held a meet and greet with a noted American novelist. Sophie's job was to arrange the wine and light hors d'oeuvres. The invitation specified everyone's "summer finest." Jeffery had really never seen Sophie dressed for effect so she decided to take a chance and let him see her as a woman rather than an employee. The dress was mid-thigh, fitted at the waist, backless with spaghetti straps. Only women who could go without a bra could wear this dress and Sophie certainly fit that description thanks to her "DD" cup breasts. Her legs, always athletic and shapely, were now nicely bronzed and accented with a new pair of five inch strappy heels.

From that day forward Jeffery and Sophie had an intensely sexual relationship; his first since the death of his wife. Sophie continued her duties at the bookshop with the only difference being that the couple spent almost every night and most weekends together. Fortunately, they had similar interests in fitness, martial arts and firearms. Even with their physical intimacy, Jeffery remained silent about his past. She knew he graduated with honors from the U.S. Naval Academy and was commissioned in the Marine Corps as a 1st Lieutenant. Evidently he pursued further advanced training in the Seals but the rest of his recent past remained cloudy at best. How he ended up in a bookshop with his grandfather was also unknown, although it was hard to believe that he was somehow "retired" from the military. They talked at length about her plans to move to America and accept a scholarship to Princeton University. Several months before she was to move to New Jersey, Jeffery introduced Sophie to an "old" friend from his time in the Marines. Alex Sosinski worked in Washington, D.C. but graduated from Princeton. Sophie thought Jeffery was trying to smooth her transition to college life; she learned she could call on Alex any time once she moved to the States. By Alex's own admission he was but a glorified concierge working for the Foreign Service like his father before him. He was thinner than Jeffery, a bit taller with an elegant bearing and every bit as good-looking as Jeffery- but in a different way. He promised to show Sophie around Washington and New York. These offers she readily accepted.

Jeffery and she spent less time together and actually stopped seeing each other when Sophie resigned her job at the bookshop to spend more time preparing to move. Neither of them had been overly romantic about their short, intense relationship. Sophie thought the old man would miss her more than Jeffery.

Moving from London to New Jersey was immensely exciting and the university was all it was supposed to be. People from all over the world came to Princeton to be educated and to take that intellectual capital back to their home countries, most of which were hostile to America. The faculty seemed proud of the fact that America educated almost every third world politician, military leader and terrorist extant. "Not only do we educate them, we then send them back to their home with our hardy best wishes and billions of tax dollars to prop up their government's failing economies ensuring a lifelong enemy," according to her faculty adviser. Having been brought up in Cold War Russia, all of those from the former Eastern Bloc countries were bemused by the current American press and how much disdain they have for the American President, Ronald Reagan, who decimated Russian Socialism. The result would certainly have been different if the current administration had been in power then.

Sophie called Alex and he took her to lovely dinners and served as a tour guide for all of New England and even New York City. She had no other family or friends so it was inevitable that Alex and Sophie would become an item. After graduating from Princeton, Alex asked her to marry him. Sophie thought she would dread this moment when she would actually have to make a commitment to another and how much of her past to tell Alex. She decided to give up very little about her family, except their Russian heritage and that her father was a small time banker. With his government connections, she knew Alex could probably find anything about her that he wanted. Sophie asked only superficial questions about his work and he reciprocated by asking very little about her parents. It could be called their marital détente. They were married about a year when Alex was transferred to a State Department post in Paris. He became some sort of diplomatic liaison with his primary responsibility involving the Middle East. Alex said, "The travel may be quite extensive but we will get a nice apartment in Paris as our base. Most of the places I have to go, you may not want to see. It is still very dangerous for Westerners in most of the Muslim countries and even worse for women where Sharia law exists." What Sophie understood this to mean was that she would spend a lot of time by herself in Paris.

CHAPTER FOUR

*"Between man and woman there is no
friendship possible. There is passion, wor-
ship, love, but no friendship."*

Oscar Wilde

As the month of August dragged on the only
thing to do in Paris was to enjoy the outdoors.
The parks were glorious so Jess and I spent most of
their time enjoying those things that are not so much
fun in the cold of winter. The couple walked almost
every day and those days they didn't walk they would
take the RER train to the Paris *banlieue* and visit
places they had never seen. On one of those tranquil
outings was in the Porsche with the top down, Tedy

broached the subject of the Sosinskis and Sophie's rather odd but definitely doable request regarding her parents' possible plastic surgery. Surprisingly, Jess was not totally against it, but was quick to point out the inherit dangers of operating on a man wanted by the Russian mafia. "What if they found out you operated on him to make it less likely that they find him? What if they do find him and torture him to get your name?" Jess said, "I truly understand that you are quite taken by Mrs. Sosinski and I actually cannot blame you. She's a very attractive and evidently a very persuasive woman. You know I'll always support you; if you want to pursue this latest of your challenges, I'll do what I can to help from the computer side."

Sophie and Tedy agreed to meet on the steps of the *L'eglise La Madeleine* (dedicated to St. Mary Madeleine, the patron saint of Paris) to get a take-out sandwich at *Fauchon* across the street, and sit on the steps to watch the lunch crowd. Sophie looked stunning as usual, minimal makeup, her hair up and curled, no bra, a partially see- through silk blouse and a mid -thigh length tight pencil skirt. Tedy gave her the perfunctory buss on the cheek noting she smelled divine, again.

Sophie started, "Anatole, as I told you, became a very rich man in a very short period of time. Even *to* me he was and remains a powerful and mysterious man. As he aged he began to slow down physically but seemed to increase the tempo of his interior life becoming more spiritual and more imaginative and much more creative in his business dealings. His nature began to clash with his more staid business associates. He stood as a shining star with his associates in the international banking community. All was good until his spoiled mafia clients were making less money in the global recession. These were mobsters who did not care to understand global trends, currency exchange rates or international arbitrage. They only knew that Anatole was losing money for them; they were angry and in their bestial world they knew only to blame Anatole. That's where we stand and we don't know how long before they come for both of them. Anatole kept the remainder of his family a dark Russian secret even to his immediate family. Some were murdered during the revolution in 1919, some banished to a gulag in Siberia and a few were thought to now live in seclusion in Estonia. Anatole seems the only one to settle in Europe. He's rumored to have a brother that no one seems to know about," Sophie related.

"I've been thinking of you a lot since our last meeting."

Tedy had to ask, "How were you thinking of me?"

"Honestly, I've been taken by you since we met, Tedy. I hope my forwardness does not make you uncomfortable. Aside from the business about my parents, I want to get to know you much better. For now I'll leave the rest up to you."

As Sophie got up with her tight pencil skirt riding up her smooth thighs, she leaned over completely exposing her breasts to him, and kissed him on the lips prior to waking away so that every man within eyesight would notice. All Tedy could do was shrug and mouth the words, "I love Paris."

Tedy decided to walk back to *Courcelles* and consider what had just happened. He tended to believe her story about her father and knew that Jess would research Anatole Carpue, and try to get to the truth of his history. That was but one issue. There was now an entirely different problem with Sophie. The testosterone that normally courses through his system, screws with his decision- making processes and frequently causes him to revert to his more basic, iniquitous self was now in control of his actions. When he looked in the cheval-glass mirror he purchased for these occasions, to see for himself if there was a physical change to accompany his mental transformations under the effect of the cruel drug testosterone; his own reflection was younger, harder, livelier, more intelligent, physically more attractive to the opposite sex and to Tedy's mind, the more desirable man to be. He realized he was slowly, almost without conscious effort, relinquishing control to the drug (read: hormone) at an all-to- opportune time: the crisis of early middle age. Tedy knew, in spite of his best efforts, he would never be able to deny Sophie her salacious desires as he was slowly becoming a slave to effects of the drug. Tedy became obsessed with conflating his surgical self; one side virtuous and in control the other side angry, reckless and capricious, an alter ego under the influence of the drug. He was terrified that she would choose Dr. Jekyll over his dominant and more appealing Mr. Hyde.

CHAPTER FIVE

*"False face must hide what the false heart
doth know."*

WILLIAM SHAKESPEARE

Tedy told Jessica he met Alex Sosinski one morning while walking their frou-frou dog Rosie in *Parc Monseau*. Jess was initially happy for Tedy to have a friend in Paris but she eventually became concerned. As their relationship evolved it seemed less likely that his meeting Tedy was accidental. She became convinced their meeting was arranged when she learned what Alex claimed to do for a living. Easy going Tedy would have never bothered to check out his story as Jess did. Without legal access to confidential government web sites her only option was Google. Their story seemed to check out in that he was a documented employee of the federal government, in what capacity remained unknown. They were left to believe his life story as he told it, and he told it convincingly.

Alex's wife Sophie was an entirely different story. When Sophie and Jessica met it was like two lionesses' vying for the same zebra carcass. It has always been that way with two beautiful women; they immediately become their own worst enemies. For some reason the same phenomenon is not always true with attractive men. Sophie Sosinski was anything but aloof. She was uncomfortably friendly, especially to Tedy who surely noticed how attractive she was and how well she presented it. Alex was totally out of his league with this one. Being told about Sophie's father Anatole, and her mother Teresa, didn't really shed much light on her personality. It was easy to see Tedy was taken with Sophie's looks but being a plastic surgeon he had grown accustomed to being around beautiful women, and was used to interacting with them in an easy, non-sexual manner. Even with everything she knew about people and about her husband, this girl was somehow different, someone to be reckoned with. Perhaps she was just doing what she could to get Tedy to help her parents. When Tedy told Jess what he was considering, it seemed incredulous at first, but she knew if anyone could pull it off it was Tedy Merrill; he could do miraculous things with a scalpel.

Jess and Tedy had a long discussion about the Sosinskis and their unorthodox request. He reiterated the conversation with Sophie almost verbatim, except for the sexual nuances. Initially, Jess was agreeable to the idea because it did seem like a worthy surgical challenge and Tedy was usually not one to turn down a challenge, especially one that had not yet been accomplished. Several years ago Tedy spent some time researching a similar facial challenge that he mentioned to Alex during one of their morning walks. During the 1930's in the United States, plastic surgery was in its infancy with most of the new knowledge being obtained during the trench warfare of WWI. The specialty had progressed such that possibilities existed whereby surgeons could actually change the way people looked. For instance, the notorious outlaw John Dillinger, the FBI's most wanted criminal, had plastic surgery to change his facial appearance to elude capture by law enforcement. There were books written describing an actual plan supported by the Federal government to provide plastic surgery to prisoners. The idea was that by changing facial appearance, one can change criminal behavior reducing recidivism making criminals into normal citizens. Unfortunately, the criminals remained criminals, they were just better looking. Even today the Federal Marshall Service which oversees the Witness Protection Program has been known to provide plastic surgery for the men and women enrollees to help these individuals remain hard to locate.

There is a long history of using plastic surgery to hide identities, so Tedy was able to convince himself that it would be reasonable to consider the Sosinski's request. Jess was a little more practical. Her viewpoint is that once you become an enemy to dangerous people, you also become their enemy. The surgeon may be the last remaining person who knows the actual identity of those not wishing to be found. This scenario makes it necessary for the surgeon to also consider going into hiding. Jess was unsure that they knew the Sosinskis well enough to put our lives on the line. We were actually doing quite well with our internet business, so why take the risk, yet she eventually gave me her support.

In one of those "lucid intervals" that I occasionally have, it dawned on me that facial recognition software, which is what we have to defeat to have a person remain anonymous, depends on certain distinctive facial features that are not subject to changing backgrounds, colors or lighting conditions. The recent facial 3D algorithms that use skin surface analysis are dependent on bone structure to create the surface texture and shape for analysis. These more recent software programs are relatively insensitive to changes in facial expression, facial hair growth, skin color or even the use of eyeglasses. The only true limitations for 3D algorithms are the conditions under which the facial imaging was taken. For instance, sunglasses or eyeglass glare, uneven or poor lighting conditions or a lack of image resolution can obscure identification. Long hair obscuring portions of the face remains an unresolved problem. In France an issue was raised with Muslim women whose facial images were being obscured by ornamental headdresses or scarves worn for religious purposes. There has also been an issue that the images are only recognizable from the front or slightly from the side but not on profile views. It remains a fact that the underlying facial bones such as the cheeks, jaws, nasal bones and chin support the facial structures identifiable by facial recognition algorithms; yet all can be altered by plastic surgery of the facial skeleton. It has been common plastic surgery practice for years to change facial surface anatomy with subcutaneous implants rather than bone surgery, which was thought to be too invasive. Recent low intensity airport x-ray equipment can identify these implants as well as breast implants so the actual bone movement has again become necessary.

Today, surgery of the facial bones has become much more precise and the desired contour changes predictable to the millimeter. Even with such precise bone surgery the soft tissue movement is not totally predictable. This is why only surgeons with cranio-facial surgery skills and experience are able to pre-dictably change the facial bone contours and this is probably why Alex was able to find me as a likely can-didate to beat the latest facial recognition systems. Also having done some work on facial recognition algorithms, I was more likely to create an operative plan to beat the software and actually make my pa-tients look far better, possibly even more attractive.

Each operative plan should change as many of the measurable data points on the face as possible rather than simply changing one point of surface anatomy. Additionally, bone structures can be ad-vanced to increase the surface projection and en-hancing the outward appearance or recessed to make the facial part less noticeable. Another recent surgical innovation is the development of bioabsorb-able plates and screws to hold the bones in posi-tion while healing and then they eventually dissolve away. Formerly plates and screws were made of me-tallic titanium that are identifiable on low energy x-ray images and could be used to determine if facial surgery had been done to change appearance. It is therefore possible for people to work with a surgeon and through digital imaging, choose what facial features to change and roughly how they would look afterwards. Add superficial changes such as hairstyle, hair color, eye color, eyeglasses as well as minor body morphology changes through liposuction or breast surgery making the transition complete. These changes would make it hard for parents to recognize their own children. With this kind of technical and surgical accuracy our challenge may be to **not** make people so attractive that their good looks draw unwanted attention.

Jess began tinkering with the software we already possessed for digital imaging so that we could determine the number and amount of facial changes that were necessary to optimize our ability to subvert even the latest facial recognition programs. As our work progressed we both became more excited with the possibilities and became more likely to accept the Sosinski's offer. We were both now ready to hear a formal proposal and to describe to Sophie how we proposed to hide her parents "in plain sight."

It was still in the down month of August when we contacted Alex through Sophie to plan a short trip to Luxembourg City to discuss our proposal. The Air France flight to Luxembourg City was short; a direct flight to a medium sized airport without the usual AK-47 armed airport security guards. Alex met us at the airport about four miles outside a city of approximately 70,000 people. Luxembourg seemed more German than French. It also borders Belgium, but nobody seems to know how to describe the people of the Belgium republic. Luxembourg City seemed like one large banking district vaguely reminiscent of Zurich or Vienna, without the geographic beauty or compelling history. Alex, upon greeting us, was a storehouse of information about Luxembourg City. The only information I retained was that there are 155 banks, the highest individual income of the European Union countries and the highest rate of cell phone ownership in Europe. The entire country has but half a million people and is thought to have the highest per capita income of any country in the world that does not sell oil. Alex put us up at the Chatelet Hotel in a two- bedroom suite with a dining area. It had to be arranged for Anatole and Teresa to meet us in the room and for a room service meal to maintain privacy; Anatole was already making plans to leave Luxembourg and was not sure that he wasn't already being watched.

Jess decided to slip off to the lobby to stretch her legs and do some shopping while Alex told me in more detail about his in-laws. He previously mentioned that Anatole and his family were from St. Petersburg, Russia. The Carpue family was reasonably well off in the post-Stalin Soviet economy, they were party members but not really politically active.

For years the Carpue family was in the banking business. There was not a great deal of banking to be done in the post-WW II Soviet economy. Most of the accounts of any size were government accounts overseen by corrupt bureaucrats. As the Cold War with America continued to grind on the ruble became almost worthless and the suffering of the Russian people led to more drinking and more corruption. It also came with more hatred of officials which came to include anyone with a desk and office in a building. The economic realities of communism were predictable as the entirety of the post- war Eastern Bloc economies were failing along with the Soviets.

Russia's primary expenditure was on the military. They simply could not keep up with the massive American economy and the military spending during the Reagan years. The Soviet economy went into free fall, the military expenses bankrupting the country resulting in the dissolution of the Soviet Union and the breakup of the Eastern Bloc countries. During the decades of Soviet decline there arose an active subculture of criminals taking advantage of the weakening government and a generalized breakdown in the society. As Russia stumbled into a Western- style free market economy, the best organized and the most ruthless "entrepreneurs" in the new Russian system were the most economically successful.

Unfortunately, most of these new "business" men were raised in the so- called Russian mafia and laundered their ill-gotten gains through the legitimate banking and finance industry. Alex explained that Anatole started as a legitimate banker in a corrupt system that was trying to practice some sort of rudimentary capitalism without an instruction book. Basically Anatole had to "go along to get along"-and thus began Anatole's trip to the dark side. Initially small accommodations were made to these new investors who seemed awash with cash. Early in the infancy of Russian capitalism the governing institutions were new and were not well- versed in the free market forces leading to lax, if any, regulation and oversight of currency or international banking. Anatole saw this problem with the infant Russian laws and knew it was the central government that he had to please for his banking manipulations to work. The old Soviet businessmen and the new Russian beaurocracies seemed to think fraud and abuse were a necessary part of financial institutions in the new capitalism. One of the new Russian twists to unbridled capitalism was the addition of violence into the business plan. This was the Russian Mafia's unique addition to business practices of the time and they truly believed it justified and necessary.

Initially, Anatole was a minor figure in the new Russian economy but became highly sought out by the *nouveau riche* of the Mafia due to his knowledge of banking and the intricacies of international financial transactions. Just as the Italian mafia found out in America, the more money created legally or illegally, the easier it is for the government to track transactions in order to claim their piece of the pie. The Italians were early to realize that the best way to stay out of jail and keep most of their ill-gotten gains was to move their profits between different countries with different financial laws and different rules for extradition. The last piece of the puzzle is to legitimize their money by laundering through legitimate businesses in multiple countries. As these multinational businesses grew it became more and more difficult to distinguish the legal from the illegal funds. Finally, the corporate finances became so complicated and intermingled that no more than one or two individuals at the top of the organization actually knew where the money came from. Anatole Carpue was one such person in the hierarchy of the Russian Mafia.

Anatole Carpue was a man to be reckoned with, if first impressions are to be believed. He has a certain Russian look but not necessarily Slavic. He reminds one more of a Russian hockey player than a weight lifter. He stands about 6 feet 1 inches tall with a well- developed physique, broad shoulders and a thick but not fat waistline for a man of his age. His face was strong, but without distinguishing features; his hair was thick, dark, with graying temples. He was blessed with an engaging smile accented by a hint of a smirk as if he knows a secret about you that no one else knows. The overall impression is one of toughness and mystery combined with a highly developed intelligence. His intelligence is manifest by an acute sense of humor and what appears to be vivid imagination that belies his profession as a banker.

Anatole explained that for years he toiled as a mid-level banking executive, a bureaucrat if you will, at a smallish regional government bank: one daughter, one wife, no girlfriends, a two- bedroom apartment in a large Orwellian government building erected to house the "heroic" Soviet working class in St Petersburg.

He related, "Most of my clients were other government workers and a few people who made a little money on the black market selling knock- off American products. Everyone knew that the Soviet economy was in dire straits through the 1980's and early 1990's. Eventually there was a run on the banks putting me in a position to help my friends and colleagues retain their wealth while the remainder lost everything."

"What happened to those of your clients who you could not protect?"

"Never saw or heard from them again. Most are probably homeless and drunk," he said with indifference.

The story continued, "Those that I helped became my business associates who referred their friends that survived the crash. The one thing we all had in common was the initiative to do well in the new capitalist system. There was no instruction book for American-style capitalism so we got our ideas about how it was supposed to work from the Hollywood films we saw with Russian subtitles. Our favorite was 'The Godfather', with 'Goodfellas' as a close second."

It took a minute for this to sink in. These guys were using the Italian Mafia as depicted in the American film industry as the proper way to conduct business: the instruction book for American capitalism. This information made it easier to understand how and why there became a Russian Mafia and why intimidation, brutality and murder became business models. The exertion of power and even brutality over others was similar to the early business practices of American titans such as Henry Ford, J. D. Rockefeller, John Jacob Aster and others.

"In the new Russian capitalism there was a premium on making money fast as if this new capitalism wasn't going to last. The easiest transactions to understand for the inexperienced Mafia 'businessmen' were those with cash," Anatole continued. "The investment markets were embryonic: There were not enough businesses that understood capitalization in the free market arena. What was clearly understood was that the fastest road to wealth was through illegal markets, such as narcotics, prostitution, usury, or anything that could be sold to Europeans or Americans with a cash transaction. The most inimical people with the most charisma made the most money. When they finally made more money than they could spend on house, cars, luxury items and vacations, they sought out investment consultants like me."

Anatole paused for a sip of wine. This man was taking money from people who are known to do almost anything to increase their wealth; their businesses were uniformly dangerous and illegal, yet he was supposed to launder these ill-gotten gains creating the appearance of legality without coming under scrutiny and without being murdered for his efforts. Eventually this invested money was to be made available to these men who could then live anywhere in the world and appear to be legitimate business tycoons. The only lingering danger to these tyrants was the man who made the initial investments and kept the records- a man such as Anatole Carpue.

Anatole continued, "Of course, I knew there could be a downside. I was breaking a new set of

Russian laws and the government had not yet become sophisticated at the enforcement of their new financial regulations nor were they able to prosecute complex organized crime cases. There potentially could be jail time in a gulag which seemed a minor inconvenience compared to the wrath of the Russian Mafia. I was blinded by the money and held hostage by my own self-confidence. Once it was clear that the amount of money coming in exceeded my ability to hide it within local markets, I made the decision to leave St. Petersburg and relocate in a country with more access to the international banking community. The small European country of Luxembourg was chosen and has proven to be a lucrative choice." Anatole and Teresa Carpue have been living under the radar yet in league with the Russian Mafia for the last ten years.

Anatole's world began to falter as the American and European economies tanked. His Russian business partners began to question his investments, ultimately threatening his life. It is with this background that Alex and Sophie recommended their new friend, Tedy Merrill, MD, an American plastic surgeon, as a possible cure for Anatole's problems.

Our consultation continued, "Exactly how dangerous are these Russians you fear and how much money are we talking about?" Anatole's reply was staggering, "These people are known to be ruthless and have killed as a matter of business many times. I have invested 3.2 billion Euros. Two- thirds of that is gone due to the global recession, a fact these men can't and don't want to understand."

"Can you walk away with enough money to last the rest of your life?" I asked.

His answer was, "Yes, absolutely."

"In that case, let's order room service, on you," quipped Tedy.

<hr>

Anatole and Teresa were set up to arrive in Paris in about two weeks. This is a short period of time considering they were permanently leaving their previous life forever. Anatole had evidently been planning his escape for months and had transferred funds to various banks around the world. I still had connections from my training days in "The City of Light" at *Clinique Belvedere* near the city's western edge in the Southern part of the *Bois de Boulogne*. *Clinique Belvedere* had been a small specialty hospital mainly used for OB-GYN procedures. During the 1980's a world- famous plastic surgeon moved his practice to the clinic. This was how I came to know this out- of -the -way medical facility. The operating rooms were world class, the doctors excellent and the patient care attentive and most importantly confidential.

I booked two ORs and scheduled two patient admissions for Anatole and Teresa under aliases. The entire admission, operating suites and postop care were paid in full, in advance and in cash. Everything but my fee was included. Anatole and Teresa met us at our Paris apartment where we had access to my modified digital imaging system. We planned to digitally image both of them so that we could finalize the surgery and the new faces and bodies both were to receive. We were interfaced with a program algorithm written by Jessica, and designed to determine from our digital images what the probability was that our changes would hide their identities from the airport security and banking facial recognition software.

Anatole's surgery was first. He had a fairly unremarkable facial structure. It was decided to take advantage of his height and natural physique which appeared much younger than his actual age. We would take Anatole back in time about twenty-five years in appearance. He had no dental issues that a little whitening wouldn't correct. On profile he had a moderate dorsal hump on his nose and a nondescript chin. By imaging we decided to slightly decrease the size of his nose, reduce the dorsal hump to a straight strong profile, osteotomies to narrow and repair a nasal fracture sustained as a teenager playing hockey and reduce his nostril size with well-planned alar wedges. This narrowed the base of his nose. Next we advanced his chin a bit to further alter his profile, tighten his neck muscles and removed any neck fat further improving his profile and decreasing his apparent age. Anatole suggested a cleft in his now strong chin. Minor malar osteotomies were planned to accent his cheek bones. Tightening of his face was planned with the standard mid-face and neck lifts.

His eyes were rejuvenated with upper and lower eyelid surgery. His eye color was easy to change from green to blue with a new procedure using a laser to remove the brown pigment from the iris, unveiling the underlying blue pigment. It would take several days for the blue eyes to reveal themselves. We colored whatever gray hair he had and suggested a more youthful longer hairstyle that would partially obscure his forehead. As a final touch we added plain glass eyewear. According to the algorithm we had achieved a 90 plus per-cent chance that his new passport photo would be for a 40 year old male rather than one in his 60's. As a final touch we planned to liposuction his waist to further accent a more youthful physique. Since we planned to make all of these changes in one operation it would be a long day for me and Anatole, with a two to three week recovery. We set up a guest room with a recliner in our Paris home, so that Anatole could sleep with his head elevated. We hired around- the- clock nursing care for both of our patients. We also provided a cooler that continuously circulated ice water through a face mask to reduce pain, swelling and to decrease recovery time.

Teresa would also be a challenge surgically. She was 5 feet 5 inches tall and already liked high heels and platforms that made her look taller. She was not quite as physically youthful as Anatole so an abdomenoplasty and a breast lift with implants were planned. She had light brown hair cut rather short which is common for older women. In her case we went blond with a shoulder- length cut. Teresa looked her age and not previously had the benefits of plastic surgery. In addition to the standard forehead, face and neck rejuvenation procedures, we needed to strengthen her chin and jawline. We addressed her slightly large Russian nose with a rhinoplasty, which was designed to make her nose smaller to fit her petite face with a contoured nasal tip and osteotomies to narrow the width of her ethnic nose. These changes radically changed her profile changing several of the usual data points. We added fat transfer to soften her features, add fullness and a pout to her lips, improve her cheeks and to fill any deep wrinkles such as the nasolabial folds. The final touch was to be a full face chemical peel which we would do in the apartment three to four days after surgery as her swelling decreased. This would take care of any remaining fine wrinkles, skin blemishes or discolorations. We added eyeglasses as we did with Anatole and easily achieved our goal of 90 plus per-cent recognition changes.

Both were happy with their new faces and bodies, so we solidified our surgical plans for the following week. Anatole was to go first on Monday as men are notoriously slow healers, and Teresa was planned for Tuesday. They would spend the next three weeks convalescing in our Paris apartment with trips to the nearby salon for hair style, color and washing and a trip to the local cosmetic dentist for a laser whitening session for both of them. After three weeks in the apartment both of the patients were getting stir-crazy so we started to get out in the Smartcar for facials with lymphatic drainage to help with swelling and several days of shopping for new wardrobes. Teresa was particularly excited with her new breasts and waistline. Teresa, Sophie and Jessica spent an entire afternoon by themselves taking in the finest lingerie shops in Paris. Teresa had the worst of the surgical trauma yet she convalesced faster and was back to normal before Anatole.

By the end of their fourth week postop our patients were ready for their new passport photos and forged documents provided by people that Alex knew through his embassy connections. All that remained was to check the quality of their facial changes while going through customs at the airport. For our test of the airport's facial recognition software and passport documents, Jessica and I would make the reservations for a business class trip on Air France, non-stop, to Miami International with "Nat" and "Terri" our new younger looking friends.

We made it through customs in Paris and Miami without a glitch. It was glorious being back in Miami: the sun, the warm tropical water, the gentle sea breezes and most importantly, the white sand beaches. The four of us checked into the Miami Beach art deco hotel Delano. The prices were ridiculously high but traveling with Nat we had access to a ridiculous amount of money. That first night we drove down to Joe's Stone Crab Restaurant on the southernmost part of the Miami Beach peninsula to taste the best seafood delicacy on earth- the venerable Florida Stone Crab (Menippe mercenaries). The restaurant has been a Miami Beach must for half a century yet they miraculously cling to their old ways; waiters in tuxedos, mostly male, and no reservations. We thought a $100 bill might move us up on the waiting list and maybe our two hour wait was a reflection of C-note status. At least there was a bar where we could wait. As recently as 10 years ago the bar at "Joes" was an afterthought only accommodating a couple dozen diners, leaving the rest of the waiting crowd to cool their heels outside the restaurant: not a bad idea on a warm, breezy Miami evening.

During the 1950's and 1960's, a time many considered the heyday of old Miami, it was a well-known fact that the Italian Mafia owned and/or operated many of Miami's finest hotels. Miami had been the stepping off point for future mafia investments in pre-Castro Cuba. At that time Havana was like "Miami Beach South," except a bit more risqué with the added benefit of legalized gambling. With the history of mafia presence in the Miami tourist industry, Nat (nee Anatole) arranged for the Russians to invest in Miami Beach property and the tourist industry in South Florida. In fact, the hotel we were in, The Delano was renovated with funds from the Russian mob, and currently was partially inhabited by select wealthy Russians and their families. It was with this knowledge Nat and I had chosen this hotel for our stay to test our surgical remakes hopefully erasing any hint that Nat and Terri were even Russian. To further test our results we took the highest profile possible, occupying the most expensive suite, interacting with all of the hotels employees, tipping lavishly, shopping in the lobby businesses, using the concierge services for expensive rentals and reservations at all of Miami's hotspots, attracting as much attention as possible to ourselves. We knew that all high-end establishments used sophisticated internal security measures and ran security checks on its wealthy customers. We also knew the Russians were particularly security conscious and hoped our display of conspicuous consumption would garner their utmost attention. It was good business to know as much about good customers and their spending habits as possible.

Noting that the entire security staff was male, we knew they were probably monitoring every step Jessica and Sophie took. Besides being a world-class computer geek, Jess possessed a "Victoria's Secret" figure except she was in her 30's and bit more curvy-not necessarily a bad thing. Her breasts were some of my best work but the rest was God-given and almost devoid of faults. She has always had a petite waist accenting her other curves stretched out over a 5 feet 8 inch frame (6 feet tall in heels). Her hair was natural blond with nice highlights out in the sun and so thick it actually feels heavy. Her facial features are dainty like her waist with full pouty lips that look more like a teenager. The eyes are a pretty blue that on occasion she will highlight with startling blue contact lenses. When you add a skimpy bikini, not quite the South American thong variety, but small with a disturbingly tiny triangle top, then you can imagine why the security staff probably has lots of footage of us walking to the pool and lounging in our beachside cabana.

After a couple of days parading around the hotel, working on his tan poolside and drinking rum drinks like Hemingway, Nat decided to take a day with the golf pro at Donald Trump's refurbished Doral Country Club and play the "Blue Monster" with a couple of guys hoping to relieve him of a few thousand dollars by betting on their golf game. Every country club has its version of the pool shark, guys who play golf every day, probably played professionally a few years unsuccessfully, yet they somehow always show up when a "whale" needs a partner for a round of friendly golf. I can imagine pro golfer Ray Floyd in his early years taking a few thousand from many an unsuspecting 10 handicapper at Doral or at Indian Creek Island where he resides. Floyd always had a roughhewn swing that seemed self-taught and was not indicative of the accuracy or power he possessed. He was also one of the best "shot makers" of his or any era. Whether in the rough, sand or behind a tree he could always find a way to hit the green and make a bet or two on the way to a miraculous birdie. Nat would be fodder for a pro like Floyd, but a real challenge for the local talent. It wouldn't surprise me at all if Nat were to actually take a few dollars from these guys.

Not golfers, Jessica and I headed out for a day-long tour of Miami's beaches all the way North to Hallandale and Ft Lauderdale. The hotel concierge set us up with a new Bentley GT convertible for a day long test drive. There was nothing but blue skies, the temperature in the low 80's with a slight breeze and low humidity We were driving a brand new blue Continental Bentley GT with tan interior and Jessica's blond hair flowing from the passenger's seat. The growling 12 cylinder engine provided a nice verbal accompaniment to the Bentley's commanding curb appeal. Everywhere we stopped on South Beach there was the predictable red Ferrari but very few Bentley GTs. We stopped for lunch in Coconut Grove at a nice bayside restaurant and got a premium parking spot out front and the attention of the entire valet staff. The restaurant was the typical waterfront establishment in existence since the 1970's. I recall eating there during my time in Miami in the early 1980's. At that time "Miami Vice" was all the rage and one could frequently run into some of the television crew drinking beer and partaking in other "party favors" such as they existed back then. The menu hadn't changed much either: We ordered conch ceviche and sautéed filet of yellowtail snapper. We turned down more stone crab as we were spoiled by the fare at Joes. After lunch we had a few Mojitos out on the dock as we watched the big boats slid in and out of port. I've always preferred diesel power over the sails and catamarans. Two thousand horsepower Detroit diesels seemed to be the most reliable method of powering a boat regardless of weather or wind conditions. I happen to like the smell of firing up those diesels in the morning, and I enjoy traveling the intrarcoastal, a place where you rarely see sailing yachts.

After lunch we cruised up US 1, stopping at areas such as Bal Harbour and Aventura on the way to the famous Ft. Lauderdale Beach. At dusk we jumped back on I-95 to Miami to meet Nat and Terri for dinner on our last night in Miami. Jessica and I were flying back to Paris the next day. Nat and Terri had been so taken by Miami that they decided to stay in Miami and make it their new home. Unknown to us they had been house shopping and found a waterfront home in the ultra-exclusive Indian Creek Island community. Apparently houses rarely come on the market for this area and Nat had no problem with the $8 million dollar price tag. What also intrigued them was the fact that this small island in Biscayne Bay was incorporated as its own city within the Miami-Dade community and had at last count a population of thirty-three souls. With a high density of very wealthy individuals, the island security was iron-clad. This was the number one selling point for the property.

Prior to the surgery we had only discussed payment in general with no specifics agreed upon. Both Nat and Terri were tremendously pleased with the way they looked and it was apparent that we had successfully changed their appearance so that they were not recognizable to facial recognition software. I knew Nat was a wealthy man but I had no idea how generous he could be. Nat knew that we had rid ourselves of currency and kept our retirement in gold. We had even showed him our storage vault during his convalescence at our apartment in Paris.

"I noticed you seem to have a thing for gold," Nat said.

"You know full well my thoughts on the subject of printed money," I said.

"Yes, I know and happen to fully agree. You probably didn't know that I came to the same conclusion several years ago and have managed to amass quite a bit of physical gold also. With that in mind I had a little bit of gold bullion and coins transferred to the *Societe Generale* Branch that you mentioned as your local bank in Paris," he said. After an unnervingly long pause he announced, "There is 100 pounds of gold for you to pick up on your return."

I was flabbergasted as I tried to calculate how much money that was. Let's see a 100 pounds is 1600 ounces, the current price for gold hovers at $1700 per ounce, that's roughly two million two hundred seventy two thousand dollars!

Nat seemed amused as I went through my calculations. His only words were, "Our lives our worth that and so much more. We both will forever be in your debt, thank you both."

━┼ ┼━

Once back in Paris in our daily routines, it didn't take Jess long to begin to feel a sense of foreboding, of dread, female intuition some call it, that we were being watched. Comparatively speaking there are very few Russians living in Paris. Yet we always seemed to be in their presence at every sidewalk café, brasserie and restaurant that we normally frequented. It was surprising to Jess that Tedy didn't notice their Russian shadows. Jess secretly hoped that she was just being paranoid which is what Tedy would have said if it were mentioned to him but she kept her council. Whenever we were around Alex and Sophie as couples, our Russian shadows tended to disappear. It was like they didn't need to know what we were doing when the Sosinski's were around; I couldn't help to think that Alex was doing their job for them. Alex and Sophie insisted on meeting any new friends we made and Alex tended to give them the third degree: Where did they live? Where were they from? What did they do for a living? It seemed to me more than friendly banter, yet Alex came off as a friendly and interested conversationalist.

Every day was a moveable feast (homage to Hemingway) in Paris. Tedy and Jessica enjoyed a good life with the only exception being Nat and Terri Wolfe, whose mere existence in Miami left a shadow over them where ever they were in the city. Tedy was convinced we would never see them again and Jess hoped that he was correct, but as long as we were involved with Alex and Sophie, the new "Nat and Terri" were never far away. Jessica was becoming surer that Alex and the Russians were watching; she had no real proof except female intuition. There eventually came a weekend when Tedy was in Bergamo, Italy for a medical conference and Jessica was alone in Paris for five days. We mentioned the trip to Alex and Sophie but no one else. On a beautiful Paris day Jess took the Vespa down to the Shakespeare and Co bookstore, parked up the street at the fountain and walked toward the bookstore.

She noticed a blue van just like thousands of others that do road and utility work around Paris. It was just then she saw Alex with several other Russian-looking men, who insisted she get in the van. Alex was trying to make it seem as non-threatening as possible but Jess knew she had no choice except to go along. Alex sat in the front leaving the back of the van to Jess and the two other men. The rear window was taped and there were no side windows. Even though she had been taught to take care of herself, these men were clearly professional in that they were featureless, cold and without emotion. They were used to people being afraid of them as they quietly exerted their physical dominance over her without actually touching her. No one can truly prepare oneself for moments like this, but she thought the less fear she showed the more respect they may have. Jess was fairly certain they were outside the city but had no idea in what direction. They finally pulled off the main road, drove a short while and pulled into what appeared to be a large warehouse.

Although not restrained in any way, she felt they were in total control of her physical self. They led Jess into a medium- sized room with a gray metal table and two chairs. On the wall was a floor to ceiling mirror, which seemed to have no function other than to provide a monitoring room for observation. The room and probably the entire warehouse seemed designed for the purpose of interrogation and probably worse. She was left alone, probably to consider the things that could happen. Her intent was to remain calm, keep her mind engaged and to not give in to the fear that was engulfing her. Recalling a bit about Alex's job, she surmised that this was probably a government building, which government she had no clue. It became obvious that these people knew that Tedy was gone for five days. Those were five days when no one would miss her if she was gone. The longer she sat there alone, isolated, the darker her thoughts were as they percolated to the surface.

There was only silence and the buzzing of that damn fluorescent ceiling light. The human mind can be a scary place where silence creates the loudest noise, mostly white noise like the drone of a thousand bees. The images come fast, in a blur like a projector running too fast. The only images that make sense are the dark ones. Jess had to stop the projector and begin to slowly count each breath, concentrate on each one as if each were its own living entity. She was intent on keeping her eyes open to counteract the claustrophobia and to study the interior of the room. She finally stood up to examine the room: the locked door, the mirror, the floor, walls and ceiling, desperately searching a way out of her own personal hell. It seemed like hours sitting there: She understood why they took her watch. It may have been only thirty to forty minutes as her mind rapidly scrolled through the images of her life. If they were waiting for some kind of reaction, Jess would not give them one. She focused as much as she could on her increasing claustrophobia. Eyes closed, she could barely control the heaviness in her chest and the feeling that each breath wasn't working to transport oxygen and that any moment she was about to die if she didn't claw her way out of the room to outside air.

Jess tried to remember if she told Alex about her claustrophobic tendencies. Her first indication of claustrophobia was during an MRI (magnetic resonance imaging) exam looking for a reason for the headaches she was having. To have an MRI one is bound and strapped onto a hard, very uncomfortable table and delivered into a tube barely wide enough for her rather narrow shoulders. Once in the tube a loud banging begins that is only partially mediated by the ear plugs provided. With one's head bound in position, there is barely six inches of space for breathing and the recurrent thought that if something happened one would surely suffocate. That frantic feeling was coming back except there wasn't anyone that could get her out of the tube. It was all returning in spades: the pressure, the tingling hands, the suppressed hyperventilation and the feeling of impending doom. At about the time when Jess was going screaming for the door, which had not even been locked, the door slowly opened and a stocky Russian-looking man who she had never seen before entered. The man vaguely resembled Anatole Carpue before his surgery. He was a bit shorter, thicker and rougher looking. His suit was a cheap, poorly fitting one, which seemed to have no other purpose than to cover his tattooed body and concealed gun. For the first time she was beyond claustrophobic and frankly terrified. As he began to speak in his accented English, he moved behind the chair.

"Do you know why you are here?" he benignly asked.

"I think so, but it would help me if you explained it," Jessica said.

"You are a very beautiful woman, but of course you are married to a plastic surgeon. I think you know why we have taken the risk to bring you here and I think you know exactly what information we need to have."

"Are you friends of Anatole? What exactly do you call yourself?" she said with as much attitude as she could muster.

"How quaint of you to think Carpue actually has friends. We both are employed by the same people but have vastly different skill sets. It is my job to see that Anatole is free from harassment by people who would harm him or see him in a U.S. prison," he paused.

"You're a smart woman. I'm sure you can see we have unlimited resources and personally have no qualms about hurting you if necessary," he said.

Standing behind her enlarged his presence as she could not watch his movements or his eyes; he was very close, close enough to feel the heat of his body and to smell his cheap cologne. Her mind was racing to find the words that would satisfy this man. She knew that Tedy may have kept records of the treatment given to Anatole and Teresa but she had no clue where he kept it.

"How do we know that you didn't keep some private documents or photos? We have searched your computers and found nothing. Once again, do you have any images of Anatole after his surgery?" he asked without malice.

"Nothing, we didn't even take his picture after surgery. Why don't you ask him?"

"How can I get you to believe me?" Jessica was beginning to get frantic.

Strategically, he placed his hands on her shoulders and massaged as gently as he could but with just enough pressure to let her know he had total control. She was wishing she had worn a turtle neck that day, it was lucky that she had even worn a bra. All she could do was keep her eyes closed and hope he didn't really want to hurt her. It was probably good that he was behind so that she couldn't see his eyes and know his intent. Jess felt his stubby, cigarette stained fingers on her bra straps as he pushed them off her shoulders. The top button of her blouse was under so much tension that she thought it would pop. It's interesting how one's mind can wander when under intense stress. Jess found herself remembering how

Tedy used to describe the blouses of his patients who had breast augmentation. He would say they had "screaming button syndrome," describing the top button of their blouses under the new tension of recently augmented breasts. Jess found herself wishing she had on a sports bra rather than the lacy, almost see-through, number she wore that day and that Tedy tended to prefer. Finally, that top button gave away and then the second. She noticed how rough and calloused his hands felt, the total opposite of Tedy's surgeon hands. She found her own hands and sat on them so she wouldn't be tempted to fight, not yet anyway. The Russian said, "You know that if I'm not convinced you are telling me the truth, they will find your naked body in some alley off *rue Pigalle*. Your husband will only know you suffered a horrible death but he will not know why."

The Russian then slowly reached down in front of her, felt the shape of her breasts and unbuttoned the rest of her blouse. Her bra straps were already off her shoulders so it was easy for him to pull the bra down exposing her breasts. She was facing the glass window and realized whoever was behind the glass could see her. Jess could only bite her lower lip and try to decide at what point to fight for her life. As time slowed down the Russian realized she could see his reflection in the window. She tried to see his eyes to determine what his intentions were, but he was looking down obviously enjoying her "DD" cup breasts. His hands moved down and cupped her breasts, he started to gently massage her nipples seeming to delight that they became erect. His front was tight against the back of the chair, it was clear that he was enjoying himself way too much to kill her. Jess caught his glance looking into the mirror as if he was looking for encouragement from beyond.

She finally confronted him, "Please stop. I swear we kept no records of Anatole or Teresa. I am telling you the truth. Please don't hurt me."

She finally felt he had enough fun and had no intentions of embarrassing her any further. As he walked toward the door he turned and with a smirk told her to "fix your shirt." As he walked out the door she pulled up her bra and buttoned her blouse. Minutes later another man entered, blindfolded her and walked her out of the room to the same van they came in. After a circuitous route back to the city they returned Jess to Shakespeare and Co. They returned her watch before driving away. It was only then that she realized that it had only been a little over an hour.

＝━┼┼━＝

Now that Terri and Nat are settled in Miami, they can move on with their lives. Alex was able to find, among his government contacts, people who would help them remain invisible to Russian enemies. When Alex first came to Anatole with a plan to change both of their identities, they were skeptical not knowing anything about plastic surgery or facial recognition software. In hindsight Alex was a genius in the way he could convince people to do his bidding. Our plastic surgeon wasn't a patsy, yet he was willing to do some outrageous things to help the Carpues. Alex, in the course of researching our predicament, found out that Anatole was under scrutiny from the U.S. Department of Justice as well as Homeland Security. Anatole really thought that he had hidden his money laundering for the Russians under layers of international banking obfuscation. Initially, Anatole thought Alex's scheme might fall apart when he noticed Dr. Merrill trying to decipher some of the faded tattoos visible under his shirt. He could only hope that Tedy had never heard of the notorious "Tambor gang" in St. Petersburg depicted in a general way on one of the more prominent chest tattoos. Sergei Kumarin, the powerful and dangerous leader of the gang known for banking fraud was recently written about in the *New York Times*.

The way in which Alex painted the picture of Anatole's predicament as being entirely a problem with the Russians and not the U.S. government made it less of a problem for the Merrills to keep their confidence. Anatole could only hope the good doctor didn't read the New York Times on a daily basis. His lovely wife Jessica seemed much more skeptical and more likely to fact check Alex's story. Alex thought she would dig deeper, but he made sure that she wouldn't find anything related to the American government. Since Alex and Sophie had befriended them, it should be easier to keep track of them after surgery should the need ever arise to further hide our past. Alex had a number of resources in Europe that could be paid to eliminate Dr. Merrill and his wife if they were forced, or paid, to give up our new identities. If the doctor and his wife stayed true to the team, we could probably use his services for other Russians needing to disappear. There had been recent events on the island-nation of Cyprus where some of Anatole's Russian Mafia clients lost millions as the Cyprus government decided to take the recommendations of the European Union and America and liberate millions of deposited Russian dollars to help finance a restructuring of the banking industry in Cyprus. The fact that most of the money was mafia money was of no concern to the Cyprus government officials, whose lives are now in danger and could possibly need to disappear as Anatole and Teresa had done.

Miami had always been fertile ground for illicit business since the years of abolition and the Chicago mafia led by Al Capone. Capone had been a very cagey businessman hiring only the best lawyers, which would have kept him out of prison except for his accountant and a Department of Treasury snoop who discovered Capone had never paid income taxes on his millions. While Capone was in federal prison in Atlanta doing eleven years on tax evasion charges, he had his lawyers based in Orlando buy thousands of acres of orange groves in central Florida. Florida government officials leaked the Disney plan to buy the land in its entirety to build its second Disney resort called-Disneyworld. Capone's acolytes sold the orchard land for millions to the Disney people helping to finance Capone's opulent lifestyle in Miami. After getting out of prison, Capone lived out the remainder of his syphilis-ridden life in a Palm Island mansion in Miami. If Miami was good enough for the Sicilian Mafia and "cocaine cowboys" from Columbia, it was certainly good enough for the Russians of today.

The Russian Mafia has been part of the Miami tourist scene for years owning and operating strip clubs, lounges, running protection schemes and operating sophisticated credit card scams through their businesses. There are dozens of Russian Mafia operatives active in Miami and have been since the 1980's with the first wave of Russian immigrants migrating to Brighton Beach, New York City. The early

Russia mafia was populated with many Russian Jews dating back to the post-WW I period when they were an outcast people, mostly poor, living in pogroms. Anatole's parents were raised in one of those pogroms and never fully recovered from the experience. There has always been a large Jewish influence in both the city of Miami and among the elite of the Russian mob. Having Jewish roots made it easier for Terri and Nat to assimilate into the Miami Beach Jewish culture which was a world unto itself away from the hip-hop music, sports and drug cultures that have become so popular. Nat's business plan for the Russians was to operate as many places as possible that the rich and famous frequented; these establishments had the highest cash flow which was used to launder illegal mafia profits. By necessity, many of these businesses were high-class strip clubs, restaurants and bars. That the Russian Mafia owned places like these was a well- kept secret and that Nat was to oversee their management was known to only a few of the operatives who would go to their death with that information.

Terri and Nat had a new life, were known to a very few people and were well insulated from the Russians in Paris who did all of the "dirty work" for the mafia in Europe. As far as anyone knew, Anatole and Teresa Carpue died in a fatal car crash in Luxembourg several months ago. Their obituary read:

The Quotien Daily in Luxembourg City:
Anatole and Teresa Carpue died in a fiery automobile crash late Sunday night on the outskirts of Luxembourg City. Anatole was a well-known businessman, originally from St Petersburg, Russia, married to Teresa Carpue, his wife of 40 years. The couple was survived by a daughter, Sophie. The bodies were cremated and no services were announced.

Miami is a city of extremes where excess is applauded in all walks of life. It is also an international city where people of all cultures are accepted with one condition: Money is the great equalizer in all cultures and especially in a city of extremes. The drug trade is still the primary driver of all Miami businesses, especially the real estate market and the bar, lounge and restaurant businesses. Even during Reagan's "War on Drugs" the illicit drug trade continued unabated but mostly under the radar rather than on the front page of the Miami Herald.

Recently the drug trade has been experiencing resurgence due to the ever widening influence of the Russian Mafia. The South Americans still manufactured the cocaine but the Russians brought a new dimension to the distribution of the drug. Drug officials were finding the Russians equally ruthless and loyal to their partners in crime as the

Columbians were. Most of the Russian soldiers had earned their stripes in the harshest environment on earth- the Siberian gulags. Those that had spent time in the gulags found the American prison system and the governing laws of America to be almost no deterrent at all. The "Brotherhood," as it was known, was controlled by the Russian "Bratva" where brutality and a complete distain for any authority ruled their lives and their business dealings. The Russians were ruthless by nature but also smart and usually educated in some manner. Their loyalty was much more intense and more complicated than mere ethnic sensibilities that held many criminal groups together.

The *"vor v zakone"* were the prisoners who emerged as the leaders of the groups in the gulags and were now the CEO and CFO's of today's Russian crime enterprises. The unknown part of Nat's past was that he was one of these men. His past was deeply hidden in Russian records that had been erased years before; he didn't even look Russian after Dr. Merrill's surgery. Merrill added a post-op regiment of human growth hormone and the same anabolic steroids that were readily available in prison for a price that mobsters were always able to pay, so that they would feel as invincible as they looked. Unfortunately, Nat Wolfe began to act like a much younger man and began to live a life of youthful exuberance, acting like he felt based on new good looks, a position of power and, of course, the money. Nat quickly gained the respect of his men; having the looks of a powerful man and the good sense to be hands on in all business dealings thus demonstrating how the business was to be handled. Nat became, out of perceived necessity, a hard, brutal man and expected nothing less from underlings. As a mafia boss, it was expected that he visit violence on rivals.

Nat frequented the late night clubs and lounges where he had invested significant amounts of the mob's money and at times violence was needed as these types of establishments had a rough, sometimes violent clientele. Almost all successful Russian mobsters emulated the boss and were therefore well-dressed, professional and used cocaine to be energized through the long, dangerous nights. They all, including Nat, were seen in the company of beautiful, young Eastern European and Russian girls most of whom were what we call "professional." Nat loved his wife dearly but business was business so he kept Terri isolated from daily life as much possible. She remained busy living the cultured existence of the rich and famous in their Indian Creek Island mansion. During the daylight they had pictures taken as much as possible with the Miami elite, sports stars and celebrities. At night, Nat's life was totally different; taking his photo was strictly forbidden and punishable by the destruction of your camera or cell phone and a significant beatdown; he traveled behind dark tinted windows with a small group of men whose only job was to maintain space between Nat, the wealthy Russian businessman and the public. Over time he even developed the affectation of the rich and famous wearing sunglasses after dark as if this would not draw attention to his presence any more than the two large men in suits that always traveled with him.

CHAPTER SIX

"The Enemy of My Enemy is My Friend"

An Ancient Proverb Attributed to
both the Chinese and the Arabic
Peoples

Paris is a city of approximately three million individuals. Considering the size of the land mass and its lack of vertical expansion in the form of skyscrapers, there are a lot of people in a relatively small area. The diversity of the city's population makes it possible for almost anybody, regardless of ethnicity or nationality, to lose themselves in Paris. And so it is true for Jeffery Rabinowitz, bookstore owner in London. The European Union borders are uniformly porous for people with European or U.S. passports, who have already made customs at their port of entry. Jeffery heard from his old friend Alex about a contract in Paris. Jeffery was semi-retired from a lifetime of contract work for various international and U.S. government entities; it was a fact unknown to his father or any of his bookstore patrons in Mayfair. His introduction into contract work was through former colleagues and members of the Navy Seals.

After Bin Laden, the CIA and Department of Defense concentrated on the drone programs and had much less use for on-the-ground operatives like Jeffery. The current U.S. administration lost the "warrior" mentality of their predecessors, deferring to the perceived sterility of drone strikes and generals who were more administrator than warrior. Drone strikes, for some reason, were interpreted as being a less overt way of killing people who were thought to be terrorists. For years, no one but the observers on the ground knew that those being killed by drone strikes were not only the terrorists that had been targeted, but included a significant number of "unknowns" also killed who were mostly women and children. Those in the anti-terrorist groups knew the truth but until the reports were leaked to the public, the warriors like Jeffery would remain on the sideline.

In the interim, ground assets had diminished to the point that all intelligence was supplied by paying the locals for information that usually could not be corroborated. The time and money necessary to fully develop ground assets and a spy network were not on this administration's agenda. The golden period of the CIA ended with the fall of the Soviet Union and the end of the Cold War. We still uncover and send home about a spy per month, half of which are employed by our "friends" in their Washington embassies. They are sent packing with a publicity fanfare making them useless as spies in the future. Leaks, mostly from the Executive branch of the Federal government, made it almost impossible to keep secrets. Congressional committees also became a sieve as bureaucrats and politicians consistently used national secrets to forward a political agenda. These developments created a large number of highly trained field operatives sitting at desks or out of work altogether itching for action. Jeffery was one of these men who had been doing black ops work for the U.S. government for years but had not been contracted lately. He had been spending his time working with his grandfather in a London book shop. The call from Alex was a welcome diversion from working in the book shop and keeping his skills sharp at the range and in the gym.

In the world of covert operations Jeffery was a known entity, equally feared and respected. Contacting Jeffery was not an easy job, except for Alex Sosinski. For the rest of the world Jeffery was only known as "the Rabbi." To reach the Rabbi one had to scan any of a number of anti-Semitic websites or chat rooms. The Rabbi would scan these sites looking for key words or phrases that would lead him to an anonymous contact and his next job. Most of his recent work came from the Russian mafia rather than the U.S. For their contracts a large, bloody foot print was required usually to send a message and create an example of the poor people designated for elimination. As the Russians became more sophisticated, their interests expanded from the street to the board room; their methods also evolved for taking care of their problems. They required less bloody extravagance and more "delicate" methods for the elimination of their enemies so that the deaths would appear natural: heart attacks, suicide and car accidents being thought of as natural. Those that cared to speculate thought that Jeffery, "the Rabbi," was seemingly Jewish, but no one knew for sure. With "the Rabbi" as a moniker, it was wrongly assumed that he had Mosad training and roots in the Israeli Army.

Over time, the Rabbi began to think of himself as a specialist. Using the London book shop as a cover, he became familiar with all things Russian and even went so far as to get a Russian employee who became his girlfriend. This same girlfriend he introduced to Alex Sosinski became Alex's wife. His Russian language skills greatly improved when he was with Sophie, he also gained an appreciation for Russian women, their likes and dislikes. Sophie was no ordinary Russian woman but she had been open with him regarding what other women found attractive in him. He was good enough at his trade to use nuances to his advantage. Sophie had taught him how to read people at a glance and how to morph instantly into a person women liked and from whom they feel no threat. Sophie started by teaching him the nuanced behavior of women, what they saw when they looked at him and what he could do with a glance to mold their opinion of him. Sophie taught him that reading visual clues was merely the fine art of stereotyping; over the time they were together he was an exemplary student and she a good teacher.

Their training sessions occurred after work; they frequented most of the high class bars and night clubs in London, sometimes showing up together and other times separately as if they didn't know each other. She taught him how to scan a room of hundreds of people and within a few minutes be able to strike up a conversation with anyone in the room, male or female. There was no real trick to it; one just had to learn how to be observant of behavior and to know everyone was there for a reason. If you add alcohol or drugs to the mix, people became even more transparent. Even after Sophie left for America and started seeing Alex, Jeffery continued to frequent every type of establishment or event, play, concert or movie and continued to hone his people skills even to the point of wearing disguises so that he could judge the relative importance of physical attributes in the equation. What he observed was that as long as one met a minimal level of attractiveness, attitude and personality could take care of the rest. The only exception to the rule was with extraordinarily attractive people; these people defied all stereotypes and can be extremely hard to read and classify. He also learned that undercover police were the easiest to read, they were casing the place just like he was. All of these societal nuances made Jeffery even more lethal in his occupation as a hired assassin.

The Rabbi knew that his next paycheck was to be earned in Paris. The why never mattered, it was who and how much that were important. He liked to spend at least six weeks creating an identity wherever he worked. He tended to work on his exit strategy first, and then he would work out the details of the contract. The Rabbi preferred his payment in two installments; the first half upon agreeing to the contract, and the remainder once the contract was certified. For years he took payment in dollars or the market equivalent but no longer. He now accepted only gold as payment to be deposited in one of several precious metal brokerage firms with which he had an account. The account number was provided, the gold deposited and the contract carried out according to a set of parameters chosen by his employer. He preferred half bullion and half Golden Eagles, which were legal tender across the globe. The downside was that there were fewer and fewer countries where his bribes assured his gold was moved under the international banking radar and that his money was also secure. Recent events in countries such as Cyprus cost him half of his holdings in that country as the government confiscated half of the deposits of its wealthy clients in order to refinance their failing banking industry. He had several open accounts in Paris with banks that had a multinational presence. He also had several hotels which he had booked rooms but he was actually staying in the *Hotel Lutetia* located off *Blvd. St Germain* at the intersection with *Blvd. Raspail.* It is a large hotel that housed many of the German soldiers during the occupation of France in the war and now housed a large tourist population. This situation made it easy to blend in and to come and go as a tourist would. He kept a low profile, traveled by the Metro, dressed comfortably and spoke fluent French. His ever-present Nikon served two purposes; it augmented his tourist persona and allowed him to photograph the movements of his target.

There was only one aspect of his current contract that was different than the dozens of contracts he had taken in the past. He rarely felt ill but Jeffery was fatigued and was having trouble sleeping. French was a second language and he had started to dream in French rather than his native English. Usually such trivialities didn't affect the Rabbi but his dreams had turned into nightmares causing his insomnia. He had started dreaming in French when he got to Paris, his dreams were now simpler and for the most part more frightening than he ever had. He was now awakening at all hours fully remembering his incubuses. His discussions with a psychiatrist he visited in Vienna frequently intruded on his thoughts.

"Dreams come to me now, lucid, almost every night. Actually I cannot distinguish deeper purpose. Freud was interested in criminal behavior and in some way that is the context of the conversations I have with him in my recent dreams. There is timelessness to the scenes in my dreams. There is only a vague feeling of time and place yet the scene together creates an almost coherent whole. The things I remember mean something to me as they are intruding on my subconscious

*without my consent. Freud thought that the nu-
ances rather than the main theme more important. I had trouble grasping Freud's world of
symbolism so his work was easy to dismiss. He,
in my opinion, made things unnecessarily complicated. The dream landscape was inherently
meaningful to me so symbolism was simply un-
necessary. Freud's questioning of the peripheral
details was a method to help his patients remember the dreams, period, serving no actual purpose. Having done before the things I am likely to
do, at no place can I find any feelings of remorse
or regret."*

As the Rabbi improved his skills over the years, there
developed a clinical efficiency to his methods. He always tested at a high level in high school and into college. Many thought he may apply to medical school.
He managed to accumulate an impressive amount of
what could be considered "clinical" experience due
to his deployments in the Middle East. Being accustomed to raw human anatomy can only be achieved
on the battlefield or in the anatomy lab. His accumulated knowledge of human anatomy, physiology,
microbiology and pharmacology made him a killer
on a totally different level than the usual psycho-
pathic miscreant that usually becomes a professional
assassin. Over the years he learned patience to add

to his already impressive arsenal. He depended on his mental sharpness to accomplish his contracts and recently, due to his unsettled sleep habits, he was not on top of his game.

The Rabbi spent the majority of his time documenting the habits and movements of his latest contract-Edward and Jessica Merrill. Even in his sleep-deprived state, he was well ahead of schedule due to the intelligence Alex had provided on the couple. He had the basic layout of the Merrill's residence including the details of their state -of-the-art security system obtained from the contractor that was referred to them by Alex. He would need to break into their safe to get the gold that Alex assumed was there. The gold could be a bonus if he chose their residence as the killing field.

Jessica had not told Tedy about her interrogation by Alex and the Russians. Since that day she noticed that the omnipresent Russians were gone. She had no intention of seeing Alex and Sophie, but she was still afraid that the situation would arise when she would have to tell Tedy who would surely display his surgeon's temper and do something that could get them both killed. Jessica knew the loss of their Russian entourage could mean one of two things; they got the information they needed or they have hired someone to get rid of them. Her intuition told her the latter was the case and that she and Tedy were in danger.

Jessica had always been the more deliberate of the marriage partners, calculating and intuitive. Tedy was more spontaneous, temperamental and more likely to go off "half-cocked" when he perceived a threat to his family. Jessica knew this and as she always did, she started to develop a plan- this time for survival.

A thorough internet search yielded much more information about Alex, Sophie and Sophie's parents. Jessica was able to track most of Alex's recent career working for the U.S. government. Previously unknown to the Merrills, Alex's recent career had been up-and –down, mostly down. According to his work evaluations, in recent years Alex had gone "off-the-rails" as those in the intelligence community called it. The Americans continued to find him work to keep track of his Middle Eastern contacts. The extent of his work with the Russians since the fall of the Soviet Union had been carefully crafted by Alex to appear innocuous. His marriage to a Russian had gone unnoticed. It's hard to believe the Americans didn't have a clue about his extracurricular activities; it was just assumed they were willing to overlook some transgressions for the benefit of the overall picture. The idea that Alex might make some money on the side was not important to his superiors. These facts meant that Jessica couldn't depend on the Americans for any help with Alex or the Russians. This also meant that they wouldn't miss Alex if he were to go missing. His handlers would probably think he had double-crossed one of his Middle-Eastern contacts and was in their hands. Jessica tried in vain to find out if anyone at Interpol was interested in a Russian national by the name of Anatole Carpue who was assumed dead in a fiery car crash back in St. Petersburg. Evidently, everyone is comfortable with Carpue being dead and out of sight. Jessica's encrypted file with pre and postoperative photos of Anatole and Teresa would only be important to the Russian Mafia who wanted him dead and not the people who would jail him. The feds in Miami had not even heard of Nat Wolfe. Jessica was slowly beginning to formulate a plan: "the enemy of my enemy is my friend."

There was no listing for the Russian Mafia in the Paris directory. The best Jessica could do was to find where in the city the Russian expatriates could be located. Just like New York City, every cultural group tended to accumulate in neighborhoods where their language was spoken and they could go to church. In many cases these immigrants gave into the comfort of their own people and never fully assimilated into city life making them easier to find. It turned that "little Russia" was located surprisingly close to the Merrill residence near *Parc Monceau*. The *Cathedrale St- Alexandra- Nevsky* on *rue Daru* was considered the epicenter of the Russian community in Paris. Jessica began to visit the church with Tedy on their morning walks. Jessica insisted she needed the exercise and she didn't want Tedy walking with Alex any longer. The easiest route to the church was off *Blvd. Courcelles* at *rue Pierre-le-Grand.* Even before seeing the five golden domes of the church you could smell the incense wafting out of the cathedral.

After a few weekday visits and several Sunday services the Merrills introduced themselves to several of the friendlier worshipers who all spoke French and Russian. After an invitation to the *L'Epicerie Ruses* for caviar, blinis, salmon and good Russian vodka, Jessica was able to question a few of the Russians about the Russian mafia as it exists in Paris. Most of the worshipers Jessica met, with or without Tedy's company, were well-to-do and seemed to have plenty of cash. Within a few weeks Jessica had befriended several Russian men who had the look of the Russian mafia in that they all had the tattoos to prove it. Jessica, being a tall blond American, was thought to be a "movie star" and immediately was popular with the Russian men. It was difficult, at first, working through the Russian men trying to find out who was who in the mafia hierarchy. There was one man that stood out both physically and as a man the others respected. Jessica knew from talking to Anatole that respect was the most valuable currency among these men. Respect was gained through ruthless behavior and making money.

Sergei was younger than most of the mafia men Jessica met, about mid-forties, with more class, better dressed and a steely look that told one why he was a man of respect. Jessica turned most of her attention to Sergei who seemed pleased to have the pretty American ask about "mother Russia" and tangentially about the notorious Russian Mafia. One night after a lot of expensive Russian vodka and a gourmet meal at the *Caviar Kaspia,* Sergei particularly full of himself and trying to impress Jessica, admitted to knowing Russians from St Petersburg and alluded to large money transfers on the international money markets. Sergei told an interesting story about an "accountant" from the old days who was thought to have stolen a large amount of money from his colleagues, and had died in a car crash with his wife several years ago. Sergei said that before he died, this man was being searched for by virtually every member of the mafia and eventually would have been found and eliminated. After a few more rounds of vodka Jessica asked if a man in Sergei's position would be held in high esteem if he were to provide information that the Russian accountant that stole the money was actually not dead. As Jessica asked the question you could feel the change in Sergei's demeanor, his eyes darkened, his body stiffened and he said that information on the accountant would be greatly appreciated. Jessica would feed the information to Sergei in increments to determine the depth of his interest. Jessica told him the man's name was Anatole Carpue and that he and his wife were living the high-life in America spending the stolen fortune. Even in Sergei's inebriated state his eyes flashed again and he turned dark evidently considering the possibilities that could arise for his personal advancement in the organization with this information. He knew enough to know that if the name Jessica gave him was correct, so the rest of the story could possibly be true also. She had set the hook; all that was left to do was wait until a sober moment to reel in her Russian "fish."

Sergei called the next day anxious to talk to Jessica. They agreed to meet at a secluded café at *Place de Ternes.* Sergei, now in full business mode, wanted, no demanded to hear details from Jessica. He was both a gentleman and a bully at the same time. She understood why he wanted to meet her without Tedy, he was hoping she was the stereotypical American female who he could either persuade with his good looks or intimidate if necessary; he wanted the information about Anatole Carpue badly. It was difficult to play the vulnerable female and at the same time negotiate with this man who had killed many according to his tattoos. He would probably earn a new tattoo if her information was accurate. She had to play this just right; first demure, then frightened of him, attracted to his power and finally agreeing to give up the information about Anatole and Teresa but only under certain conditions that were not negotiable. Sergei planned to ignore the conditions, there was nothing he could think of that would keep him from getting the information he desperately wanted. Jessica knew as soon as Sergei had the information he would be on the next flight to Miami so she had to string him along a little longer. Maybe she was an American actress after all. She agreed to meet him the next day at *Angelina's* where she would provide him with their location, new names and photos. Sergei thought to himself that the American lady probably wanted money; he would be more than happy to pay, he thought.

The next day at *Angelina's* they were seated in the back of the main dining room so they could talk in private. Again, Jessica thought she could get his attention better if Tedy were not there. Sergei was well- connected in Paris, especially the underworld, so Jessica ventured a guess that he would know if anyone was working on his turf. Jessica began by telling him how she and Tedy met Alex and were introduced to his wife's parents, who turned out to be Anatole and Teresa Carpue. She explained how Anatole came up with the car crash cover story and the plastic surgery Tedy performed on both of them to outwardly change their appearances and help them escape to America and a new life. Sergei seemed amazed that such things could be done, he was a believer when she showed him their before and after photos.

Once Jessica had his full attention, she asked if he had heard anything about a contract on her and Tedy. She explained, "Alex kidnapped me for an afternoon with some Russian buddies to find out if I had given Anatole's photos to anyone. That was the moment that I knew our lives were in danger. I don't know who or how but I know he hired someone and before I give you these photos and the rest of the information you need to find Anatole in America- I need for you to make some inquiries and find out if there is someone in town that could have been hired to find these photos and eliminate Tedy and me." Sergei knew for a fact that no Russian had been hired to kill them. He was a little less sure about others, but had heard that a guy known as "the Rabbi" was in town and probably not on a vacation. Jessica, not a believer in coincidences, got as much out of Sergei as possible about the Rabbi. Jessica told him point blank that if they were dead the rest of the information about Anatole would vanish. She kissed him on the cheek hoping he was as well- connected and ruthless as his reputation led her to believe.

Jessica and Tedy tried to maintain their normal activity level even though they both knew they were being watched and there was a guy out there called the Rabbi who was hired to kill both of them. Tedy wanted to arm himself, as if that would do any good against an unknown assailant who would more than likely not approach them in broad daylight with a gun. If the Rabbi was out there he was very good at his job as they were acutely aware of their surroundings and nothing seemed out of place, especially since the Russians disappeared.

Unknown to the Merrills, Sergei had a couple of his best men follow the couple as if they had the contract; doing what the Rabbi would be doing. Sergei was sure that they would surely spot anyone who would be following the couple. It took less than a week for the Russians to spot a nondescript man checking up on the couple. They were lucky to spot him with the tourist crowd occupying large parts of the city. That was what eventually gave him up; the Merrills spent most of their time in areas of the city where you usually don't find tourists making the Rabbi a bit more obvious with his Nikon camera and sensible walking shoes. Sergei related the news to them when his people spotted the Rabbi. They were able to keep close tabs on him because people that are trying to follow someone are not as careful to make sure they are not being followed. Sergei described it in terms of the follower being more vulnerable when in the surveillance mode. His men had followed the Rabbi back to his nest at the *Hotel Lutetia* and awaited instructions.

The Rabbi continued to have trouble sleeping and he refused to take any medication that might dull his senses. He knew the Merrills rarely went out after 10 p.m.; he had nothing to do except work on his plan during the long night ahead. And he still had those dreams when he did manage to close his eyes. Sergei told his men to stand tight and keep track of the Rabbi who had settled down in Room 322 at *Lutetia*. Unexpectantly the door of Room 322 opened at about 10:30 and the Rabbi exited abruptly, skipping the noisy, slow elevator and left the hotel turning right, walking briskly to the Metro station across the street. Sergei's men managed to follow him without being detected. He entered the Metro system at the *Solferino* station which was fairly busy at that time of the night and took the train north toward *Porte de la Chapelle*. The men waited in the next train car having no idea where he was going. Sergei had given his men the Merrill's address in case the Rabbi headed that way. Since north was the relative direction of their residence the men paid strict attention to which station the Rabbi exited. He stayed on the train past the Merrill's stop and eventually exited at the *Pigalle* station. The *Pigalle* station was at the top of *rue Pigalle* in one of the seedier areas of Paris. There were strip clubs, sex clubs and dozens of XXX video stores. They had no idea where he was going until he was outside the *Moulon Rouge*. Evidently he bought a ticket from the hotel concierge for the late show. The theater was emptying from the eleven o'clock show and in the crush of people they almost lost him but luckily picked him back up as he was talking to one of the theater guards before entering. The show would last until well after midnight so the men found a run- down café within eyesight of the theater's exits to relax and drink several *café-au-lait*. If the Rabbi had detected the men this would be the perfect opportunity to give them the slip as there was no way to cover all of the exits with just two men. All Sergei's men could do was sit, drink coffee and wait until the show ended. Sergei decided to join his men to take advantage of the situation that had presented itself. The Rabbi was obviously out of his normal routine for some unknown reason. Sergei figured the Rabbi was about to make his move on the Merrills at any time. How lucky can he be to get an opportunity like this to kill one of the most notorious contract killers in the world? Sergei saw these events as his destiny; especially the information on the Russian accountant to the mafia who was the most wanted man in the world by the Russians. It was past 1:30 a.m. and the show would be getting out soon. Sergei had already decided that he was the one who should take down the Rabbi. Each of his men was carrying a 9mm Sig Sauer with a suppressor and various other weapons that each man was proficient with. Over the years, Sergei's signature weapon had become the U.S. armed forces Ka-Bar knife, fixed handle and a 7- inch serrated blade. He bought the weapon on-line through the Ka-Bar Company. It was truly amazing what one can get over the internet with a stolen credit card.

Sergei's plan was to use the crush of people leaving the *Moulon Rouge* as cover so he and his men could get close to the Rabbi without being detected. Sergei was to take him down with the Ka-Bar and only use the suppressed 9mm Sig as a backup. The Russian mafia tended to prefer the more traditional ways of killing a man; they preferred close contact killing, hand-to-hand or the knife were the preferred methods. This particular nuance was learned in the Russian prisons and translated into their usual routine once outside.

The show finally let out, hundreds of patrons who had been drinking rolled out onto the wide sidewalk and even onto the street. One of Sergei's men spotted the Rabbi as he was leaving the theater. He stopped to talk to the armed guard at the exit, which gave everyone with Sergei a chance to reposition so he couldn't escape. They hoped they wouldn't have to kill the guard also. As the Rabbi turned away after talking to the guard, he rounded the edge of the entrance in front of the large poster pictures of the dancers in their revealing costumes. The crowd had thinned somewhat but there still remained dozens of patrons who stopped to smoke their *Gitanes* French cigarettes. The Rabbi noticed Sergei's man straight ahead of him at about ten feet away. He slowed and turned around to go down the street in the opposite direction. Just as he passed in front of the theater entrance on the opposite side he almost ran directly into Sergei. Sergei had already unsheathed his Ka-Bar and as the Rabbi was passing on Sergei's right hand side he plunged the knife deep into the Rabbi's body under his rib cage, directing the penetration upward to the left. He held the Rabbi up for a quick moment to twist the knife that was in up to its 7- inch hilt. The pathway of the knife Sergei knew exactly; it transversed the upper stomach and esophagus, the diaphragm, the left pleural cavity and finally the right ventricle of the heart. It took about four heartbeats for the heart to empty, start to fibrillate and then to stop altogether while Sergei spoke in the Rabbi's ear, **"вашей вонючей жизни-**your stinking life has been ended by a better man."

The Rabbi was dead and Sergei let him slowly slump to the ground. The men walked briskly to the *Pigalle* Metro station where they caught the train heading south and effectively disappeared within minutes of the crime. Once Sergei settled into a seat on the train, he texted Jessica telling her that "the deed is done" and suggested a time and place the next day for them to meet and consummate their deal. The next day Jessica met Sergei at *Parc Monseau* in the rotunda and gave him a zip drive with the pre and postop photos, the Carpue's new names and their address on Indian Creek Island, Miami, Florida. Sergei was on the next Air France flight to sunny Miami to meet Nat and Terri Wolfe for the first time.

CHAPTER SEVEN

"Seems to me there is a fine line between insanity and dedication...I call that line commitment"

JEREMY ALDANA

Flying into Miami International Airport from colder climates for the first time is a shock to the senses. This is especially true for the winter months in the Western Hemisphere, February being the favorite month in the subtropics. It starts as the aircraft begins its descent over South Florida, usually following the path of I-95 if you are coming from the north. If you can see both sides of the interstate from the airplane one can't help but to notice that every house, every neighborhood looks exactly the same. There are no gaps where you can actually see the earth except where there is water. What distinguishes the landscape from the north is that there are virtually no buildings while looking down from 10,000 feet. It seems like way too many people are living on the limited amount of South Florida peninsular land.

You don't feel it on final approach but as you taxi to the terminal it starts. When you look out the window the men and women working on the aircraft and the baggage handlers are wearing shorts and are sweating; everyone has on a hat of some sort, many with Miami Dolphins caps and they all look hot. It doesn't hit you personally until the flight attendants crack the exit door and the hot air washes over the cabin. I'm usually in business attire flying to Miami: a long sleeve shirt, a wool blend suit and the standard suit jacket. By the time one steps on the jetway, which never has air conditioning, everything you have on is stuck to you; your tie is loosened and all visible skin glistening but not yet dripping with sweat. Finally, you reach the terminal and some air conditioning. It immediately becomes apparent that few businessmen travel through Miami; everyone is on vacation with shorts, sandals and an impressive array of t-shirts advertising ever bar and restaurant from Florida to South America. The terminal is a stark contrast to Atlanta or Chicago O'Hare where there are a few families on vacation and a huge number of men and women in business attire carrying briefcases with laptops. The other distinction is that the travelers in the Miami Airport have an exotic flavor, mostly a Latin influence, and the people seem to be happy to be there. Even in Atlanta, a Southern city with its roots in the antebellum South, the airport travelers walk fast, look down mostly to minimize eye contact with other humanoids, and don't appear happy to be there yet in Miami everybody seems to be on vacation.

The ambient temperature may only be in the 80's but for a large part of the year the humidity is also in the 80's so that it feels more like 100 degrees. There are very few places in the country where sunglasses are absolutely necessary. In Miami it is bright, the sun is high in the sky, and the days are long. It is almost impossible to drive without sunglasses as the brightness reflects off of everything. High quality sunglasses with polarized lenses are not just for the rich and famous, if not for sunglasses Miami would be a town of perpetual "squinters." Sunglasses are a large part of Miami culture since the hit television show CSI-Miami devoted most of an episode to the circumstances around star David Caruso(Horatio Caine) obtaining and wearing a pair of stylish titanium framed sunglasses that he has worn in every subsequent episode. For the Londoner visiting Miami, top coats give way to t-shirts and umbrellas are replaced with sunglasses.

Sergei arrived for his first trip to Miami on a typical bright mid-winter day. He always traveled light so there was no checked luggage. He hoped to be able to accomplish his mission within a few days; finding the "new" Nat Wolfe shouldn't be all that hard with the information Jessica provided him. The glorious Miami day made no difference to Sergei as he did his best work after dark. He had never been to South Florida and was overdressed as were most businessmen who traveled to Miami for the first time. The heat and humidity made him uncomfortable and he thought a nice rain shower might help. Little did he know that a rain shower in Miami was like throwing water on the rocks in a sauna; it would cool for a brief second, then there was hissing and steam followed by even more humidity.

He reserved a rental car, but didn't know that the rental offices were miles away from the airport. He was instructed to catch the "Avis" bus to the rental area. On this particular day the "Avis" bus seemed to be the only one not running. Thank God he could wait in the shade. After what seemed an eternity he sincerely thought about either going to the parking deck and stealing a car or catching a cab to the rental lot. The bus finally came and was full, but he had no intention of waiting for the next one so he created a spot where he could stand pissing off several people at the same time. When they finally arrived at the rental lot the airport was nowhere to be seen and they were in a dilapidated industrial area of Miami. By the time he sat in his mid-sized rental his nerves were frayed, his clothing wet and there was no way he could follow the map instructions leading him to his hotel on South Beach. He reserved a suite at the art deco hotel Delano, which he knew was owned and operated by the Russian mafia. Jessica told him that was the hotel they stayed in when visiting with Nat and Terri last year. Sergei's contact was to meet him there tonight so he could purchase a few necessities for the job at hand. He didn't expect his contact to know Nat Wolfe but the man did know the strip clubs thought to be run by the Russians. Sergei would choose from the list the one or two that are the most likely to be the biggest money makers and the ones known for having the most credit card fraud.

It was early afternoon when he finally arrived on Ocean Drive and located The Delano where he checked-in and asked for the concierge desk. Sergei was provided a map and shown how to find Indian Creek Island. He knew Nat and Terri lived on the island in Biscayne Bay in a well-guarded neighborhood and was not surprised it was a gated community with a 24/7 guard presence or the continuous armed patrols on the streets mostly there to keep the paparazzi away. There was no easy access to Nat's property except by water. As a backup plan to eluding the armed guards who were probably not well-trained he could enter the property from Biscayne Bay at night. He'd probably have to use RPGs or explosives to take out the rear walls of the house which were mostly glass to accent their view of the water. Hopefully, he would catch the two in bed: not a very elegant plan but one that was definitely possible. Sergei thought to himself that Nat had good taste in Miami real estate. He read in some magazine that Al Capone's Star Island property had recently been sold again for $10 million.

Driving back to Ocean Drive, Sergei let his mind wander back to the 1980's in South Florida. The entire city including the upper keys was awash with cocaine. He thought the Columbians were basically backwards people when it came to crime and drug smuggling, and that they were not smart enough to take full advantage of the drug monopoly they had. For the people living in Miami it became very complicated with the "Cocaine Cowboys" who were Columbian and the influx of criminals from Cuba. The drug trade and Hispanic criminals made Miami easy to stereotype as it was in 1984 in the movie *Scarface* starring Al Pacino. Sergei had very little direct business with the Columbians even though they continue to provide two-thirds of the cocaine sold around the world.

The next stop would be a small shop he passed on South Beach to buy a good pair of sunglasses. When he walked in the door it was clear by his business attire that Sergei was a tourist. He spent years trying to camouflage his native Russian accent, but the sunglass dude recognized immediately that he was Russian. Sergei was glad to be able to speak Russian to the sunglass salesman who was an immigrant from the Ukraine. The little sunglass dude was an expert at fitting sunglasses to faces and within ten minutes Sergei had chosen an expensive pair of titanium frames that fitted his face nicely. He now and had the absolute best polarized lenses available to battle the Miami sun. His choice of frames was very similar to the sunglasses worn by Horatio Caine, which were a big seller in Miami according to the sunglass dude. He noticed immediately two benefits to wearing expensive sunglasses; first, he looked good with them on and secondly, they made it easier to watch the young girls in string bikinis without being detected. The only place he had ever been where the girls were so scantily dressed was on the French Riviera near St. Tropez where tops were considered optional. The girls were dressed like this year-round in Miami while St. Tropez had a rather short bikini season.

The area of South Beach across from the sunglass shop was about a 100 meters wide with girls occupying almost every available piece of sand. Thinking as a businessman Sergei immediately understood why there was such a huge business in strip clubs; the amount of bare, tanned skin and topless teenagers led the men from the beach to the strip clubs where most of the topless girls worked at night. This would give the guys the possibility, no matter how remote, of hooking up with a dream girl from the beach. The more Sergei thought about it, the more impressed he was with Anatole's choice of a semi-retirement location and choice of vocation-strip club owner/operator.

That night after he met his contact to purchase a 9mm Glock 43 and a 4 inch switch blade, he ditched his tie and walked a couple blocks to the Versace store on Ocean Drive. He spent the late afternoon tanning his face so that he would blend with the other tourists. He told the gay salesman at Versace that he preferred white shirts with texture and soon found out they had several in his size. The theme of the clothes in the Versace store ran toward black and white so he was in luck. He didn't have time for a fitting so he bought all of the white shirts they had in stock and walked back to the Delano. He thought he looked quite stylish in his new Versace shirt and his recently tanned face. He certainly looked good enough to frequent Miami's best strip clubs. His contact had given him a list of the most notorious strip clubs in Miami. After looking them up on Google, he picked the one that would most likely be Anatole's place. His Google search also told him the strip club he had chosen had the most complaints about credit card fraud.

He knew that in addition to prostitution, Anatole's place would also be selling drugs and with the income from the VIP area credit card fraud there was a lot of money to be made in one place. While using the internet in the business office of the hotel he made sure the $100,000 he transferred was available on his credit card. He also withdrew ten grand in show money so that he could buy his way into the VIP area of the club. The eyeglass guy told him that the prettiest girls went for $1,000 for the night, a lap dance was $100 and house champagne was $200 per bottle from which the girls received a split. Once you spent enough money and they checked your credit, you might be offered cocaine at a grand for a quarter ounce, cash only. Sergei was amazed at the enterprise **Anat**ole ran, and especially the credit card scam. From a strictly business point-of-view choosing the right mark to be scammed would be important, but that should be easy in that most of the men with high credit card balances were married businessmen, travelling for work. They had no interest in legal action, which meant having to admit to the little woman at home that he was even in a Miami strip club paying for sex. For reasons of self-preservation most men just ate the loss and kept quiet. The more Sergei studied A*nat*ole, the more he realized that "Nat" was no sciolist, he had thought out carefully his business in Miami even to the change in his name, extracting the N-A-T from the substance of his previous moniker. It must have been his small way of acknowledging his past.

It would be hard to stand out in a club with Ferraris parked out front so Sergei's challenge was to be noticed. Besides being 6 feet 4 inches and weighing 220, Sergei had the uncommon bearing and demeanor of a man of new wealth. The nature of his work meant he had to keep in top physical condition; he learned in the gulags that it was just as important to appear imposing as it was to actually be imposing. His tattoos told his story, but he rarely showed off his ink in public, not wanting to have to explain that which was unexplainable. He knew there was a certain group of women that found tattoos in some way exciting, irreverent and maybe a little dangerous. He also knew that the women working in a strip club would be those types of women. He did fear that one of the male employees might know the meaning of some of the tattoos, which would tend to give away his cover. In addition to his tattoos he had the scars of physical confrontation, which at times was necessary. One of the things Sergei learned that separated him from others of his ilk was that the legitimate threat of violence was in many ways more threatening than the actual thing. As a result, Sergei rarely took his shirt off in public and if he did it meant something bad was about to happen.

The "lap dance" is a mainstay money maker in all strip clubs. The best way to describe it would be cuddling with your first middle school girl friend where the clothes stay on but the friction leaves the guy with a mess in his pants. Now consider the lap dance where the beautiful, young Eastern European girl with a 32 inch waist and "D" cup breasts is allowed to rub on you as you stoically sit there knowing if you touch the girl you will be dismissed to the parking lot, erection and all. It really is quite a brutal experience yet it is like schizophrenia, the girl does the same thing over and over again and each time you expect something different to happen. Other than the Franklin leaving your hand and entering her G-string the same unfulfilling experience happens every time. Naturally, Sergei chose the prettiest and best endowed dancer for a lap dance at one of the side tables hawked by the big Russian bouncers.

The girl he chose had long blond hair and went by the stage name "Monica." The name was probably homage to Monica Lewinski of Presidential blow job fame. Monica spoke with a pronounced Russian accent and related she was from Kiev and was now an exchange student on a temporary student visa at the University of Miami. He had to endure at least five lap dances to wrangle an invitation into the VIP room just as the sunglass guy told him. With each successive lap dance, Sergei became more and more familiar with a different part of Monica's fragrant, smooth, perfect body. She finally asked him if he would like to go in the VIP room where the "rules on touching were not as strict." She left to talk to the bouncer who seemed to run the VIP room in addition to his other of duties keeping the girls safe and untouched by the drunk and rowdy patrons. Sergei made sure she saw his roll C-notes which Monica hoped would end up in her G-string. During the evening Sergei noticed the occasional well- dressed guy exchanging guy hugs with the bouncer before entering the VIP room. He had a pretty good idea how big the room was so he could calculate that each girl was given an adequate amount of privacy in the room to entertain the high-end guests.

Judging from the amount of security and the quality of the girls this had to be Anatole's primary hangout and that he would probably want as few patrons as possible in the VIP room while he was there. Sergei knew that he would have to flash serious cash if he expected to be in the VIP room at the same time as Anatole. There was one other guy in the VIP room who Sergei pegged as the one who handled the credit card information. He was dressed to the nines in a tuxedo, cummerbund and elegantly tied bow tie. He was the only small guy in the building, presumably to be less intimidating as he fleeced your credit card. All of the men overseeing the action were Russian and seemed very protective of the girls.

When Monica returned she led Sergei to a prime table hidden in a far corner of the VIP room. Sergei couldn't spot any video monitoring as what happened in the VIP room, stayed in the VIP room- all of it was illegal. The lighting was more intimate and the music not quite as loud as the thundering bass beat in the main room. He was not in the direct line of sight of the bouncer, the tuxedo guy or any other of the tables, giving the illusion of privacy. Once Monica led him to their table the tux guy emerged from nowhere to offer the couple a bottle of their finest champagne and to take an imprint of his credit card as they didn't take cash in the uber-exclusive VIP room. Additionally there was a $500 minimum, which was rarely necessary according to the tux guy. In the meantime Monica had insinuated herself next to Sergei, as close as she could possibly be. She had raised her arm to play with the hair on his neck as she talked seductively in his ear, her lips brushing his ear as she spoke. Sergei thought it a rather odd interlude in distinction to the previous sexually grinding on his crotch in the main room.

After a short interlude, he noticed tux guy peeking around the corner giving Monica the thumbs up sign. Sergei assumed that meant his credit limit passed scrutiny and they were ready for the fleecing to begin. Sergei figured that every dance, every bottle of champagne, every "courtesy" provided by Monica or the tux guy was recorded on a sheet of paper and itemized to document the evening's festivities. This was to discourage men from requesting a bill of services which would include sexual favors documented in pornographic detail. Monica started by offering Sergei a lap dance, on-the-house, as a gesture of good will and to unlock Sergei's alligator wallet. She took off what little clothing she had on to once again reveal her perfect breasts, smooth bottom, shapely, long legs and her exquisitely groomed body without a single hair visible. She was perfectly manicured, pedicured and sported a seductive full body tan; she was a perfect anatomy specimen.

The music was more of a "slow grind" rather than the frenetic music in the main room. Her perfect tan made one wonder on which beach she was when she got it. She wore five inch stiletto heels, which provided no issues of balance even with small, round -top table dances. The VIP version of the lap dance was an all- together different animal than the lap dances in the main room. The grinding part was about the same, her perfect bottom grinding on ones crotch; it was what happened next that was surprising. She was leaning back, full body contact, completely na-ked, breathing in his ear when she took his hands and cupped her breasts, massaging her already erect nipples. Breathing in her ear that this was way past brutal, she responded at the end of the song that she would end the brutality in a good way-soon. Sergei excused himself to the restroom to regain his al-ready depleted composure and to check and see if the Glock 26 was still strapped to his ankle. The at-tendant in the restroom offered a towel and asked without hesitating if he would like some cocaine. Sergei asked if he could pay cash laughing that this is the only cash transaction allowed in the VIP room. Sergei tried a couple of "hits" from the small gram bottle he bought thinking it would probably be me-diocre stuff, but again, he was totally wrong.

When Sergei returned from the restroom with renewed vigor due to the cocaine, Monica had also gone to the restroom to recharge with the white pow-der, too. The tux guy in charge of the room came to Sergei's table asking if Sergei had everything he needed and was he happy with Monica as his "escort" in the VIP room. Sergei replied that he couldn't be happier. He also ventured to ask if there were any more patrons coming to the VIP room tonight. The question seemed innocuous enough since Sergei obviously wanted more private time with Monica. It was getting late at this point, but the tux guy said they were expecting "the Boss" later on that same evening. Sergei asked innocently if he knew a guy named Nat Wolfe, the tux guy said he had never heard the name. He excused himself as Monica returned from "powdering her nose." Her perfume was French, a fragrance that he had smelled before but it never smelled as good as it did on her. As she sat down Sergei offered her the small opaque bottle with the top also functioning as a small spoon. They both then snorted small amounts of the high-grade product. It's amazing how the night immediately became younger, the music better and Monica even more seductive than before. They say cocaine makes you horny which is an understatement. Sergei had to continuously remind himself why he was at this club and that his credit card was being defrauded even as he sat there; his erection was not totally controlling the situation quite yet, but the little head tended to outsmart the big head in most instances. Sergei was impressed how the people in the club had maneuvered him to a place where cleaning out his credit limit was of no consequence. From this point forward the night was to be fueled by champagne, cocaine and the little head running the show; it was a potentially dangerous and expensive combination.

He and Monica finished the first bottle of champagne and the first gram of cocaine and ordered a second of both. They were feeling the effects of the drug and the alcohol. Monica wanted to give him another lap dance as much as Sergei wanted the dance. She began the "slow grind" as before again taking his hands and massaging her breasts, making her nipples hard again. As she moved her bottom pressed against his crotch he had to reposition himself to accommodate his growing erection. He knew that she knew exactly the effect she was having on him as she smiled as an acknowledgement that her bottom was caressing him perfectly. When the song ended she turned around straddling him front-to-front as the next song started. She leaned forward, her breasts against his chest, breathing seductively in his ear. She then out of nowhere kissed him, deeply and passionately. Sergei couldn't help but to think that she was probably a professional doing her job, but he couldn't help but think she was actually turned on. He was sure that everything she did was probably being itemized and added to his credit card. He tried to imagine how his credit card statement read: hump, rub, kiss and who knows what else. She repositioned herself so that she was grinding on his erection when she apologized that her wetness might stain his pants. She was rubbing him with more vigor to the point she reached down and started rubbing her clit as she rode up and down on him. She put her finger inside herself and then put her finger in his mouth. It was by the grace of God and the alcohol that he had not had an orgasm by now. She was thinking the same thing and whispered in his ear that he must have tremendous self-control. She then offered him another bump of cocaine and took one herself. She took the next spoonful and rubbed it on her lips and tongue. She then slipped down to her knees between his legs as he sat. As she unzipped his pants she said that she promised him an orgasm, she just didn't know how much it would take.

He made no motion to stop her and actually helped by taking his erection out of his pants. Monica was caught a little off guard as she looked up at him smiling as if to acknowledge how big he was. She held him gently in her hand as if judging his size relative to her mouth. She snorted another bump of coke and took a second and put it in her mouth and followed by swishing a mouthful of champagne to wash it down her throat. Her lips were naturally full and colored with hot pink lipstick. Men being visual creatures would notice her lip color as she rubbed them up and down the length of his shaft, both kissing and sucking intermittently. She flicked the end of his penis with her tongue and gently sucked the head and let her teeth drag across where her lips had been. Sergei took this as long as he possibly could before he forced himself into her open mouth, expecting to gag her as punishment for her prolonged foreplay. Much to his surprise, she took him all the way into her throat without even a hint of a gag reflex. He held her behind the neck and thrust several more times to the hilt without anything but a smile.

She knew she had a special talent even if it did depend on champagne and cocaine. She continued doing it without his encouragement, taking him again and again deep into her throat without even a hint of a gag reflex. She knew all of the tricks; using her hand to accent the friction, twisting her head almost violently as she took him all of the way in and then slowing the tempo, slow and deep, gently rubbing her teeth along the shaft. At times she sucked and others she would just open her mouth and throat to create a vaginal feeling orifice. Finally he thought he would orgasm so he warned her that the next decision could be hers. She looked up at him with her big blue eyes and said "do it." As he was thrusting in her mouth he grabbed her by the hair and came deep in her throat; she patiently swallowed until he was spent and she finished by gently sucking the last bit of semen so that the only mess was from her saliva. When she finished she left to go to the restroom to compose herself and reapply her pink lipstick. Sergei needed the time to regain any semblance of composure as he wondered how the best blowjob he ever had was itemized on his credit card; he knew it was probably expensive but didn't care what it cost.

As the night wore on, fewer men entered the VIP room. Monica stayed with him, but they were both spent on the champagne and cocaine. Sergei was beginning to sober dramatically as the time neared for the boss to show. He asked "the tux" if the boss was still expected and his answer was yes. Sergei had downloaded the postop photos of Nat and Terri so there would be no chance of killing the wrong man. He didn't expect to see Terri; he was sure she wouldn't present a problem later. Sergei was trying to wean himself from the beautiful Russian girl but she was still nude and he was still a man. It was 3 a.m. before the staff started to awaken to the fact that "the Boss" was just a few blocks away. Evidently Nat preferred a choice of girls so there were suddenly three new girls present that he had not spotted earlier. He thought to himself that if Nat knew about Monica's oral talent the choice of which girl to choose would be easy. Waiting for Nat to show up, Sergei again excused himself to the restroom where he checked his weapon, chambered a round and let the hammer down gently. He re-taped the weapon with it's suppressor to his leg and on the way out he checked the back door to make sure it was unlocked and that his escape route was clear.

Monica noticed the change in his demeanor, but thought he had become tired of her company. Sergei and Monica were the only other people left in the VIP room when Nat entered with his small entourage. He sent his men back to the main room to be entertained by the dancers on stage as he sat down with the three girls that were waiting on him. He immediately retrieved a bottle of coke from his coat pocket and took three or four hits before passing it on to the girls. Nat talked to the tux guy before sitting down, looked Sergei's way and nodded slightly as if to give his approval to Sergei. Nat ordered a bottle of champagne and started drinking as if he hadn't had a drop all night. Nat and the girls were running through the cocaine at a surprising rate making Sergei want to give Nat some time to get smashed making him an easier target.

After about an hour Sergei decided to make his move when Nat and one of the girls got up heading toward the restroom. Sergei couldn't believe his good luck as the two entered the men's room. Evidently Nat liked a little privacy for his oral sex. Sergei waited until the attendant left the restroom and gave the couple a few minutes to get started before he quietly entered the men's room. They had chosen the stall at the end. The noise emanating from the stall indicated that Nat was enjoying an enthusiastic blowjob. Sergei peeked around the edge of the stall with his gun drawn. Nat's eyes were closed, the dancer was on her knees in front of him as he sat on the toilet not having a clue that anyone else was in the room. Sergei quietly moved directly behind the girl on her knees, pointed the Glock 43 over her bobbing head and fired directly into Nat's forehead. The round blew out the back of his skull. Sergei aimed at the dancer indicating she needed to be quiet if she wanted to live even though he had no intention of harming her. Sergei turned, walked to the back door and exited before the dancer sounded the alarm. As Sergei got in his rental he began to realize that his life had just taken a turn for the better; he would be known as the man who killed Anatole Carpue.

CHAPTER EIGHT

*"Being a woman is a terribly difficult task,
since it consists principally in dealing
with men."*

JOSEPH CONRAD

Jessica and Tedy were enjoying one of the first clear days since the onset of winter in Paris. The weather had been perpetually overcast with rain that tended to come every morning and afternoon. Everyone carried an umbrella everywhere they went. When not in use for the rain, the umbrella became a useful weapon to keep the Gypsy children and other pickpockets away. Very few women carried large bags unless they were carrying food and men rarely kept their wallets in their back pockets. The city dwellers act much like New Yorkers as they always walk with purpose and rarely notice the others occupying the same sidewalk. The exceptions are the people in the parks where people watching is the same as Central Park. Jess had just entered the *Bazar d'hôtel de Ville* (BHV for short) to do some shopping for hardware needed for the house when her cell phone rang. The number was a U.S. 305 area code so she knew it was from the Miami area and it might be Sergei calling.

"Hello," she answered.

"Hey, this is Sergei calling. I have some good news for you."

"Is it something you can tell me on the phone?" Jess asked.

"Not really. I just wanted to thank you because the information you gave me turned out to be fruitful," Sergei responded, talking in a code he knew she would understand.

Jessica understood exactly what he meant; Anatole was dead and a threat no longer to the Merrill's or anyone else. Suppressing a huge smile she finally answered, "That's good, we'll see you when you get back to Paris."

Jessica was beside herself, the deal with Sergei the Russian mobster had actually worked and she had arranged all of it. She thought she should keep in touch with Sergei as he would now be even more notorious and more powerful among his colleagues in the Russian mafia-a good man to have on your side. Jess knew that they would probably need to deal with Alex and Sophie who would probably re-act poorly to Anatole's demise. Jessica didn't think they could trace his murder back to the Merrills but if they thought about it, they may figure out that there were few people who might know how to find Anatole and the Merrills were on the short list. As Jess wandered the floors of the recently renovated *BHV*, she couldn't help but think that Alex would eventually put one-and-one together coming to the ultimate conclusion that Tedy had given up Anatole to the Russians.

Jessica noticed that the *BHV* had become more of a "high-end" store than it used to be. She worked her way down to the basement where the hardware products were located; everything was there as it had been, the prices were simply higher. In the base-ment with the hardware is a one-of-a-kind shoe store where you can actually make your own shoes. You choose a style, choose the leather, choose the sole and heel and from there you can assemble your own sensible foot- ware. In a city like Paris where there are few taxis and only the rich ride in them, biking, motor scooters, walking and the Metro are the pri-mary modes of transportation. The expensive shoes sold in the upscale stores such as Weston, Churches and Tedy's favorite *Berluti's* on *Blvd St Germain* have recently taken a backseat to shoes costing less and providing more comfort. Even the expensive stores now are offering a selection of less expensive shoes built for comfortable walking, yet still having a certain Parisian style to justify the cost. Jess thought to herself that she would remind Tedy about the *BHV* shoes.

Tedy was spending the afternoon at the kitchen store *Dehillerin* on *rue Coquilliere* trying to finish their kitchen. *Dehillerin* is a huge store and had just about every pot, pan, skillet, doodad or widget for the kitchen. Tedy had chosen a new skillet and a couple of pots and was in the process of checking out when he got the call from Jessica. She talked in code but made it clear that Sergei was successful in his Miami trip and they would talk about it at home that evening. It had been necessary to talk in code since the American NSA recently was accused and then admitted to collecting data on cell phone calls of Americans living in Europe or the Middle East. It was easier for the NSA if the Americans kept their cell phone provider from the U.S. - which the Merrills did.

Jess and Tedy spent the evening inside that night. Tedy picked up a fresh baguette and stopped at *La Ferme Saint-Hubert* for a selection of regional cheese and then to *Fauchon* for a couple of prepared dinners of chicken *cordon bleu* with *haricots verde* that they could heat up in the oven at home. After dinner, accompanied by a good bottle of Meursault, Jess told Tedy exactly what Sergei told her. They would see Sergei tomorrow and talk to him in person about the gritty details but tonight they would celebrate. Before they got too comfortable they discussed in detail that Alex Sosinski was now their primary issue. Jess took the opportunity to finally tell Tedy about the "road trip" that Alex and his associates had taken her on leaving out some of the sordid details of the experience so that Tedy wouldn't fly off the handle in one of his surgical rages. Even without the details, Tedy was furious that Alex would betray their friendship after all that he had done for Anatole and Teresa. Because of his trusting nature, Tedy found it hard to believe that Sophie would be a party to Alex's deception. The news that Anatole had been murdered would soon reach the Sosinski's in Paris. It seemed inevitable that Alex, with his government training, would sooner rather than later put the pieces together and figure out that the Merrills were the only people that could actually identify Anatole. They talked late into the night about their options. It was after midnight before they narrowed the possibilities to moving back to the States where they could blend into a big city environment or they could go straight at the problem. Jess reminded Tedy that it was Alex who hired "the Rabbi" who came within hours of completing his contract to kill the two of them. Tedy thought of Alex as a cancer that needed immediate resection before it had a chance to metastasize and cause real damage.

The next day the Merrills tried to keep up the appearance of normality in their daily routines. Jessica was in her antenna- up mode where she was hyperaware of her environment. She hopped on the Vespa and took a short trip down to the Shakespeare and Co. bookstore where she had first been accosted by Alex and his Russian associates. She purchased a couple of paperbacks from 20th century American novelists: **The Torrents of Spring** by Ernest Hemingway, the most famous of the expatriate artists from the U.S. living in Paris during 1920's. This novel was written and published during the time he lived in Paris circa 1926. The second novel she chose for Tedy was **Madame Bovary** by Flaubert. She purposely bought the French version to tax Tedy's French reading skills. At the last moment as she was in line to pay, Jess noticed a shelf with "spy" novels. As she perused the books she was drawn to a group of novels by John le Carre (the pseudonym for David John Moore Cornwell). She had read his novels before and had always been drawn to his "super spy" George Smiley. Smiley was always able to stay several moves ahead of his Cold War Russian counterparts.

Jess chose **Tinker, Tailor, Soldier Spy** published 1974. Maybe Smiley would give them some ideas on how to deal with the Russians.

It was too early in the year to go to the coast for sunbathing but the Merrills decided to leave Paris anyway. They wanted to get away for couple of weeks to let the shock of Anatole's death settle down. They met with Sergei before leaving town, a couple of days after his call from Miami. He related to them how he found Anatole using the information they provided. He described exactly how Anatole was murdered including the lurid details surrounding his death by gunshot wound to the forehead. Sergei's story left no doubt that Anatole was dead and that Sergei had escaped town cleanly and there was no way any of it could be traced back to the Merrills. The credit card that Sergei used was from a stolen identity and he had emptied the account before he left Miami. His escape seemed complete. Sergei mentioned that even in the short period that he had been back in Paris his closest colleagues in the Russian mafia were already showing him renewed respect even though Anatole's death was still just a rumor on the street. Sergei was a man who paid his debts and he thought he owed the Merrills for the information they provided. There was no way anyone would have found Anatole and Teresa without them. The only remaining loose end was the daughter, Sophie and her husband Alex. Sergei and his colleagues would keep an eye on the couple. Sergei encouraged our plan to get away for a couple of weeks as the Russians gaged the temperature of the situation.

Jess and Tedy decided to do a car trip to the Loire River Valley and a tour of the castles and chateaus along the river. The wine grown in the Loire Region was also a good reason to explore that part of France. They loaded up the Porsche cabriolet, dropped the top and headed out of Paris heading southeast toward *Chartres, and* then south to *Tours* where they found a beautiful little hotel with a fantastic restaurant serving great local cuisine. For the next week they slowly meandered westward along the Loire River stopping to taste the local wines as often as possible while also loading the car with cases of the best they tasted. The most impressive castle was a short drive south out of *Amboise* toward *Chateau de Chenonceaux* near a small village of the same name. The chateau was built in the 16th century by an unknown architect and remains today as one of the prettiest examples of renaissance architecture. The couple spent a romantic several days exploring the village and the area around the River *Cher,* a tributary of the *Loire* River. They continued east along the river then angled north to *Dijon* and then to *Nancy* where they visited an old friend of Tedy's from his training days in Paris. The next day they went north again toward Paris but decided to do a side trip to *Reims* to see the *Cathedrale Notre-Dame de Reims* where the kings of France were once crowned. The cathedral was particularly interesting to Jessica who was a student of the Middle Ages in Europe.

Finally back in Paris, they talked to Sergei who had been working on their behalf. Sergei, through his network of Russian mafia members, started the rumor that the Miami people thought it was probably Anatole's daughter and son-in-law who gave up his location. The rumor made perfect sense as Sophie and her father had not been close over the years and Alex worked for the American government and had arranged for Anatole's disappearance from Paris. Sergei in one move had directed attention away from the Merrills and had laid the blame for Anatole's demise on the Merrill's only potential enemies. Sergei felt justified in his plan to silence the Sosinskis before the truth could be revealed. Jessica thought to herself that Sergei's move was reminiscent of something George Smiley would do.

As the days turned into weeks nobody heard from Sergei or his men. Alex left the city, probably renewing his contacts in the Middle East somewhere. One early fall afternoon Tedy bought a sandwich at the *Fauchon* delicatessen and walked across the street to the front steps of *La Madeleine* where he enjoyed sitting in private with his gourmet sandwich. Much to his surprise Sophie Sosinski walked up the twenty or so steps and sat down next to him.

Sophie started the conversation after a pregnant pause," What's going on Tedy, it's been awhile."

"Just living the good life here in the City of Light," Tedy said. "Where's Alex, did he really head back to the Middle East without his beautiful wife?"

"You know Alex; he's secretive about his Middle East dealings. He's been gone for a week and will be gone for a couple more. I can't even reach him because his cell doesn't work where he is," Sophie offered. She was wearing her usual stylish clothes, a wool blend dark pencil skirt; a stylish top unbuttoned half the way down the front showing the upper outline of her black lace bra and just a hint of her "DD" breasts. Her porcelain legs were bare and visible to her midthigh due to the necessity of sitting on the steps next to Tedy. Her red hair was up in a tight French twist showing off her long neck; no jewelry was needed. Tedy assumed this was Sophie's "professional" look, even with that she was beautiful.

Every time Tedy saw her he felt like a school boy lusting after his teacher. She felt this response from Tedy and her attitude varied from supercilious to flirty depending on what she thought was necessary. Today she was definitely flirty. Tedy was smart enough to know that Sophie always had a reason for the things she does; this begged the question, "What is Sophie up to today?" Tedy knew he had been obvious in the past that he thought she was attractive. After all he is only a man.

Tedy finally asked her, "What is it that I can do for you today?" What followed was another pregnant pause. She finally gave Tedy that luscious smile and coyly said, "I have a medical problem that I would only trust you to fix. You can't tell by looking at me but I think my breast implant is deflating and I need you to look at them." Tedy was taken completely by surprise; he had no idea if this was some sort of ruse or if she really had a problem. He caught himself looking at her chest. She noticed and said, "You can't really see it with my padded bra on. If you would come over to my place I would be happy to open a good bottle of wine as payment for your expert opinion." Tedy knew this was probably a big mistake but he didn't have it in him to turn Sophie down. "Sure I'll be there in about thirty minutes," Tedy said.

He finished his sandwich and decided to walk the ten blocks or so to Sophie's place. Along the way he tried to figure out how to get out of this predicament. He thought to himself, *Just be professional, act like a doctor and I should be okay."*

By the time Tedy arrived at Sophie's place she had changed into a Japanese silk robe cinched at the waist. "Come on in Tedy, have a seat and relax. Let me open a bottle of wine to relax both of us. I'm surprised I'm so nervous about this. I guess I don't want you to see me naked with a problem in my breast." Tedy was hoping she actually had a problem otherwise Sophie was playing him: To what end he had no idea. She returned a few minutes later with a nice *Pomerol* that he opened and poured for both of them. They both sipped their wine without saying a word. Tedy started the conversation, "When do you expect Alex back?"

"I'm not really sure. Alex has been out of the country ever since we got the word father had been killed in Miami. You did know about your patient, didn't you?"

Tedy was a little unsure how to respond. He hadn't seen Alex or Sophie since they got the word from Sergei. Actually he hadn't seen Sophie since Anatole's surgery and recovery. "We heard something about it and Jess meant to call but couldn't reach Alex. We actually didn't think it was true because we were so certain his new identity would keep him safe. I guess it was the Russians who figured it out," Tedy said as earnestly as he could.

"He lived a dangerous life. That's probably why he sent me away to school when he did. I guess in his own way he was trying to insulate me from his life style but I hated him for it. He gave me plenty of money but wasn't there as a father," Sophie told him as she started to tear up. "I'm sorry Tedy but he was my father even though I knew what kind of man he was," she said as she blotted her eyes trying not to ruin her perfect but minimal eye makeup. "Excuse me for a minute Tedy, I need to fix my makeup and I'll be right back."

Tedy thought to himself after she left that she didn't seem to have any idea how Anatole was found by the Russians or she had just given an Oscar-worthy performance. She was breaking his heart to see her cry. Tedy tended to believe the best of people so he resolved that she was truly upset about her father and that she had no idea that he and Jessica had anything to do with his death.

Sophie returned after a few minutes refreshed, smiling and beautiful as usual. "I'm sorry Tedy I didn't ask you here to watch me cry about my father. I really need your expert opinion about my breast implants." She stood up in front of him and opened her robe exposing her magnificent "DD" cup breasts. Tedy had only seen glimpses of her porcelain skin before. Even though he had seen thousands of breasts in the course of his work as a plastic surgeon, he had never seen skin like Sophie's. She also had perfect areolas; in fact their pink color perfectly matched the color of her thong panties. As he was looking her up and down she let the robe drop to the floor. He noticed for the first time she was barefooted and that the color of her toes also matched the color of her panties and her now hard nipples. Tedy was nothing if not observant; it was during his moment of pink ecstasy that Sophie broke the spell directing his attention again to her breasts.

"Up here Tedy, I'm most interested in your thoughts on my breast implants. "

"Sorry but I was momentarily noticing how beautiful you are."

"Coming from a plastic surgeon that is a wonderful compliment," she said coyly. "Stand up and let me show you the problem with my left breast. Give me your hand." She placed his hand on her left breast, on the outer part where the breast blends into the chest wall. "Can't you feel the rippling in the implant?" Sophie asked. Actually, he could feel the slight rippling that saline implants tended to get over time. He asked professionally, "How long have you had your implants?"

"About five years Tedy. Does that make a difference?" she asked.

"Actually it does. Even the best saline implants tend to lose volume over time even though they are not actually leaking. It seems they lose about ten percent of their volume by something like evaporation," Tedy told her while struggling to keep his professional composure and simultaneously fighting the growing erection in his jeans. He removed his hand from her left breast and shifted slightly to be more comfortable. Sophie knew exactly what she was doing to him.

"So Tedy, is it your professional opinion that my implant is okay?" she said in a manner that made him think that she knew all along that her implants were fine. All Tedy could do was smile as he stood in front of this almost totally nude, tall, beautiful, seductive woman. The little head was now in total control of his decision making processes. Tedy put both of his hands on her breasts judging their weight, size and shape just like a good plastic surgeon. Sophie moved closer, put her hands on his shoulders and pulled him against her, pressing her breasts on his chest and kissed him, open-mouthed, searching for his tongue with hers. She was deliberately pushing her pelvis against his erection. As they kissed he lowered his hands to cup her perfect, round buttocks drawing her body even closer into his. Tedy was in sensory overload; her smell was intoxicating, her skin porcelain and silky smooth, her red hair up revealing her long elegant neck and she was almost his height on her tiptoes. When they finally broke she began unbuttoning his shirt. She was going too slowly for Tedy's' taste so he helped to finish the buttons. He slipped his shirt off and she again pressed her breasts against his bare chest and kissed him again. Unexpectantly, Sophie grabbed him by the belt buckle, unzipped his pants and pulled his jeans and underwear down to his knees releasing his already painful erection. She wasted no time and took him into her perfect mouth.

"Dam Sophie, you're killing me." There was no immediate response as she kept taking him deeper and deeper into her mouth expertly suppressing her gag reflex. The only sound was the slurping sound she made as she salivated from her mouth onto her chin, finally dripping on her ample breasts. She finally looked up with his erection still in her mouth. She disengaged with drool covering her chin and her breasts, "I've never had a guy last this long. Aren't you enjoying this?" she purred as she wiped off her chin with his shirt that was on the ground next to her.

"Frankly, I've never felt anything so wonderful. Whoever taught you to do that is my hero," he said smiling and hoping she wouldn't stop. She still had him in her hand when she reached over to the table and downed the rest of her wine. Then almost abruptly she took him back in her mouth. She seemed to be taking his lack of an orgasm personally. She was deep-throating him almost immediately. She was salivating again; she used the saliva to add lubrication as she was aggressively using her hand and mouth on him. He finally grabbed her red hair and forced himself deep into her throat as he spasmed again and again until he was spent. "I was wondering if

I was doing it right," she grinned sheepishly. They both dressed in silence. That was when Tedy realized his shirt was a mess and more importantly smelled like sex. Sophie took his shirt and washed it in the sink and put in in the dryer for 30 minutes. In the meantime the two chatted like old friends, which they were not.

Tedy was beginning to wonder why she had him there as her breasts were fine and he thought she knew it. He began to think that she now had something on him that she could use to modify his behavior. Yet he had the same thing on her with what he could tell Alex about their tryst. Maybe they did this sort of thing all of the time. As he got deeper and deeper into his thoughts the dryer timer went off signaling that his shirt was dry. Sophie was back in her silk robe as she smoothed out his shirt. It was good enough so he put it back on kissed Sophie one more time and headed out to the Metro. He took the train toward *Le Defense* exited at *Charles deGaulle* and took the Number 6 line to *Courcelles* where he exited to walk the streets toward home. He was intensely guilty that he was not faithful to Jessica and was afraid he may have compromised their safety somehow. If Sophie had played him like she had probably played dozens of men before him, he had no idea what the end- play was. Self-reflection was not one of Tedy's strong suits as he usually did not like what he saw when he looked inside that complicated brain of his. What he called his "dark side" had released itself at Sophie's; it was a side of him that he seemed to have less and less control over.

That night Tedy mentioned to Jess that he ran into Sophie while he was having a sandwich at *Fauchon*. She didn't seem all that surprised but asked how Sophie and Alex were.

"She talked mostly about what had happened to Anatole and seemed genuinely upset that he was gone," Tedy related.

"Did she have any idea how he was found?" Jessica asked.

"She seemed ready to blame the Russians and his dangerous lifestyle. Interestingly, Alex was in the Middle East again and was out-of-pocket since they found out about Anatole. She didn't seem to know or care where he was," Tedy related.

"Do you really think that's it? Don't be naïve Tedy; he is probably in Miami right now doing his own investigation into Anatole's death. Remember he has extensive resources in the Russian mafia as well as the American government. I trust Sergei for some reason but I don't trust Alex at all after that little ride he took me on with his Russian associates. I think he thinks he can scoop me up on the street anytime he wants to extract information from me. It really makes me angry that he takes so much for granted. I will never be put in that position ever again," Jess said with the conviction that one gets from fear.

"You need to stay close to home until we figure things out. Work on the web site, check the account for the fed's money that they wire for our services, count out our Golden Eagles, but don't go out without me or Sergei. I'll talk to Sergei about hiring a few men to watch our backs until we can take care of Alex and Sophie. We can't get a conceal carry permit in Paris unless we work for the U.S. government like Alex does. We'll have to be careful but you should carry your Glock 26. Since I got the extended magazine it fits your hand better. The suppressor may be a bit much but you do seem to shoot well with the suppressor as it seems to balance the weight of the gun when fully loaded. If you do venture out like I know you will, make sure your bag is big enough for the gun, but small enough to keep it away from the pickpockets. This time of the year an umbrella is necessary to fend off the child pickpockets and also can be used as a lethal weapon."

Jessica felt Tedy may be a little over-protective since she told him about the ride with Alex. Sergei had no reason not to be on their side and Russians tended to be loyal to a fault with those they trusted. Sergei had proven a good friend with his work on the Rabbi and with Anatole, Jessica felt comfortable with him on their side. Jessica was much more of a realist than Tedy and knew that in the future Sophie and Alex would become problems: Sophie probably more trouble than Alex. Jessica knew her husband was smitten by the long-legged red head with the porcelain skin and the big boobs. If Jessica had learned one thing over the years, it was that when her instincts were strong she was almost always right.

CHAPTER NINE

"I became insane with long intervals of sanity."

EDGAR ALLEN POE

Finally, Alex returned from his travels in the Middle East. He called Sophie from Istanbul giving her his flight info into Paris. Alex traveled with a diplomatic U.S. passport allowing him to walk through customs with barely a notice. He was reasonably sure that his employers knew very little about his small arms dealing to the Syrian insurgents but they knew enough to let it proceed as long as his goals did not conflict with the policies of the U.S. government State Department. For the most part the rebels fighting in Syria were Muslim and had the specific and often stated goal of creating an Islamic caliphate across the Middle East, North Africa and eventually the entire world. Alex did the best he could to assure the "right" people received his weapons even though he knew that many of the weapons were resold once they entered Syria to whoever had the cash: Sunni, Shia or Kurd, it made no difference. After Anatole died, Sophie lost her stipend making Alex the bread winner for the family. Due to Alex's competence and notoriety as a gun runner came large sums of money and no uncertain amount of danger. That danger existed primarily from Alex's main competition in the Syria arms market: The Russian military supplied the Assad regime with arms for many years causing Syria to become Russia's only stable ally in the region. Being former KGB, Vladimir Putin maintained his surreptitious connections with the Russian mafia, while allowing his government to have the appearance of neutrality in the region.

The increasing volatility in the region was fueled by the vacuum created by the injudicious withdrawal of the American armed forces and American leadership in the region and the increasing isolationist policies of the current American administration. The balance of power in the region took a dramatic turn when the Americans allowed the UN to relax sanctions against Iranians just enough to allow for the completion of their uranium enrichment program. Once Iran became nuclear capable, Israel was forced to acknowledge that they were also a "nuclear state" by American proxy adding to the nuclear family already including both Pakistan and India. Saudi Arabia was now actively negotiating with the Pakistanis to become the next nuclear state. The hope that rational rulers in the Middle East would understand and believe the concept of "mutually insured destruction" and would be deterred from using these weapons was the basis of the American foreign policy. As was the case during the Cold War, an uneasy "peace" settled over the now nuclearized Middle East. Just beneath the surface the "Arab Spring" slowly evolved until the entirety of North Africa, the Middle East and large portions of Asia came under the control of extremists Muslim leaders and was to be known as the Islamic Caliphate.

Alex saw the possibilities of doing business with these new Islamic governments and was in the early stages of making deals for arms delivery when all of his contacts started drying up. Working behind the scenes, Putin's men made it known that they were going to be the supplier of armaments not only to the Assad regime but to the other members of the Caliphate. Working out of Paris, Sergei and his Russian mob had become the most effective mafia organization in Europe and in the Middle East, with Anatole gone. The first job of the Russian mafia, now under Sergei's control with ties to the Putin government was to consolidate the market by getting rid of the competition. Sergei had only recently learned the name Alex Sosinski. He was quickly able to put together a dossier on one Alexander Sosinski: a low level intelligence operative, husband to a Russian native, American expatriate living in Paris, and a competent small arms trader who had big ideas and someday could become a competitive danger to Sergei or his people. After making a few calls including one to Jessica Merrill, Sergei was able to piece together Alex's organization. He would use the inherent danger of gun sales in the Middle East to cover Alex's demise. Sophie was a totally different problem. She and Alex have been married seven years, but she never traveled with her husband on his business trips to the Middle East. Sergei thought it best to leave Sophie to her friends in the city of Paris- the Merrills. Sergei was committed to the fact that both Alex and Sophie needed to be dealt with.

Once back in the Middle East, Alex renewed his risky arms transactions which seemed insane to his colleagues and to Sophie. He was buying weapons from the arms cache left unattended after the fall of Libya's government. The new government, while on its face appeared supportive of the U.S., was actually weak with no significant support from within the country. Our CIA remained in place providing support for the remnants of our embassy and State Department. As a side operation the CIA was tasked to protect and maintain the cache of weapons we had provided their former leader Col. Muammar Gaddafi. Working through the CIA, Alex was the front man for the sales and distribution of these armaments to our allies in Syria. As Sergei researched Alex's operation he became more and more impressed. Alex leased freighters that were docked at Sirte, Libya near to the place where Gaddafi had warehoused the weapons. The arms are shipped out of Sirte to Cyprus where they are again warehoused until the negotiations are concluded and payment rendered. It is a short hop from Cyprus to Turkey or even directly into Syria. Alex never really cared which fighters actually obtained the weapons so long as Alex was paid.

During the late fall and winter months the weather in Paris is typically atrocious; cold, damp, overcast and bleak. Not as many tourists walk the boulevards and occupy the outdoor café seating still available to the strong-willed. Inside the cafes are warm and inviting, the acoustics terrible and the air permeated with the ubiquitous cigarette smoke. Coffee or slightly chilled or warm beers are the preferred libations. Jessica was truly living the expatriate life.

She spent most of the day exploring, usually alone. During the months with the worst weather she traveled by the Metro using her *carte orange*. Sitting in the Paris Metro stations is warm and usually comfortable. During the busiest hours there can be all sorts of street entertainment including musicians of all type. There are certain Metro stations noted for their entertainment value and the quality of their musicians.

Once outside the Metro tunnels, Paris continues to entertain. The *bouquinistes* or book sellers with their green stalls along the Seine ply a trade that has been part of Paris street life since the Middle Ages. Over the years the *bouquinistes'* stalls have served as rallying points for citizens and students needing to vent discontent, anger and frustration over the current state of affairs. *Bouquinistes* have been afforded a unique status as the only street vendors allowed to work the pavement without paying a tax for the privilege. Jessica was certain that Sergei was developing an extensive dossier on Alex. She recalled that Alex had mentioned trading information with some of the *bouquinistes*. Jess had befriended several of the merchants over the years and thought nothing of inquiring about Alex.

Daniel became her favorite *bouquiniste*. He was young and well educated at the *Ecole Normal Superieur*. His stalls were in a prime location on the river at

Quai Saint- Michel. Daniel seemed to like the attention of the older, attractive American lady and was willing to do anything she asked as long as he got her attention. Jessica explained that she and her husband, Tedy, needed to locate a former acquaintance that traveled extensively outside of the city but had no known address while in Paris. She gave Daniel a detailed description of Alex and a cell to call if he turned up. Daniel kept his finger on the pulse of the city from his perch as a *bouquiniste* during the day and at night frequently holding court in any of a number of cafes surrounding *Blvd Saint Michel* at its intersection with *Blvd St Germain.*

Jess ran into Daniel sitting outside by himself at *Le Depart Saint Michel* on *Place Saint-Michel.* This area of Paris is usually populated by students of the *Sorbonne.* Daniel was holding court with the undergraduate students although he didn't look much older. Jessica was enthralled by him. She maneuvered herself to get his attention and at the same time ran off the coeds as Jess was easily the prettiest of the group and by far the smartest.

"I think you know that my name's Daniel. I'm a former student and instructor here at the *ENS (Ecole Normal Superieur).* I don't think I remember an American so well spoken on French issues."

"Daniel, I place your age closer to mine than your adoring students."

"You are very observant. I only come down here after work for the academic stimulation. My primary job is as a *bouquiniste* up on the quai."

"I detect the underpinnings of a true French renaissance man, selling subversive pamphlets during the day and rabblerousing at night with the students who are rapidly reaching their tolerance for wine. Am I getting close to the real Daniel?" Daniel thought to himself that he would be anything she wanted him to be.

Jessica spent the entire Metro ride home considering the options on how to deal with Sophie and Alex. Jessica believed in her heart that Tedy was probably too naive to be able to deal with the beautiful Sophie as he typically tried his best to find the good in people he came into contact with: a noble trait unless those people pose a serious threat. Later that night she and Tedy had a chance to talk.

"Tedy, I've given a lot of thought to our relationship with Alex and Sophie. It seems pretty clear that Alex could be a dangerous man. With that said, I think Sophie is the more dangerous of the two," she said.

Tedy was pensive at first then answered in measured terms. "I have been giving this a lot of thought. I've come to the same conclusion as you. I believe the Sosinski's are devious and dangerous people with Sophie being the more destructive of the two."

"You don't know how good it makes me feel for you to say that," said Jess." I was afraid you may not agree with me about Sophie. I don't see any way we could deal with one and not the other." I think Sergei believes that he owes us. Let's see what he thinks about the Sosinskis.

The next day Jessica tried Sergei's cell number. He agreed to meet them at *Le Cafe Soufflot between* the Pantheon and Luxembourg gardens for a late afternoon cup of café. Jess and Tedy spent the day deciding exactly what they wanted to ask of Sergei. Alex being an employee of the U.S. government could prove to be more complicated than his wife. When they got to the café Jess took the lead. She thought the best idea for Sergei was to let Alex do what he did for a living which was inherently dangerous. Should some sort of accident happen to Alex no one would be the wiser. Sophie was going to be trickier problem as she rarely left Paris but she did have behaviors that made her vulnerable. Evidently she has been known to entertain men other than her husband when Alex is away.

Tedy called up his most genuine look," Really, she seems like such a friendly person."

Jessica went on, "I've heard that she and Alex both have problems with fidelity."

Sergei showed up at the Café an hour late. Tedy could only guess what issues a Russian mafia boss might have that would cause him to be tardy.

"What do you two love birds have in mind? Maybe Tedy needs to know where to get a sensible set of walking shoes," Sergei offered after noticing Ted's American stiff leather footwear.

"That would normally be a good idea but today we have more pressing issues to deal with. We have a couple of friends that we thought we could introduce you to. We have reason to believe that you may actually have met Alex or heard of him in your business dealings."

"That's quite interesting that you would mention Alex Sosinski as his name has come up recently in my business. How well do you know Mr. Sosinski?"

"We met Alex and his wife shortly after we moved to Paris. It is Alex's wife Sophie who was the daughter of Anatole Carpue: the mafia kingpin who you took care of in Miami."

"It appears that we are closing the circle on these people. It would probably do my smuggling business good to eliminate Alex as competition. Sophie appears to be a problem only because I killed her father, a fact she may or may not know."

"Tedy and I think it would be a big mistake to underestimate Sophie. We think that Alex may have already tied us to Anatole's demise."

Sergei held his cards close, "Seems to me that gun running is a dangerous business. Whether you and Tedy know it or not part of my business is to provide armaments to the Syrian government in Damascus. The Russian government under Putin has been our benefactor for the last several years. We have been given "carte blanche" to handle this business without oversight from Moscow. That your Mr. Sosinski has interests that conflict with mine is reason enough to eliminate him. His wife is another matter which I think you and Jessica can handle without interference from my people. I understand Mrs. Sosinski rarely leaves Paris. I really cannot afford any unwanted attention to my organization so close to home. You two should know much more about her than I do. Perhaps she will remain your problem while I take care of her husband."

"Well it looks like we have a plan of some sort," Tedy responded. "I'll see if I can get in touch with Sophie and find out Alex's travel plans. The next time he is out of town we will try to get Sophie to vacation with us somewhere out of town." After their meeting with Sergei, Tedy and Jessica strolled through the Latin Quarter and brainstormed.

"How do you think we should handle Sophie? You seem to get along better with her than I do. She is not very comfortable around other women, especially if they pose a threat, and it seems that I definitely am a threat to her. If she agrees to travel with us we must be extra careful as she will be working her own agenda."

Jessica said, "I've always thought that she had her sights set on you since we first met. She and Alex lead a bizarre lifestyle which, Sophie told me, lacked intimacy. She certainly is interested in plastic surgery giving you guys a lot in common. I think she's a street smart girl and cannot be duped easily. Do you think you can be deceitful enough to lead her where we need her to be, away from the city and comfortable with the two of us as traveling companions?" Tedy was now walking a thin line; he couldn't let Jess know that he had been with Sophie yet he must agree to some sort of seduction scenario to get her out of town. "I think I can talk her into a vacation with us."

The couple was now walking without a destination. They decided to cross the Seine at *Pont Neuf* where they marveled at the scenery and how lucky they were to be living in such a glorious place. They crossed *Ile de Cite* within sight of the *La Conciergerie* and *Ste- Chapelle*.

Once on the right bank they grabbed the *Pont Neuf Metro* heading toward *Charles de Gaulle Etoile*. At *Charles de Gaulle* they changed to the No. 2 line toward *Nation*. The second stop was *Courcelles* where they lived.

That night Tedy brought together a nice pasta dish to go with a baguette and a nicely chilled Pinot Noir. The general concept on how they were going to take care of Sophie was in place. After talking all night they decided on a road trip to the coast for a long weekend of sun, sand and drinking on the beach.

It was several months before the Merrills heard from Sergei about Alex's presumed travel schedule. Sergei related that Alex was scheduled for a trip to Libya then Cyprus on his usual gun running route. He was scheduled to leave the next week. Tedy still had Sophie's cell, she answered on the first ring. They agreed to meet at a café at *parc Monceau* the next day.

The day they were to meet was one of the first warm days of the spring season. Tedy was early and chose a table outside on the sidewalk and ordered a *café-au-lait*. When Sophie showed up she looked stunning as usual. Tedy kissed her on each cheek in the European fashion and she kissed him square on the lips in return.

"Sophie, you look marvelous as usual. I'm glad you could make it."

"It's no problem. Alex is busy getting ready for his trip. I think he is headed back to Libya but you know how secretive he is about his work. Regardless, he will be gone for the next two to three weeks. You called at exactly the right time to relieve me of my impending boredom. You mentioned you had something to ask me."

"Jess and I want to invite you to drive down to the coast for a long weekend at *St Tropez*. I know Jess would appreciate having another woman along for the shopping. The two of you have very similar taste in clothes and are about the same size. Jessica saw no reason why we couldn't get a suite so we could stay together and defray some of the costs," Tedy offered.

"Tedy, I was really hoping we could spend some time together away from Jessica."

Tedy looked down cupping her hands in his. "I was hoping the same thing. We'll have to see how it goes once we are down there." The two agreed to get together in the next several days to solidify their travel plans.

The next couple of weeks passed quickly. Jess booked *trois billets* on the *TGV (Train a Grand Vitesse)* from Paris to Toulon on the French Riviera. The trip was smooth as silk; the train known as the "fast train," traveled up to two hundred kilometers per hour making the trip to the coast in four hours. In Toulon Tedy picked up the rental that Jess had arranged for the drive to *St Tropez*. The three of them piled into the obsidian black Mercedes CLS 63. Jess must have sweet talked the owner of the car rental agency as the car was brand new. The luggage easily fit in the trunk leaving the almond mocha leather interior to the three of them. The day was glorious so they drove slowly down the coast road to *St. Tropez*.

By the time they passed through the small coastal city of *Hyeres* both of the girls had changed in the car into their cut off denim short- shorts and bikini tops. With the windows down and the sunroof open, Tedy drove as slowly as their 550 horsepower Mercedes would travel.

They arrived at the hotel *Le Residence de la Finade* in the late afternoon and were taken to their two bedroom suite overlooking the water. The hotel was charming; most of the guests seemed to be well off and on vacation from Spain or Italy. The hotel lobby was open, bright and airy, all of the patrons holding champagne cocktails while in their swim attire; the women in expensive cover-ups, dripping in jewels and all of the affectations of the *nouveau riche*. There was still time in the day for some exploring so the three took off for the waterfront. The "yacht" parade was in full bloom. There must have been a hundred of the ships moored in the harbor. The girls and Tedy shopped along the boardwalk finally ending up in a quaint bar on the waterfront. The specialty drink was a local concoction called a *kir royale*. The bartender told us it was made of champagne and a currant liquor called *cassis*. Simply sitting at the table and drinking, the girls generated a lot of wanted and some unwanted attention. The French and Italian men seemed to think all attractive American women were models or famous actresses which wasn't all bad as we drank for free for the rest of the afternoon.

The three ultimately found a little restaurant around the corner, recommended by their waiter, whose signature dish was *bouillabaisse*. The chef came to our table when our *bouillabaisse* order was recognized. Chef described the dish as the traditional version of the recipe from the *Grand Bar des Goudes* in Marseille rather than any Americanized version we may have had before. They ordered a round of aperitifs and discussed their plans for a full day on the beach and in the water tomorrow.

When the *bouillabaisse* arrived to much fanfare by the wait staff, the presentation was beautiful and the dish would have fed eight of us. The seafood broth with a delightful *rouille* and fresh bread was served first. The *rouille* sauce was exquisite with just the correct proportions of garlic, saffron and day old bread crumbs making it an excellent accompaniment for the fish. The fish, shell fish and vegetables were served as the second course. The compliment of fresh fish was excellent. The *rascasse* was particularly good; the *langouste* freshly caught by local divers that day was superb as was the *pieuvre*. We were all full, happy and content walking back to the hotel. The next day would be a big day on the water so we all turned in early.

Tedy leased a sailboat the next day. He and Jess were accomplished sailors. Sophie was an amateur but hid that fact by drinking a lot and talking a good game once on the boat. They were all having a grand time sailing, drinking heavily and trying to teach Sophie a little bit about sailing. Regardless of their instructions, Sophie refused to wear her life vest as it may have been too small to fit over her breasts and was not at all stylish. The weather was perfect so Tedy plotted a course up the coastline requiring Jess to be first mate. Even as they worked to keep the boat on course they continued to drink. Tedy and Jess had no idea if Sophie was a good swimmer or not as they never had a chance to anchor and take a swim since the start of their outing. Tedy turned over the helm to Jess for the return leg of their trip. It was late in the afternoon as they were heading back to *St. Tropez* when a strong wind gust hit them broadside tipping the boat over with Jess at the helm. In a manner of seconds wine bottles and debris were everywhere floating in the rough seas except there was no Sophie. Tedy called the coast guard and helped search for hours with no success. Sophie was gone. There was no doubt in Tedy's mind that she had drowned even though it was less than a mile to the shoreline. The entire plot was bordering on the insane, had too many working parts but had managed to turn out fine. For Tedy and Jess there were no regrets.

Back in Paris no one could locate Alex in the Middle East to notify him that Sophie had drowned. After a couple of weeks it became clear Alex was also missing. Sergei kept his council claiming no specific knowledge about Alex but everyone seemed to agree that Alex would not be heard from again. The State Department was afraid he had been captured like other Americans and he would show up on an ISIS video with a hood over his head. Until that time he was considered missing, presumed dead.

CHAPTER TEN

"People's realities are the result of their perceptions."

KAREN WOJCIK, *UNTIL MY SOUL GETS IT RIGHT*

Back in Paris the Merrill's sphere of acquaintances remained unchanged except for the loss of Alex and Sophie. It was several weeks before Jess was able to reconnect with Daniel, the *bouquiniste*. The weather had warmed and the streets once again became congested with tourists rummaging through Daniel's stalls and seeing the sights of Paris along the river. Daniel usually had three or four folding chairs around his three stalls for friends and colleagues to sit and converse about the issues of the day. This is where Tedy and Jess found him one glorious Saturday afternoon. Most of the talk centered on the American President who had lost the international "rock star" status that he enjoyed during his first term. The students and intellectuals in Paris as well as in other European capitals were initially pleased with the "kinder, gentler" image portrayed by the American President and his progressive view of foreign policy. The countries of the United Nations that depend on America as their protective big brother were not pleased with the manner in which previous administrations had provided that protection; mainly protection from the former Soviet Union. As long as the current Russian policies were non-threatening to the countries of the European Union and NATO, those nations were pleased with the American policies. But, as the topic of today's discussion indicated, the Russians under Putin were becoming more aggressive in their dealings with the Ukraine and had essentially overrun the Crimean peninsula without firing a shot, gaining a cold weather port for trade and for their warships. Daniel led the discussion on what Europe should do and more importantly what position the Americans should take.

The oldest and best- known of American foreign policy schools, one taught to French students at the *Ecole Superieur*, is the policy of isolationism. Of the foreign policy schools, isolationism is the oldest and makes the most sense for a country bounded by two oceans. The "isolationists" held sway even after several years of war raged in Europe prior to the Japanese attack on Pearl Harbor. It took an attack on Americans on American soil for President Roosevelt and the isolationists in congress to finally enter WWII. The isolationists would probably control the policies of today if it were not for our export driven, global economy. Our foreign policy today can be described as a "liberal internationalism." Daniel described our policy under the current administration as one of passivity with a disdain for the projection of American force overseas, especially in the Middle East. Our aversions seem particularly strong when the projection of our military power is for reasons of purely national self-interest. Otherwise, we act only when we have attempted to gain the moral high ground by some form of moral suasion which succeeds only in weakening our position. Daniel quoted America's Charles Krauthammer regarding our need for multilateral foreign policy, "The whole point of multilateral enterprise is to reduce American freedom of action by making it subservient to, dependent on, and constricted by the will and interests of other nations."

"Russia's new-found power was due to the fact that their once dormant economy was being stimulated by the sale and potential sale of millions of barrels of oil and gas to Europe. They are providing, by contract, all of Ukraine's natural gas and their pipelines deliver oil and gas directly to Germany and the Eastern European countries. It is easy to see why the Ukraine is important to the Russians but history tells us that once a country begins down the road of expansionist policies it is very hard to stop without being forced to. Unfortunately there is no one in a position to challenge the Russians. Many think Putin is trying to recreate the 'Old Russian Empire,'" according to Daniel in his latest blog.

According to Jessica, "the only positive aspect of the Russians new power is that they dislike the Islamists just as much as we do. In fact, their number one competitor in the sale of oil to Europe is from Saudi Arabia. It is clear from the American response to the Syrian civil war that we have no intention of confronting Putin's new Russia."

Tedy added," Without America as a real deterrent Putin could recreate the entirety of the Russian Empire by selling oil and gas and without firing a single shot. Most people believe that the global expansionism of the Russians is a direct result of the loss of American influence and most importantly American military power. The American foreign policy team was the architect of this debacle and seemed perfectly willing to "spin" the situation and watch from their gilded thrones as the power of the world is reorganized into something just as bad as an Islamic Caliphate. Russian dominance will be bad for freedom as we know it, bad for liberty and will surely be a threat to all free thinking people of the world."

Daniel was in the middle of the global discussion and seemed the most disappointed in the decline of American influence. He and millions of Americans were snowed by the uplifting "hope and change" rhetoric coming from the White House. Jess and Tedy had seen this coming and acted accordingly after The President's reelection becoming expatriates and interested observers of the global situation from afar. The only time they were upset or disappointed was when they watched a country of low information voters cast ballots for the incumbent because of the promise that they would receive a reward for voting. They were promised that money in the form of new entitlements as well as cash (cryptically known as Obama Stash) would redistribute income from the successful to the poor. Of course, the taxes were raised but the money to raise the poor never materialized and the electorate felt duped. From the dissolving middle class point of view the thought was, "you people voted for him, so it's your mess." Mostly young people were the most disappointed that every promise turned out to be a lie, not a few promises but every single one. It also was obvious that every promise was part of his first campaign and had already been exposed as lies but a majority of voters still voted for him a second time.

Being French, Daniel understood how the dynamics of the voting population could be hard to explain. Even after a yearlong campaign and six years in office the general population continued believing the slogans and had little or no idea about the scandals that were beginning to plague the administration. On this beautiful day surrounded by friends Daniel finally understood how an entire government could function without accountability for so many years. He asked himself and Jessica, "What is the difference between this government and previous American administrations?"

The answer came as an epiphany to both Jess and Daniel. The answer came as the answer to a question; who or what in our country is responsible for keeping an eye on the government so that excesses are challenged? It was clear that the press had failed the American people. The so-called Fourth Estate whose job it was to report on the government, to provide oversight and an honest evaluation of what the policy makers are doing, had failed miserably in their jobs and seemed proud of it. It happened slowly over time but it is clear that the mainstream press had become politicized. It probably started in a subtle manner with the main reporters that read the nightly news adding nuance to the news that supported a progressive point of view. Nuance became a change in wording to push a point finally leading to what we have today where an agenda is reported with coverage of the "talking points" of one candidate or party. It has become so one sided that most people choose a specific network's news to watch because you know which party will be featured on their news broadcast. Everybody by their nature wants to hear opinions they agree with. News broadcasts have become so skewed that important news will simply not be covered if it is negative for their party or candidate. Daniel had newspapers and magazines in several languages from several countries but the only publications that screened the news were the American news publications. The light that came on was that reporting was real in every language but English. The Fourth Estate had failed the American people dramatically because the press liked the President. They were unaware how much damage one administration could do in six short years, even if they liked him personally.

Later that night Jess and Daniel at *Au Deux Magots* decided that the only answer to America's dilemma that could be affected by individuals was to create an internet broadcast which covered all of the news and also oversaw the mainstream press and their coverage of events. The idea of a "Fifth Estate" to cover the American press had been floated several years ago but didn't seem necessary at that time. Daniel, being a French national, had a unique perspective on American culture and politics. Jessica had extensive internet skills and was the better writer of the two. They figured truthful discourse was the most desirable thing that they could provide as the country had slipped into the Nazi version of marketing where all one had to do was repeat a lie enough times until it becomes the truth. In many instances the wrong questions were being asked and no one seemed to be responsible for checking the veracity of the responses. Jess and Daniel could also look at the issues from an international perspective leaving out the party affiliations and the prejudices that tainted most mainstream publications. Commenting on issues a short period of time after the actual event allowed for the truths to become more obvious and allowed for less hyperbole and "spin" in the news presentation. Jess and Daniel wanted to reconcile the presentation of the news with a restatement of information based on what was known to be true. As part of their restatement process they asked Tedy to dissect The Affordable Healthcare Act and explain why the restructuring of the entire medical system could only end up creating a massive bureaucracy run by non-medical appointees whose primary goal has nothing to do with patient care. Judging from the administration's count of the number of new people who now have real insurance, not Medicaid, we could have bought all of them a standard Blue Cross policy and saved the country billions of dollars without dismantling what was the finest healthcare system in the world.

Once Jess and the guys applied themselves to the task at hand, the internet was soon permeated with the day's news as seen from an international viewpoint. Having the blog emanate from outside the U.S. gave it instantaneous validity. Since there was a very short lag time between the events and their reporting, there was no need to "scoop" each other to report first; events were usually reported days ahead of the American media. The trio received a lot of American media criticism even though they tried to remain as anonymous as possible. The new bloggers were hard to criticize since they reported events that had only recently occurred; many from the mainstream media were trying to create a revisionist history to change a narrative they thought wrong because it was contrary to their own political beliefs. The European print media started to print their blogs keeping the less than internet savvy people informed. It took several months to determine how popular their blogs would be. As a group they had no idea how to turn clicks into Euros but soon

Jess was able to make all of the connections allowing their blogs to become enormously lucrative in a short period of time.

Since they first met, Jess and Daniel found much in common while enjoying their intellectual discourse on multiple levels. Being European made Daniel's contributions slightly different in content and tone than Jessica's. Jessica was American as were her parents. They carried much different expectations and were much more animated in their disappointment for the American government. Jess tended to wear these emotions on her sleeve. Coming from these divergent viewpoints caused Daniel to be more lenient of the administration's mistakes as he could compare them to the history of European governments who tended to behave just as badly. Jessica, on the other hand, had only previous American administrations to compare and found the current administration's behavior off the rail when compared to the administrations during our lifetime (even the Nixon administration). This divergence in viewpoints and sensibilities made for an interesting writing style which was entertaining to more people and had a wider audience than other reporters.

Tedy was acquainted with a small but eclectic group of physicians who thought as he did and recognized what was happening to medical care. Medicine had stepped away from patient care as the core objective of doctor's efforts. Doctors were now spending the majority of their time assigning CPT codes to patients and then plugging patients into practice parameter algorithms. The algorithms were extracted from available clinical data that was not always good enough for the purpose of creating these all or nothing parameters. The entire practice of medicine as applied to disease was being rewritten such that all decision making was done by algorithm. That is not to say clarity of thought was not an important goal, working through protocols does make the practice of medicine simpler as the number of choices for treatment are fewer and the possibility of mistakes lessened. With the centralization of medical records the data was available to evaluate the outcomes. All that had to be done was that the right questions had to be asked causing many of medical careers to be based on data manipulation and software development rather science and biology. Medicine once drew the best and the brightest of our students but the challenge of medicine was becoming more of a clerk's job or at best a data engineer.

Tedy's blog on The Affordable Care Act was an attempt to tell the American people the unadulterated truth about the legislation that now was the cornerstone of the American healthcare system; a system that at one time had been the envy of the world. Nobody doubted that the American health-care system had become too expensive and too inefficient to be sustainable over the long run. Since the Clinton administration in the 1990's and the attempt at a socialized healthcare system, it should have been clear what the legislation would look like. This should have given legislators twenty-three years to figure out how to implement the restructuring of seventeen percent of the economy. Yet the rollout was one of the biggest debacles in American history. It took several years for the perfect political storm to occur providing the opportunity for dominance by one party and a leader with the hubris to govern well outside the mainstream of American thought. Many think he was given carte blanche because of our collective "white guilt" wanting at all costs to see our first African-American President to succeed. Everyone probably knew there would be some price to pay but few realized until it was too late precisely how steep the price would be.

The perfect political storm predictably would last the two years while the Democrats had both the House and the Senate. In addition to The Affordable Care Act, it is still uncertain how much of our borrowed money the President spent in those years. The estimates are somewhere in the $4 to $5 trillion per year range; more money than had been spent by all of the previous presidents combined. Tedy's blog tried to tell the entire story as it related to healthcare. There were dozens of "mandates" each accounting for a new tax on businesses and individuals. All policies backed by the remaining insurance companies increased their costs so that under no circumstances was health insurance less expensive. The policies were tailored so that after including all of the administration's requirements the only way to keep the costs from skyrocketing out of control was to offer a range of very high deductibles and narrow the illnesses covered. The tragic part of the entire mess is that exactly the same number of people remains without health insurance as before the dismantling of the American healthcare system and roughly seventeen percent of the economy. Tedy's blog kept track of the massive The Affordable Care Act bureaucracy and the dozens of political appointees chairing a multitude of committees directing the flow of healthcare dollars through the system; and as all governmental bureaucracies, the committees are corrupt to the core. Their meetings are supposed to be open to the public but their strict notification processes are rarely followed. Tedy has assigned specific individuals with the duty of keeping track of each of the committees and their elusive chairmen and women. Even with Tedy's diligence the monster bureaucracy is consuming American tax payer dollars at an alarming rate, which will soon encompass a quarter of the national budget.

Daniel became a constant source of stability for Jessica as Tedy became less and less approachable due to his work on The Affordable Care Act blog. Daniel continued his surveillance work for the French government, occupying his place as a *bouquiniste* and keeping an eye on anyone identifiable as Muslim. He received daily updates by way of the internet from the French equivalent of the "State Department" called the *Direction Centrale du reseignement interieur* (DCRI). Jess helped Daniel identify those Muslim men flagged by the DCRI as being high risk as Islamic extremists. Jessica was valuable to Daniel in one other way; she maintained her relationship with Sergei and his colleagues in the Russian mafia. Sergei was willing to provide intelligence to Jess and Daniel about the Muslims as the Russians tended to dislike the Muslims as much as the Americans and Europeans. Sometimes he would inform on their plots to Daniel and sometimes he would take care of a terrorist threat himself. Either way Sergei stayed in the good graces of the French government and specifically their intelligence apparatus while being allowed to continue his mostly illegal black market activities. The Islamists were a part of the French underground community but are uniformly disliked because of their rhetoric, their unbridled hate for Christians and Jews, and the unwanted attention they drew from the Americans and Israelis.

CHAPTER ELEVEN

"Information is the new currency."

Unknown

Tedy, Jessica and Daniel were becoming the 21st century version of the Fifth Estate. For the last decade the mainstream media had become willing to be a conduit for their personal political beliefs utilizing their position to influence political change. It has always been known that the media tended to be progressive in their politics but it has only been in recent years that media members, especially executives, producers and their talking heads were willing to become more transparent in their liberal politics. This has led to the publication of political opinion rather than providing information and overseeing political excesses. The so called mainstream media has gotten drunk with the power of political influence they wield over their viewers. They no longer monitor the political process; they have become the gatekeepers for one political view over others. Accuracy has been compromised both by the reporting itself as well as the decisions regarding which stories not to report.

It is only fitting that our "free" media outlet, the internet, should become the vehicle for the resurgence of the Fifth Estate. It is not uncommon that in order to see the political landscape accurately one must see it from a distance in order to obtain perspective. It is perspective that is necessary for vision to be accurate. Knowing details may be necessary in some instances to understand the reasons or the historical perspective on events but it is through a wide angle lens with full field vision that provides enough information to honestly assess and report on events in context.

Jess, Daniel and Tedy have taken internet blogging a step further and are using short view historical data that has already met scrutiny, it is repackaging reportage into historical context, available for free. And it has met the criterion for accuracy such that the information and its meaning are irrefutable. In the reporting of historical events, the future can many times be extracted from the past but only if the reporting of the past is accurate and has not been subjected to revisionism.

While the Fifth Estate rose from forces outside the established power structure of the First, Second and Third Estates, it has been established as the independent press and is slowly taking the place of the mainstream media in America. This new internet realm creates a broader perspective where individual citizens (or expatriates) can contribute to the global discourse by merely owning a computer and web access. Most people now understand that the once revered "Nightly News" broadcasts from the three major networks have been reduced to "entertainment" rather than being an important source of information delivered to the living rooms of America. With loss of relevant content from the evening news, the era of the respected, superstar evening news anchor has passed. The same is true for the print media where each paper's politics is evident on the editorial pages and in the stories that are chosen for the front page and above the fold. The economics of the newspaper industry has almost ended honest and accurate reporting by reporters working for the newspapers except maybe the **New York Times** on rare occasions.

Thus, the advent of the Fifth Estate, not government, not clergy, not the press but a separate entity based in cyberspace, unable to be bought or sold or regulated, populated with the new blogger-journalists. It is able to deliver the news of the day visually and by print revealing the bias of the news we do receive and the political slant to which we have become accustomed.

The alphabet soup of government agencies are surveilling the bloggers as if something may ring true and therefore become dangerous. Our present government has successfully pressured the American news media to do their bidding by offering unprecedented access to the White House while leaving the media members they dislike out in the cold. As the years of governmental malaise marched on, the government continued to fumble for a policy even on the simplest issues; and it could only find traction on the major issues only if they could step out front of the parade, which had already left the station effectively, causing the administration to perpetually lead from behind. The government used the NSA to monitor internet activity they disagreed with which meant there was not a thing the feds didn't know about Jessica and Daniel. The two bloggers were too proud, to right in their cause, and too stubborn to shut down the blog under government pressure. The three of them were walking a fine line between freedom and incarceration. As a precaution Jess and Daniel had contacted a trusted attorney outside of

New York City and forwarded all of their contact info including the veiled threats. If anything should happen to any of the three their attorneys would release "the Hellhounds" on our Federal government. Having to live in fear of our own government was a new phenomenon that came to light after an employee named Snowden released volumes of secret information that was accumulated by the NSA spying on our own citizens. The checks and balances to be provided by special federal courts and federal judges offered little comfort as even the judges were political appointees. Jessica and Daniel were certain that the NSA probably had an extensive file on their lives and their blogs.

PART 3
"THE MIAMI YEARS"

CHAPTER TWELVE

"It is one thing to show a man he is in error, and another to put him in possession of the truth."

JOHN LOCKE

There is no simple formula for success in any field of endeavor. After unofficially retiring as a plastic surgeon and spending the last number of years living on the largesse of contracts with the federal government and the occasional command performance challenging the world's latest facial recognition software, we lived with the implicit understanding that our lives could be in danger at any time. This was due mainly to the work I had done for the

Russian mafia in Paris. Sergei, who we considered a friend, was a dangerous, volatile man who ran the Russian mafia in Paris with an iron fist. He had evidently decided that Jess and I were no threat to him or his business and thus decided leave us to our lives as long as we were not in conflict with his people or any of his businesses that were all illegal. Such was the tenuous nature of our lives for several years. Our relationship with Daniel remained active as he continued to provide intelligence for their blogs from the DCRI where Daniel continued as an undercover asset. Both Daniel and Jessica thought the nature of their work as the old "Fourth Estate" had given rise to the "Fifth Estate" emanating from cyberspace.

Daniel provided a unique perspective of global events that no other bloggers had access to. As their internet presence expanded and more and more news outlets subscribed to their feeds, Daniel spent more time with Jessica. Tedy's contribution to the debacle that was The Affordable Care Act and how it affected not only the American healthcare system but also how it affected both European and Asian healthcare systems. This caused him to spend a great deal of time on the road providing an international perspective on the administration of current healthcare. Tedy discovered through his travels in many countries such as Taiwan and Germany were more thoughtful and more successful in their administration of limited healthcare dollars; they had governmental systems to deliver healthcare we as a nation should study.

Tedy decided it was time to move back to the U.S. His relationship with Jessica had been deteriorating for a while as she and Daniel worked more closely together during Tedy's absences. Since they never had children their divorce was uncontested; a 50-50 split of all assets leaving both well off for the foreseeable future. Tedy would, from that day forward, fear for Jess and Daniel's safety both from our American government and Sergei as long as they continued to live in Paris.

Tedy could have afforded to live anywhere in the world with the gold accumulated over the years. He decided that of all the places he had been, he would choose the place where money couldn't buy its number one commodity: sunshine. Miami is expensive and in some ways difficult because of the drug trade and crime but overall the sun, sand and beaches trumped the minor difficulties one faced living there. After all he could always fly to experience winter and autumn elsewhere.

Soon Tedy found a recent short sale of a condo at the Setai on Miami Beach. The view was extraordinary and the building had the amenities he was looking for including a full service spa with a world class weight room. He inquired at the desk for anyone who Tedy could hire as a training partner. The personnel at the desk only knew of one member who lived in the area and who was big enough to train with Tedy. They gave him the name Clint. He left a message at the desk for Clint to call him regarding a training proposition.

Tedy spent the afternoon on the Ferrari website trying to decide on an appropriate car for Miami Beach. After much study he decided on a red 2014 Ferrari 458 Spider. Luckily he found a virtually new car at a Boca Raton dealership which he bought with cash and drove off the lot as he had no other form of transportation. The valet service at the hotel parked the car out front during the day to draw the attention of the other building occupants, particularly the single females.

Tedy and Clint talked by cell the next morning and agreed to meet at the gym that afternoon at 3:00. In the meantime, Tedy logged on to several web sites to see what he could find out about Clint. Evidently he had been around in his younger years. He had a juvenile record for misdemeanor drug possession, had been in a few fights where the other boy spent the night in the hospital with a broken jaw. He was fired from a couple of gyms and a couple of menial jobs where he worked as a trainer and in one instance he was accused of distribution of small quantities of ecstasy. In his late 20's and early 30's he was a body

builder of some repute, never quite good enough to
go pro. Since arriving in Miami several years ago his
record was clean except for a few beefs as a bouncer
at a South Beach night club. Clint always had some
form of income as he lived in reasonably nice studio
a block or two off the beach and drove an almost
new Range Rover. He charged $90 an hour for his
training services, which was on the high side. This
indicated he probably has a small but elite clientele
of patrons for whom he provided much more than
weight training. According to the valet guys at the
condo, he was well- connected around South Beach
and probably knew the main Columbian cocaine
dealers. He also occasionally hung out with several
high- profile Russian mobsters. Tedy knew that Clint
could be a dangerous companion but he would be
a necessary evil until Tedy could make his own connections around Miami.

The last five months in Paris had been tough on
Tedy as he had become soft mentally and physically
in distinction to the tanned, hard bodies that thrived
in the subtropical Miami heat. That afternoon Clint
was introduced to Tedy. He saw immediately that
Tedy, with the right diet, nutritional supplements
and chemicals wouldn't take long to get into fighting shape.

"What's up big man?" Clint offered when he saw
Tedy who stood a full four inches taller than Clint's

six feet. Even at that height Clint weighed in at a bulked up 235 pounds.

"You come highly recommended as a trainer. I need a proper protein rich diet as well as supplements. What do you think?" said Tedy.

"We need to get you a cook to prepare your meals for the next six weeks and get you a protein supplement. If you are truly serious about your training, I can get you some testosterone and a good human growth hormone regiment." Clint offered as nonchalant as one would offer a slice of pizza.

"Let's train an hour a day three days a week. I'll do my own cardio after we have worked out," said Tedy.

"Sounds good to me bubba. You probably know that I charge $90 an hour. If you don't show you pay anyway." Clint smiled or was it a smirk. He knew the hell he was going to put Tedy through. "I'll bring the stuff by your place tonight. You'll need about $1500. Is that cool?" Clint asked.

"I will trust you to be discreet. By the way, don't bother with that shitty black market 'grow' that you get on the internet. I always prefer American products when possible."

"A man of discriminating taste; I can appreciate that, it just costs a bit more. I'll see you tonight big man. I know which unit you are in."

With the afternoon free Tedy decided to dive into to the thick of things and take a stroll down South Beach. The weather was perfect; the temperature was in the low 80's, the sky a cloudless azure blue and a gentle breeze coming off the ocean making it feel like there is no humidity. South Beach oozes with glamour and the definite feeling of decadence-like anything was possible. The beach was covered with tanned sunbathers, the girls in skimpy bikinis including a preponderance of thongs. Almost all of the girls were topless lying on their towels. Tedy's newly purchased Wayfarers were just dark enough so that the girls couldn't tell if they were being ogled or not. Tedy made a mental note to return later after dark to one of the art deco hotels with outside seating to see what the night- life offered after spending the day on the beach. He walked back on Ocean Drive scoping out which bars would be the best location to show off the Ferrari. He thought his 458 Ferrari probably the most eye- catching vehicle he had seen, almost as eye- catching as the Bentley Continental GT he and Jessica had rented years before. All the better to fit into his new home turf; he realized there were too many clubs and bars to choose from, so he would need some guidance from a local. At this point he thought of Clint, who would be stopping by later.

Clint rolled up just after sundown, his silk shirt open at the neck, linen pants and loafers without socks; it seemed like nobody in Miami wore socks. He had a small gym bag from which he produced two boxes with 1cc vials of prescription growth hormone, two 20cc bottles of testosterone cipionate, several small 50cc bottles of saline to mix with the growth hormone and an assortment of needles and syringes.

"That'll be $3500 due to the prescription growth hormone," smiled Clint.

"Why does it feel like I'm being ripped off?" Tedy asked.

"If you want the best you have to pay top dollar."

Tedy grinned at Clint, now understanding where at least part of his income came from, and peeled off another grand. "Here's your down payment on the training. I truly hope you're worth it."

Tedy ambled over to the bar and opened a bottle of high- end Russian vodka he had procured in Paris from one of Sergei's friends. He set out two lead crystal cocktail glasses and poured each of them three fingers over ice.

"Here's to new friends. Let's see what kind of damage we can do to South Beach." Tedy asked if Clint had plans for tonight.

"Nothing solid," he said.

"Well then, I need some local information about the bars on Ocean. Why don't we head down there and have a few drinks and meet some of the local talent?"

"Why not?" I know most of the valet guys and all of the bartenders down there. We can take my Range Rover; the valet guys all know my wheels."

"Did you happen to see the red Ferrari parked out front when you came in?" Tedy asked with a sly grin.

"Yeah, I saw it; how could you miss it? Why do you ask?"

"That's what I'm driving these days. Do you think we can get more attention in the Ferrari?" Tedy asked, already knowing the answer.

"Holy shit Mon, we've got a chance to be stars." Clint knew for an absolute fact the cache that accompanied a Ferrari on South beach.

There was one concession that was necessary to live in Miami. Tedy had always carried a firearm since he was a teenager learning how to handle guns. He owned a 45cal Sig Sauer P227 and a 9mm mini-Glock 26. The Stone Hart Gun Club in Kendal offered a course necessary to obtain a concealed carry permit in Florida. There were very few cloudy or rainy days in South Florida in the winter months. On the first such day Tedy drove to Kendal and joined at Stone Hart to take the course. His skills with the Sig had not diminished much but he still tried to go weekly and maintain his marksmanship.

Although he was now carrying his Sig, he had very little anxiety concerning the run of the mill drug dealer or gang- banger, but he was constantly watching his back in anticipation of running into the Russians who would probably want to see him dead. He was very sure about the clubs he frequented so that he didn't inadvertently walk in a club operated by the Russian mafia. It was his understanding that the Russians mostly owned strip clubs but one never knows where they will show up.

One day Tedy was strolling at the Lincoln Road Mall when he stopped at an outside seated restaurant to do some people watching. That's when he noticed two men with darkish complexions that seemed out of place; they were wearing wool blend suits in the Miami heat. As they got closer he recognized one of the men as being one of Sergei's men from Paris. He knew if he could see the man's chest and arms there would be the usual mafia prison tattoos. Tedy was wearing a baseball cap and sunglasses so he was probably unrecognizable. Even so Tedy was shaken to the bone worrying that he was being searched for. He didn't move until the Russians were out of sight. On his walk back to the Setai he decided now was the time to take care of the problem. Leaving Miami was out of the question so he dialed the number of his Professor who taught him plastic surgery at the University of Miami. The next day he was in the office of Dr. Anthony Miller, Professor of Plastic Surgery at the University of Miami. Tedy explained his dilemma to Dr. Miller, who agreed to do the necessary surgery to rejuvenate and maybe camouflage his face a bit. They decided on a rhinoplasty, fat removal from his neck, fat injections augmented with stem cells and liposuction of his lower abdomen and back both for contour and to obtain the stem cells. Postoperatively he would change his hair- style to one a bit longer; he would grow a goatee, lighten his hair color and get some gray- tinted contact lenses.

A date was chosen and Tedy had the surgery which went as well as possible. He spent the next few weeks convalescing at his condo. Clint brought food every day and helped him keep his face iced 24/7. Two weeks later with his sutures out and his nasal splint off, he and Clint agreed it would be difficult to recognize him and the surgery actually made him look younger and better. After six weeks convalescence Tedy restarted working out with Clint and spent as much time as possible tanning and buying new clothes to fit his new waistline. Because of modern chemistry, Tedy put on twenty-five solid pounds lowering his body fat to six percent. At 6 feet 4 inches and 230 pounds Tedy was a sizable man to be reckoned with. Tedy and Clint spent at least an hour a day with stretching exercises and full contact martial arts training. Mostly what Tedy knew was the

Marine style of fighting, not elegant but absolutely fatal if performed correctly.

A couple of months later he and Clint decide to test the results of his surgery by going to a bar that the Russians were known to frequent. There may be a few women he and Clint had met previously who would probably not remember his name or recognize him due to his change in looks. He would go as a new friend of Clint's. He knew one of the doormen at the Star Club on Washington which was their destination that night. It was thought to be owned by the Russians, who had mostly taken up residence in the Sunny Isles community on Miami Beach. Tedy and Clint had rarely frequented the place in the past before Tedy's surgery. The girls including the waitresses were mostly of Eastern European origin and were uniformly tall and attractive. They ran into several of the patrons and bartenders who were familiar and recognized Clint but had no idea who Clint's friend was. The boys stayed for several hours until they were sure Tedy's new look was not challenged. Tedy made several new Russian friends that evening who knew nothing about Paris or Sergei or the Russian mafia.

Tedy and Clint were seen together several nights a week. Clint continued to supply Tedy his testosterone and growth hormone. Tedy trusted Clint so he never asked where he got his supply. He assumed

Clint bought a lot of product as he had many more clients than Tedy and he was known as a full- service trainer even to his female clientele.

Clint left Miami for a couple of weeks not mentioning where he needed to be so urgently leaving Tedy to his own devices for their now daily workouts. Tedy did his usual Monday routine, rode the stationary bike for about an hour and ended by going a few rounds with the heavy bag. As he was finishing a nice looking brunette, maybe part Hispanic, stopped him to ask about his workout and where he lived. She seemed a bit forward but not too much and Tedy guessed she probably came from old Miami money. When she asked what he did he said that "I just live in Miami" and she knew exactly what he meant. She told him of a Latin dance club that he hadn't heard of up the beach away and asked if he would be her date for the night. There was something odd about how she asked him but he just assumed it was some sort of cultural difference this Southern boy knew nothing about. He agreed to pick her up at 9:00 at her place in Coconut Grove; she introduced herself as Angie.

Tedy was a little late picking Angie up due to congestion on the causeway. When Angie answered the door she looked very pretty in her summer dress and strappy heels; he bet she was a dynamite dancer. She introduced Tedy to a young ten year old girl who was her daughter, Lila. She offered her hand like she was trained and said *"Ola"* to Tedy who responded in kind. As they walked to the car Angie was a little taken back by the Ferrari. She said," I've never ridden in one of these, how does a lady get in? You just sit down and slide you're legs over. It's a bit more difficult in a miniskirt," Tedy grinned.

"Top up or down? I brought a scarf if you want to feel the entire experience."

Angie said, "The weatherman said it might sprinkle later tonight, let's leave it up for now." They chatted for the thirty minute drive up I-95. She directed Tedy to get off at Julia Tuttle, go to US I take a left and go until you see the people. The club was evidently very popular as the parking lot was full but he immediately spotted a young valet who motioned them his way and let Tedy back in right at the door. Almost everyone going in ogled the car, but acted like they had seen plenty of those and had one at home in the garage. Tedy gave the valet a Franklin to watch over his baby, they paid the door charge and walked into the loud sound of Pitbull (Armando Christian Perez) singing. They were seated at a pretty good table and ordered tequila and a cerveza for each of them. They danced and drank tequila and talked and were having a wonderful evening until sometime after 2:00 a.m. A Cuban man they had seen on the dance floor walked up feeling the effects of too

much tequila, and leaned over Angie to say something in Spanish that Tedy could not quite make out.
Whatever it was it made Angie furious. Tedy ques-
tioned her and she said it was local guy who didn't
want her to be seen with a gringo. The crowd in the
room was too big to notice the developing storm.
Tedy started to stand up but Angie tried to pull him
back down. The Cuban saw Angie occupying Tedy's
right arm; he moved to strike at Tedy who saw the
punch coming. He deflected most of the force off
his left shoulder and simultaneously used the back
of his left clinched fist to break the man's nose rendering him stunned, bloody and his eyes blind with
tears. As the Cuban tried to fight back blindly, Tedy
blocked his right hand easily and to make sure this
idiot went away he snapped his thumb at the knuckle
rendering his hand useless. It was so loud from the
music that nobody heard the Cuban scream nor did
they notice him slink away bleeding from his nose
and cradling his useless right hand. Tedy sat back
down, unruffled, needing a glass of water and a nap-
kin to wipe the blood off his hand.

"What did you do to that guy? You went through
him like he wasn't there."

"I just get a little irritated when people show their
ass around me or anyone I'm with. People let retards
like that get away with being obnoxious because they
are afraid; drunken people who act out like that

need to be taught a painful lesson to stop. I guess Pedro, not knowing his real name, won't bother you or me ever again."

"You are an amazing, dangerous guy; you must be from the chivalrous South. I'd hate to see what you could do to someone if you were really mad." Angie thought about what she said for a moment and realized just how inimical Tedy might be. Tedy took her home without a word spoken between them. Once back in the Grove, Tedy got her number, gave her a soft kiss on the lips and found his way back home thinking they had a wonderful date except for "Pedro's" nose.

The next day the thought never came to Tedy that the idiot from the night before was some sort of dope dealer in the Cuban community. That next morning Tedy did his routine; he walked a couple blocks toward South Beach, stopped at Starbucks and ordered a Grande latte and took his coffee down to the cement wall overlooking today's sun worshipers on the beach. Tedy was pretty laid back with shorts, loafers and a Rolling Stones t-shirt from the *Sticky Fingers Tour in the early 1970's.* After an hour or so of girl watching three large Hispanic enforcer-looking guys showed up; one of which had black eyes and a cast on his right hand. Tedy assumed this was the same idiot from last night looking for some payback.

Tedy knew exactly how this would go down. "How are you gents doing this fine morning? Looks like your little buddy there had a rough night of it." The two larger men seemed to be carrying short bats or batons or something. After cursing in Spanish at me, not a word of which did I understand, the bigger guy on the right seemed most willing to move so I stepped closer to him inside the swing radius of his baton and flattened his nose with the heel of my right hand. Then at the same time, I struck the left guy across the face with my key chain, which was loaded with keys and Swiss Army Knife. The big guy seemed to clear his vision. He came at me but was a little tentative, worried about what I may do to his face; so I collapsed his right knee and simultaneously relieved him of his weapon, which would do him no more good. The second guy seemed to have been temporary blinded by my keys strafing his eyes so I just hit him on the back of his head with the baton. I finally remembered to address Pedro. "If you bring any more of these thugs around me or Angie, I'll kill them, and then I'll kill you. I'm sure the police would appreciate you loading these broken guys up and going back to the barrio."

CHAPTER THIRTEEN

*"The Russians are crazy. They'll shoot you
just to see if their gun works."*

RETIRED NYC COP IN "RED MAFIYA..."
ROBERT FRIEDMAN

Sergei continued to live in Paris and managed to keep track of Jessica who he has not seen since their business with Anatole. He followed her blog and enjoyed her take on American and international politics. Lately she was more and more interested in the situation going on in Russia and its Ukrainian neighbors. She couldn't leave well enough alone knowing the number of patriotic Russians who live in Paris, and they did not appreciate her making unflattering editorial comments about Putin or the motherland. Sergei seemed willing to overlook her blog for the time being but he seemed sure one day he would hear from Moscow about the internet traffic condemning Russia's behavior and the so-called negative effects the American sanctions are having on the Russian economy.

The Russian mafia's hierarchy wasn't upset when Anatole was murdered in his own club. They suffered through a short period of decreased income which would not right itself until new leadership emerged. Brighton Beach decided to step in and sent its most notorious enforcer to take control of the situation in Miami. Nikki Volkov was a ruthless taskmaster known for his violent outbursts usually resulting in a severe injury to the nearest person. All of the Miami soldiers knew of Volkov and sincerely feared the man.

Volkov wasn't simply a beast; he had risen through the ranks because he was also clever. When he reached Miami he did a much unexpected thing: He made a social visit to Teresa, Anatole's widow, just to let her know she was in no danger and never would be as long as he was around. He gave her his numbers if she should ever want for anything. This was a kindness that he was not required to do. Yet someday he may require a favor from her and she would be obliged to consent.

Nikki started with the club where Anatole was shot. He reopened the club with a million dollar makeover; more beautiful Easter European and Russian girls, discounted cocaine for the VIP customers and more computer people to run the credit card fraud hopefully making it more discreet and therefore less likely to be busted. The "new" ownership lavished champagne on the opening day crowd; Nikki wanted to be the new king of South beach. Nikki notified his colleagues in Paris that he didn't want to see Sergei in Miami at all. The men thought there might be too many cooks in the kitchen or more appropriately, too many roosters in the henhouse. There were still plenty of Russians dispensing concussions and broken bones while collecting debts at the behest of Nikki Volkov.

Tedy never heard from the boys from the barrio nor did he ever hear from Angie again. She must have thought that Tedy's methods were a bit extreme for her tastes or she actually knew Pedro and wasn't as offended by his boorish behavior as Tedy was. Regardless, Tedy was becoming known as a man who could take care of himself in a fight so most of the time the bad people left him alone unless they wanted a shot at the South Beach title.

Tedy knew that the Russian mafia was a presence in Miami but he was informed through Clint that they were infinitely stronger in Miami than in

Paris. Clint told Tedy the story of a Russian mafia guy who was arrested trying to sell a Russian submarine to the Columbians. The sub was to come equipped with a seventeen man crew. The Russians were taking over organized crime where ever they lived and Miami was one of their most popular locations now. Offering slightly used Russian military equipment to the Columbians was easy for Volkov; now the undisputed head of the Russian crime syndicate in South Florida.

There had been a several year lull in the Miami real estate market which Nikki immediately took advantage of. He began buying up houses, condos and art deco real estate near and on South Beach. He opened several more nightclubs and even a few sleazy strip bars on more isolated property, more inland. Even Anatole would be amazed how fast Nikki worked. The coup de grace was his deal with the Columbians, who he distrusted and thought were weak, for speed boats, helicopters and even small two- man submarines to facilitate the import of drugs and weapons into Miami. The outward bound subs delivered tons of money to various Caribbean and South American banks to be laundered before returning to Miami in the form of low cost real estate investment loans. Nikki took care of these deals himself as he also had a degree in International Finance from the Sorbonne in Paris.

Nikki's chest and shoulders were covered with tattoos he received in a Russian jail. He was careful not to have any ink which showed outside a dress shirt as his plan from the beginning was the business end of the mafia. He was about 5 feet 11 inches tall but built stocky from years of working out in prison. About forty-five years old with short blond hair and azure colored blue eyes, he would have been an attractive man except for his teeth, constant scowl and look of disapproval. He tended to dress like a wealthy man of leisure yet his hands betrayed him; they were those of a manual laborer, thick knuckles, several damaged and crooked fingers, and a thick callous on his palm mostly from lifting weights. They were the hands of a man who did manual labor and used his hands as weapons.

Tedy and Clint kept up their work- out routine pushing each to get the most out of their time in the gym. They frequented all of the hot night spots, mainly on the weekends, and during the week they frequently went out on Tedy's 50 foot Bertram sport fishing yacht docked on the intracoastal not far from the Setai. Tedy hired a sixtyish year old boat captain named Ernie mainly because he could find the fish when no one else could and he also had great stories about old Miami and even a few about Papa Hemingway in the day. They were probably all lies but he was an enormously entertaining old guy and he was honest. Tedy let him sleep on the boat as partial payment for his services; and he allowed him to partake of the Cuban rum he stocked on the boat called Havana Club, but only when Ernie was off the clock.

One Saturday at the gun club, Tedy met a former Delta Force guy. The conversation finally came around to personal defense, in particular knife fighting. Tedy learned that the Delta Force guys and the Navy Seals were the two branches of the military where the almost lost art of knife fighting was still taught. Since Tedy was by trade a surgeon, Mac thought he would be a good study and may even help to clarify a few of the finer points of the human anatomy.

Mac started, "We will be training with the United States Marine Corps Ka-Bar knife identified by the leather handle and the 7 inch straight, non-serrated blade. As Mac showed Tedy the details of the knife, weight, balance and the feel of it in one's hand, it looked like a musical instrument, both left and right hands were equally facile. He started with a few basic concepts; no fight is fair, it is best to strike first and strike hard, try to maintain distance and use your feet as much as possible to attack your enemy. Finally, it is to your advantage if you know some basic human anatomy; people will try to protect their face at all cost, so keep your knife movement from the shoulders up pulling his defense up opening you for a devastating kick to the groin, chest or knee, any of which could allow you to escape. If you cannot run and escape then know the areas of the body that are vulnerable to a knife wound and those that are not. Your most vulnerable areas are your face, hands and chest area. The wrist, elbow, neck are areas where small wounds can incapacitate because of their superficial location. Mac showed him how to quickly get out of his shirt or t-shirt and wrap his left forearm to use as a defensive weapon against your opponent's knife.

Mac and Tedy spent the afternoon at the outside combat range practicing both stationary and non-stationary shooting techniques with both the Sig 45 and the Glock 9mm.

Tedy finished the afternoon at the indoor range killing paper targets with bad guys printed on them. After about 300 rounds his groupings were consistent so he packed up his shooting glasses, ear protection, and headed back home to shower off the smell of cordite and gunpowder.

Tedy spent the evening cleaning his weapons just like he was taught. After an exhausting day with Mac, who was quite a taskmaster, Tedy decided to stay in and listen to some classic rock music, throw together a crab quiche and open a nice slightly chilled *Meursault*. He set the table outside on the patio and enjoyed another beautiful Miami evening; the temperature in the low 80's, a slight breeze off the ocean making the humidity feel low and dispersing the mosquitos. The quiche had a nice flaky crust with a tasty filling of large lump crab meat, leeks and Parmigiano reggiano cheese. Tonight was to be a Led Zeppelin concert until it was time for bed. He doubted the neighbors were Zeppelin fans, but they would just have to get over it tonight. The music always created calmness in his thoughts that Tedy desperately needed tonight. He remembered the good times with Jess and actually missed her from time to time as he did tonight. He looked carefully at his hands, stretched his fingers out and cracked his knuckles, contemplating whether or not he could still perform the delicate plastic surgery procedures he performed for years. His hands felt well, no arthritis yet and his brain seemed to work as good as or better than ever. He thought through the steps of his favorite operations, seemed to recall every detail, and felt even more relaxed than usual as he worked through the operative details again and again. He thought about his old friend Sergei and the Russians wondering what they were doing to terrorize the citizens of Paris and how Jessica and Daniel were doing. He actually wished them the best. In that place just before sleep takes over, Tedy recalled a Miami Herald article about the "new" Russian mafia in

Miami run now by Nikolai "Nikki" Volkov, who the feds and Miami Police knew virtually nothing about except they thought he was from St. Petersburg and had spent some time in Cyprus and then Brighton Beach. Most in the know thought he was the top enforcer in the U.S. for the Russian mafia. He was ruthless, powerful and untouchable: a formidable foe for anyone.

CHAPTER FOURTEEN

"Isn't the human body a miracle?"

Shane Flynn

The nights are clear and warm, the sky liquid black with a kaleidoscope of stars, planets-the Milky Way. There is always a slight breeze and the smell of the ocean, humidity and the fragrance of the myriad of sea creatures both dead and alive. It was February and the Miami International Boat Show was on full display along the Intracoastal Waterway directly in front of Collins Avenue. The boardwalk was busy with couples strolling and dreaming of owning one of the glorious yachts moored along the dock. Tedy loved the smells and sounds of the waves buffeting the sides of the yachts as locals plied the waterways in their smaller motorboats to see the yacht parade with boats totally out of financial reach in this life or any life. Just out of the shower after a day on the beach, Tedy was leisurely walking the boardwalk; just a hint of burning from a day in the sun, wondering if he would ever own one of these behemoth vessels. His common sense always prevailed: too big, too expensive, too much upkeep and easy for Tedy to borrow or lease. He thought his Bertram was enough boat for him.

His silk shirt clung to his damp skin as he walked into the nightly breeze. The incandescent lamps lighting the boardwalk emitted a rainbow of colors, there was always a slight mist coming off the inter-coastal waters; the water droplets became a prism, diffusing the incandescent light creating a rainbow around each bulb. Tedy's attention was on the yachts and pretty girls in bikinis and tropical wraps worn to protect their nubile bodies from the night breeze. The hawkers were beautiful models in revealing sun dresses, inviting the passersby on board. It was at this moment he first noticed a single man who stood out because almost everybody else was coupled and because of his out- of- place Hawaiian shirt and his sheer size. Tedy was about half way between the lights where there was a slightly darker area when the man, who was now about ten feet in front of Tedy, raised his right hand holding a gun. He heard the gunshot a millisecond before he felt the searing pain in his side and abdomen. The walkway was fairly crowded so the man luckily didn't have the opportunity to fire a second round into his body. Tedy's first thought was that the man wasn't a very good shot or he would be on his back with a hole in his forehead. There was some pain but not much. He thought that the shot may have only grazed him until he reached down to his abdomen and side and felt the sticky ooze from the hole he found there. He looked at his hands seeing the amount of blood leaving his body, and felt his entire body shutting down even though he was mentally trying to walk and seek help. He simply sat down as the crowd surrounded him trying to provide aid and comfort, but actually occupying the space he needed for air. A woman who obviously had some medical training knelt next to him and used her wrap to put pressure on the gaping wound and calmly told a man to call 911. He felt someone place something under his head as he raised his head momentarily trying to focus his eyes but seeing nothing but shapes moving about, no details, no colors: just ghostly figures. The woman helping him was talking at him but he couldn't understand what she was saying. All he could hear was the frenzied talking and the high pitched scream of vehicles in the street. For some reason the wound ceased to hurt and instead he felt the wetness from his blood on his shirt and pants and even the pooling blood underneath his body. As he thought he would close his eyes and give in to his body's wishes, he was besieged with men in blue jumpsuits, which he thought odd clothing at that moment, placing a mask on his face, taking his blood pressure and speaking loud and urgently to each other.

Usually needle sticks hurt like hell but he felt nothing as they penetrated both his arms with large needles. He felt the coldness of the fluids going up his arm. His mind kept telling him to fight but nothing would move. He gradually realized he could move his fingers and toes, which seemed a good thing. He was turned on his side and felt the blue men feeling his back, evidently looking for exit wounds or maybe another gunshot wound. A hard board was placed beneath him and he was briskly lifted off the ground. He had the sensation of movement almost like he was flying above the scene. He was lowered quickly to a gurney and shoved quickly into the waiting vehicle where there was constant chatter among the blue men, one on the telephone, one fumbling with his wallet and reading his driver's license and unceremoniously noting out loud that he was an organ donor. He could feel the urgent movement around him and the urgent pleas to take a deep breath, again and again. He noticed the movement of the vehicle, side to side as we rounded corners at a high rate of speed, the braking and sirens and horns as we went through intersections, and finally braking at the emergency room of which hospital he had no clue. While barely conscious he heard the blue man telling the woman in the bright white coat a brief synopsis of who he was: BP 90 over 50, pulse 150 respirations 10 per minute and oh yes, the guy's a doctor, evidently a plastic surgeon, name Edward Merrill. The white coats were now in charge, giving orders that Tedy had given hundreds of times as a resident. The key word was "blood," getting it, giving it and then movement again as the main guy bent over, telling Tedy he was going to be alright as he lost consciousness – finally.

There was a three day gap that Tedy would never recover. As his head began to clear he felt something being ripped from his throat and the white coat and nurse encouraging him to take deep breaths and he, by reflex, coughed. Words cannot describe the pain he felt in his abdomen realizing for the first time the extent of the incision from above his belly button to his pubis. He promised himself not to give in to another cough reflex for a while longer. They were letting him wake up slowly as Tedy started to take inventory of his situation. He had a beautiful nurse who was in control of his entire existence, most importantly his pain control. He had the urge to pee, the nurse noticed him squirming a bit and told him he had a catheter in his bladder that may give him the impression he needs to urinate. Tedy looked down to confirm and was surprised by the amount of blood in his urine. The nurse noticed his concern and said it was getting better every day and that it was there because the surgeon had to remove his left kidney. He noticed she called him Dr. Merrill thinking it may get him preferred treatment; a thought that was probably untrue but it calmed him anyway. She was also in charge of all of his bodily functions and the myriad of tubes and devices monitoring his every orifice.

His doctors and nurses begin to slowly remove the tubes and devices that had kept him alive for the last five days and with their removal his brain began to function again. The fog of trauma, surgery and the narcotic haze was lifting as he required less and less pain medication. To recover fully, Tedy knew he had to get up and start walking. Initially, the nurses had to help him keep track of his IV pole and catheter drainage bag. Later in the day he told his doctor that he would pull the catheter out if they did not. His urine was still slightly blood tinged but they took his threat seriously and removed his bladder tube. This would give Tedy another reason to get out of bed.

When he was discharged several days later, Tedy came to grips with the fact that somebody tried to kill him. He was clear enough to understand that whoever it was would now know that they had failed to end his life. Until he was functional, Clint, who was the only person to visit Tedy in the hospital, agreed to stay with him at his condo until he could protect himself from further attacks.

The Miami-Dade cop who spoke to him in the hospital showed up to finish his interview with Tedy about the details of his shooting. Tedy had little recognition of who shot him except to say it was a rather short, stocky guy, Caucasian with no facial hair and possibly a low, simian hairline. Everything else was fuzzy and the man was partially in the shadows on the walkway. Tedy kept it to himself that he knew it was a Russian Mafia hit man who shot him. He withheld from the detective why he thought the Russians would want him dead. Tedy knew that no one was murdered by the Russians if it wasn't sanctioned by Nikki Volkov himself. After the detectives left, he and Clint started to formulate a plan to get some payback from the Russians. Tedy didn't come clean with Clint about his past relationship with the Russian mafia in Paris. As he was talking with Clint, it dawned on him that Jessica and Daniel may be in danger back in Paris. He hadn't spoken to the couple in several years but he still had some numbers to call in case of emergencies. He knew Jess was a smart lady and had probably seen the page seven articles in the Miami Herald that mentioned a recent increase in gun violence in the tourist areas of Miami. No one except the mayor and his police force cared about the constant violence in Liberty City or the Little Haiti sections of the city but they always responded aggressively when the tourist areas of Miami were threatened. Tedy couldn't get her on the phone so he left a message on her Facebook page to contact him.

It took six weeks for Tedy to get his strength back with Clint's help. The eight inch scar on his abdomen was the only residual from the shooting. He continued to check his Facebook page and email daily, but there was not a word from Jess or Daniel. Tedy surmised that Daniel used his French government contacts for information about the Russians, and he had used that information to keep track of Sergei. They may have even left Paris for the time being in case there was anything going on with the Russians. Tedy knew Daniel and Jessica were resourceful people and would not unnecessarily put themselves in danger. They probably left Paris for an extended vacation as they could continue their internet blogging from anywhere in the world there was an internet connection. Tedy, keeping track of their blogs, noticed there were recent postings having to do with the global influence of the resurgent Russian mafia. He hoped they didn't do anything to pro-voke Sergei and the Russians in Paris.

❧

After about three months Tedy felt and looked back to normal. The only significant change he made was that he never left the house without his Sig Sauer. He figured he would have to defend himself against a second attack by the Russians. What he had learned about Nikki Volkov told him the man never left any-thing undone, and he would send more than one as-sassin next time. The man who failed to kill him was probably gator bait in the Everglades by now. He also learned that Nikki was a patient man who would bide his time until the police investigation turned cold to make his next move. In the meantime Clint and Tedy would frequent all of the clubs and bars thought to have a connection to the Russians to see if they could get a fix on the weekly movements of one Nikki Volkov. Nikki was nothing if not arrogant; figuring his entourage and his reputation would keep him rel-atively safe from those who would do him harm but in the back of his mind was how his predecessor Anatole was murdered in one of their clubs in the bathroom.

Tedy was lucky that he had but one friend, Clint, and no living family as Volkov was known to target any-one close to his marks. Clint was careful and could take care of himself but he and Tedy tended not to go out at night alone so that they could watch each other's back.

His body had healed from the gunshot wound and he learned that the human body could survive on one kidney with no adverse effects. He also learned the mental recovery from life threatening disease or trauma is much harder than the healing of incisions; his mind now focused on more philosophical issues such as his place in the universe and the presence of heaven or hell. Additionally, Tedy now suffers from a common ailment that post-trauma victims tend to have-insomnia. As long as the sun was out everything seemed to be normal but after the sun went down the demons tended to keep him awake no matter what he did to stimulate sleep. His mind cranked up in the stillness of the night and was uncontrollable at times; neither alcohol, pills nor Chinese herbs and tea or exercise before retiring relieved him of nights where he was up and down every hour causing him to be exhausted from the struggle. Muscle aches, shooting pain in his legs and feet, incisional pain and busy legs were attacking every night. Tedy understood that a lack of sleep for three or more nights at his age led to delusions and a frantic search for sleep. At the three day point he would do almost anything to get a few hours of good sleep. When Tedy did manage to sleep his was tortured by the succubus of his dreams.

CHAPTER FIFTEEN

"Man is nothing else but what he makes of himself. "

JEAN-PAUL SARTRE

E very major metropolitan city has its own version of the "Urban Hunter" mythology. Large, over-populated cities always have crime and on occasion crimes of violence that go unsolved for years. As these cases begin to accumulate crime reporters begin to romanticize these felons and ascribe to them catchy nick-names used only by the press to romanticize their felonies mainly because they are able to escape detection and arrest giving them an outlaw quality harkening back to "Jack the Ripper," "Pretty Boy"

Floyd and the "Unabomber." These men met their fate with a violent death except "The Unabomber," Ted Kaczynski, who to this day is rotting in a federal prison somewhere in the U.S. Over the years there have been dozens of "Cocaine Cowboys" who have emerged as the leader of the Columbian or Cuban Mariel boatlift survivors who would qualify as a romantic outlaw in the City of Miami. Today there is only one who is both an outlaw and immune to the Miami-Dade police and able to escape the feds both FBI and DEA; that man is Nikki Volkov.

If first impressions are of any predictive importance, Volkov makes most people shiver when introduced to him. He dresses immaculately, but it doesn't look good on him because his physique is square. Clothes make him look fat which he definitely is not. His hair is thick, blond and wavy with too much on his forehead making him appear simian. He has deep wrinkles from excessive sun exposure and a year- round tan. His hands are thick and calloused, those of a manual laborer in the Miami summer heat, except his nails manicured and polished, out- of- place with rest of his body. It is intended to reflect some sort of primeval version of class. Under his shirts, which are uniformly long- sleeved year- round, is an entire torso covered with prison tattoos outlining his place in the prison hierarchy and the number of heinous crimes he perpetrated on his fellow prisoners. The ink was carefully done to omit his wrists and neck, or he had those tattoos removed, so he could interact with normal people in the financial and banking worlds. It had to be quite a shock for someone to see him take off his shirt for the first time. From Tedy's point of view, Nikki's only redeeming value was that he still liked to get his hands dirty, to dole out punishment to his own men and certainly anyone else who stood up to him. This seemed to be his only weakness: one could provoke him into confrontation and get close to the man. He normally traveled in a bullet-proof Cadillac limousine which seemed to pay homage to the gangsters of old. He traveled in Miami with only two bodyguards, a form of arrogance on his part, as he thought that was plenty of muscle and he could take care of himself. It looked like, to Tedy, that the way to get to the big man was to appeal to his arrogance.

For a man who was a physician, taught to heal the sick and to "do no harm," Tedy was in the early stages of life altering decisions, now ignoring any family traditions or ethical rules that would help him define the meaning of the rest of his life. He realized that his struggle would be an internal one; inchoate yet formed well enough in the darker recesses of his mind for Tedy to feel its pull, its wrongness, its necessity in order to save his life. He knew his decisions would define his personal nature and he knew the decisions he was making were irrational when one looked at his life up until his near death experience at the hands of Nikki Volkov. He had learned in a college philosophy course years ago that "a person is at his best when struggling against their individual nature, fighting for life." He never considered himself an existentialist but he guessed that is exactly what he had become.

It had been six months since Tedy was shot; there had been no contact with the Russians. He and Clint worked out and then retired to Tedy's condo to re-hydrate when Tedy broached the subject of Nikki Volkov. "I think I'm finally ready to deal with the Russians. I've been having crazy dreams and all of them tell me that they will be coming for me soon, the Russians that is. I've been working on a plan in my head for a couple of weeks. With each iteration of the plan, two people are needed to accomplish the goal to kill Volkov."

Clint was listening carefully and replied, "I've been wondering when this day would come. I've actually thought about my answer a lot. Early on I thought I shouldn't get involved. I didn't want to put myself in harm's way because I didn't know you that well. Since I have watched you struggle and work to get back to normal, I've realized we have become friends. I've grown to respect your grit and moti-vation to regain not only your physical health, but your mental health also. I also know you are one crazy sonofabitch and have thought this through and you wouldn't put yourself or more importantly me into any more danger than absolutely necessary. In answer to your question, I'm with you all the way."

After months of surveillance, the only repetitive and therefore predictable part of Nikki's day was his stop at a coffee shop on US 1 on the way to his office. This is the only place that he would exit his bullet proof car with one of his men and pick up two coffees with milk and a double shot of expresso. He would miss a lot of days, never did he get coffee on the weekends but he was almost 100 percent on Monday morning at 7:30 on the dot. Rather than try to shoot him in a public place, Tedy thought it better to find a way to add something to the coffees realizing there would be two drinkers and therefore two deaths. Tedy didn't really care just as long as one of them was Nikki. He also knew that all of the Russians smoked in the car. Using his medical knowledge and what was available, Tedy decided that highly concentrated nicotine would be odorless in their coffee; smoking cigarettes would also camouflage the taste if any. The substance could be bought anonymously from chemical research companies over the internet. Tedy put in the order to be delivered to a post office box in about a week.

In the meantime Tedy ingratiated himself to the morning staff at the coffee shop so that his or Clint's presence wouldn't be out of the ordinary. He knew that Nikki probably knew what he looked like so the plan would be for Clint to poison their coffee while Tedy stood ground outside under cover in case Nikki didn't show or stayed in the car. If the poison didn't get into the coffee for any unknown reason, the backup plan would be a walk- by shot to the head as the Russians entered the limo. If neither was possible, they would keep their cover and come back in a couple of weeks.

The week after Tedy received the clear liquid nicotine product was, at times, full of despair as Tedy struggled with the part of his mind that was a doctor treating the maladies of mankind versus the iniquitous, homicidal killer that he soon would become.

Tedy, in a Miami Marlins baseball cap and wraparound sunglasses, and Clint arrived at the coffee shop at 6:30 a.m. in the morning, separately, and bought a copy of the Miami Herald and a Grande latte much like everyone else in the coffee shop that morning. Tedy always enjoyed the writings and editorials written by Carl Hiasson who was again on a rant about future development of the Everglades and the alligator found in his swimming pool. Just before the time they expected the Russians, Tedy took his coffee and paper to a bench across US 1 that advertised a lawyer who promised to make everyone pay for the implicit damages done by their doctor. He had Clint on speed dial and notified him the minute the Russian's limo was in sight. There were the expected two body guards and a driver in the limo. Nikki and one guard exited the curbside door and entered the coffee shop. Clint had already gotten in line and ordered another latte. His timing was such that he would be at the pickup counter at the same time as the Russians. They ordered two coffees. Clint was able to add a couple of teaspoons of the liquid to each cup as the barrister was calling their names. With his mission complete he called Tedy who fetched the car and picked up Clint. They planned to follow the limo at a distance to see if any alarms rang. About ten minutes into the ride toward Nikki's office the limo pulled to the side of the road, stopped momentarily, and then sped off erratically heading in the general direction of South Miami Hospital.

CHAPTER SIXTEEN

"We are the sum total of our experiences."

B.J. Neblitt

Reverdin was not well known outside his narrow circle of friends in the city of Miami. Among his lawyer colleagues few have actually been introduced to him and those that have hold widely divergent opinions about the man. He is variously described as a man in his 40's, maybe 50's, less than 6 feet tall, and his physical stature would be called stocky but in no way fat. He had thick black hair, which seemed his natural color, combed straight back and held in place with pomade. His square head appeared too large for his body, like the Hollywood star Robert

Wagner, although Reverdin is not as handsome. He almost always wore expensive suits and the finest silk shirts which he invariably left open at the neck and accented with a garish gold chain. His face decorated many a bus stop bench as a paid advertisement for his ability to fight for "the little man" and get just monetary compensation for injuries suffered at the hands of doctors. Reverdin maintained a full-body South Florida tan similar to Speaker John Boehner. His year-round tan was probably part Eastern European genetics and part the tropical sunshine of South Florida. While people would disagree as to his attractiveness, none doubted his mien as one of animal physicality, darkness and malevolence. The eyes of this man were disturbing; the color darker than brown, almost black, as if his pupils were constantly dilated. His dark, unblinking eyes were made more foreboding because they were partially hidden behind drooping upper eyelids. The overall effect was reptilian.

The lawyer was seen out at the finest restaurants and the most popular nightclubs with different women who all looked somewhat the same; taller than him in high heels, thin with long shapely legs and an ample bust displayed well in a low cut dress. He seemed to interest attractive women who sought his company for his money, notoriety, fast cars or they were simply being paid as his escort. Younger lawyers wanted to work for him and be seen in public with him. The beginning lawyers wanted his money, his legal connections, knowledge and power; but mostly they just wanted to be seen with the notoriously successful malpractice litigator. The youngsters wanted to look like him, act like him and have his fame or maybe his notoriety was what they wanted by association.

Reverdin made a mountain of money suing Miami doctors, or so everyone thought. Miami is the mother lode for malpractice attorneys as the city has always been highly litigiousness and is the winter home of thousands of doctors and hundreds of beauty surgeons who by the nature of their business are easy to sue; moreover, many of the doctors have sketchy credentials from overseas and many are not even licensed physicians in the U.S.; yet they prey on the Spanish-speaking community of immigrants who were well disposed in their native lands but cannot afford mainstream plastic surgery here in the U.S. The only limiting factor for Reverdin's earning potential was the doctor's malpractice insurance and in some cases the solvency of the malpractice insurance companies. Those doctors without malpractice usually just left the country when sued, returning to their native lands until their legal issues dissipated and only then would they return again to Miami with a new address and on occasion a new Hispanic surname to again fleece the same vulnerable people mainly in the large Cuban and South American communities. To this day there are still communities in Miami, like Little Havana, where the primary language is Spanish; that includes street signs, menus, newspapers, radio and television. The lack of assimilation is so entrenched in individual neighborhoods that there are older individuals who have been in Miami since the Cuban revolution in the late 1950's who cannot speak a word of English, even to this day.

Not in business to clean up the illicit doctors in Miami or to effect social change, Reverdin was in the business of making money and doctors without malpractice coverage were usually low on his radar unless his investigators could uncover a secret overseas account in a wife's or relative's name. A man like Reverdin, with few if any scruples and dozens of private investigators on retainer, is immune to the invectives that always came his way during a trial. He is good at what he does because deep down he assiduously despises doctors: the façade of their long white coats, their education he describes as simplistic and incomplete, and he mostly uses their brashness in front of a jury as fuel for his prosecution of the case as the "little man" against the rich, insolent doctors. The jury, by the time Reverdin has weaved his web, usually find the doctors guilty and their insurance companies are forced to pay "policy limits" on their doctor's misdeeds. Reverdin considers each newly minted jury a tabula rasa with his job to mold their opinions in favor of his plaintiff and to depict doctors tendentiously as money hungry, arrogant, dishonest and deceitful. His job when examining doctors under oath was to use the language of medicine, which most doctors speak in order to make themselves appear intelligent, against the doctor who do not understand that most of the doctor's "peers" on the jury find doctor-speak abstruse and demeaning and at the end of the day a cloying monotone. Most juries in Miami simply want to give the plaintiffs money if for no other reason than to "screw" the vainglorious doctors who already have enough. It's money- redistribution of wealth in its most elemental form.

Reverdin's growing fame in some legal circles was due to the fact that in today's malpractice environment where doctors were singularly hard to prosecute for their malfeasance, he had a better than average number of guilty verdicts. The only problem was that insurance companies were becoming more and more insolvent; owing Reverdin money which was discharged in federal bankruptcy court or summarily reduced by a judge kept him from being as rich as he thought he should be. Most of his colleagues weren't aware of his financial "difficulties" and still referred medical malpractice cases to him. The referring lawyers continued to think Reverdin only accepted the "slam dunk" cases and they were sure to make money from their referrals. A sure fire way to make friends with a lawyer is to make them money where they aren't required to do much work. While splitting fees is illegal in the medical profession, it is *de rigueur* in the legal field and a large source of income in many legal practices.

Now at the height of his powers, not withstanding some minor cash flow problems, Reverdin felt invincible as he continued to amass an impressive list of high profile courtroom victories. With success came the appearance of wealth, aloofness and indifference toward his junior partners. He treated them more and more like highly paid paralegals regardless of the law school from which they matriculated or the honors they received upon graduation. These young lawyers were staying for no more than a year or two and found it was advantageous upon leaving to speak poorly of their previous boss, sullying his reputation even though they had suckled at the teat that was Reverdin's practice before striking out on their own. It took some difficult self- evaluation before Reverdin realized a new strategy was needed when evaluating young lawyers for positions in his practice. Even with his local reputation as an ambulance chaser, he still received many dozens of applications for each position in his practice. The allure of money continued to draw the best graduates from the best law schools. In the past he never inter-viewed the applicants with the Cardinal Virtues in mind: prudence, justice, fortitude and temperance. He could abide the first three, but temperance was a big problem for him and therefore he thought it hypocritical to require it from his employees. As it turned out, the young attorneys had no trouble with temperance but failed miserably at prudence; watching Reverdin conduct himself in court caused the youngsters to lose sight of judgment and the dif-ference between right and wrong as it applies to a courtroom and the ultimate search for justice.

Along the road to their own practices, the young lawyers who were the future of the legal profession lost the concept of loyalty; and even though some were Catholic, all eventually stepped away from their backgrounds and emulated Reverdin, who was a non-practicing Jew, in the courtroom. They were trying to become Reverdin; very few were able to become the tyrant he was, and therefore few were as successful. What Reverdin failed to realize was that he was creat-ing a cadre of enemies in the legal profession, without loyalty and who generally despised their old mentor.

⟱

Tedy Merrill, M.D., once his divorce from Jessica was finalized, assets liquidated and split evenly between the two, lives comfortably with the Atlantic Ocean as a wall between the two. Jessica and her new lover Daniel continued to live in his native Paris. Tedy has resided in Miami for the last number of years and managed to survive an assassination attempt by the Russians. Nikki Volkov was targeted as the one who gave the order and was dispensed with by Tedy and Clint only to realize that the Russian mafia in Miami is like an amphibian; you cut off its head only to see it grow back. The new head of the mafia was promoted from within the ranks. He was a younger protégé of Volkov, much better educated, just as brutal and twice as ambitious. Ivan Kasparov earned his position of power within the mafia not only by being brutal but by making his bosses and his colleague's a lot of money.

He started by re-evaluating the methods by which the mafia made its money in South Florida. First cost-benefit analyses were performed of their drug, credit card fraud and human trafficking businesses without considering intangibles such as danger, death or criminality. Ivan, with an M.B.A. from Wharton's School of Business, decided that their most lucrative move would be to find a country in South America (the South Americans, mainly the Columbians, were their most dangerous competitors in the drug trade because most of the cocaine emanated from their countries) and begin cultivation of the cocaine plants themselves thus eliminating the Columbian middle-men. As it turned out their motherland Russia and Vlad Putin had good relations with the socialist gov-ernment in Argentina and there existed terrain in Argentina similar to that in Columbia and Peru where the coca plant had been cultivated for centuries.

The Argentina government with its socialist pres-ident would allow cultivation in his country and pro-vide security for a small cut of the profits. There were already a small number of acres of coca plant culti-vation which the central government of Argentina could easily usurp for their own usage and the usage of the Russian mafia. Once the acreage was in full production the profits could be in the billions. The Russian mafia, working with agents in Colorado, studied the horticulture of the marijuana plant and were successful in creating a more weather resistant and a more potent coca plant with similar techniques used for marijuana. Their hybrids produced twice as much cocaine per individual plant immediately doubling their profits with a more potent product. Their research also widened the range of weather and soil conditions that would support the growth of the coca plant to include a large part of remote eastern Argentina. Although they were only half way through their first growing season, the rumors on the street in Miami were that the Russians under Kasparov were making a move into the drug market in a big way. The rumors only enhanced the position of the Russian mafia amongst the street dealers in Miami. Tedy spent several years keeping a low profile after Volkov was murdered. With plenty of money in the bank, his only motivation to return to work was that he was still a relatively young man and had much more to contribute to the field of plastic surgery. He was also a bit bored and missed the rigors of the operating theater- he missed being a surgeon.

Those intervening years after Volkov turned out to be the darkest years of Tedy's life. After his near-death experience he turned away from his only friend Clint and kept strange hours, sleeping very little and befriending what most considered Miami low-life. Those in the bar scene recognized how much Tedy had deteriorated but no one would mention it to him afraid he would quit drinking and tipping so well. Most of the bar crowd enjoyed his company as he always bought everyone's drinks and always had the very best quality cocaine to share, mostly with the ladies. He was tall and good-looking, dressed well, drove a Ferrari and had money to burn- what's not to like? Tedy continued his risky behavior as the weeks turned into months and months into years. A typical day for Tedy began when he finally crawled out of bed at about noon feeling the effects of too much partying the night before. Every night that he made it to bed he promised himself to drink enough liquids to forestall the inevitable hangover but it never happened. He awoke with a raging headache, a hairy tongue and a mouth that tasted like a septic tank. After he chewed up three or four aspirin tablets, drank half a carton of orange juice and stood in the shower with the water running on his head for thirty or so minutes, he felt good enough to go to his favorite breakfast place called "Cholesterol Heaven." Three eggs, potatoes, bacon, sausage, gravy, biscuits and a carafe of black coffee returned him to the world of the living once again. Soon after his return home to the Setai he would change into his trunks and head out to the beach and the Tiki Bar at the pool. A Bloody Mary or two led to an afternoon of tanning and girl watching on the beach. Tedy's was an idyllic life to some but it finally began to wear on him and he slowly came to the point where he needed intellectual stimulation other than working the New York Times crossword every morning.

Realizing that he would need some time to re-acquire his operative skills, he contacted his old Professor of Plastic Surgery at the University of Miami, Anthony Miller, M.D. who had operated on him several years ago. Tedy was granted permission to work on cases with the residents. Tedy quickly found that his mental faculties were not diminished at all and that within a few short weeks he was back in the saddle, so to speak, with his dexterity and

hand- to- eye coordination. It had been well imprinted on Tedy as far back as his medical school days
that surgical techniques were learned primarily by
the student emulating the hand movements of the
teacher; much like baby ducks imprinting on the
mother ducks. Taking that bit of relatively unknown
trivia, Tedy designed a training program for himself
since medical school that included residency training by not only the best and brightest plastic surgery
professors, but the ones who were considered the
most talented operators. Over his years of plastic
surgery training their skills were imprinted in Tedy's
mind and in his hands and required no more than
a week or two to reemerge as if they had never left.
The residents that he worked with realized a once
in a lifetime opportunity to watch first- hand how
Tedy's skills returned; the difference in his movements, from hesitant to fluid, from only slightly better than their surgical skills to masterful; they were
able to witness the entire process from where they
were to where they all wanted to be in a matter of
two weeks. They learned as Tedy had known all
along that mimicking master surgeon's hand movements was the best way to achieve a physical mastery
of the art of surgery. They had already been taught
the second most important lesson of surgery; understanding the nature of disease and its natural historical progression will give rise to a decision-making

intellectual process that determines when and if one should operate. The decision, if and when to cut open into another human being, is one of the most important and irreversible decisions a surgeon can make.

Tedy hung his shingle and returned to the practice of plastic surgery with an upscale office on Brickell Avenue in downtown Miami. "Hanging one's shingle" seems on its face a simple proposition. In fact, that may be true for most medical specialties but not for plastic surgeons, especially the good ones. Plastic surgeons by their very nature are a hypercompetitive group which is why plastic surgeons to this day rarely practice with a partner. They are the last and final bastion of the solo practice of medicine left in the U.S. and they compete with each other as if plastic surgery were a blood sport.

Within a year, Tedy's practice had grown exponentially even though he had not invested much in a marketing campaign. Word of mouth flowed through the South Beach area as he had become a known entity to many of the bar owners and patrons. Since he was practicing for the love of the specialty, and was independent financially, he was able to undercut his competition's prices at first, and then when he had secured his practice base he slowly raised his prices once he became known as the "South Beach Plastic Surgeon of the Stars." The plastic surgery market in Miami was even more predictable than other places he had practiced. The one thing Miami had that many other markets lacked was the fact that malpractice insurance was outrageously expensive due to the number of attorneys plying their trade in South Florida. Every digital sign and bus stop bench from North Miami Beach to Kendal touted the expertise of a certain malpractice attorney.

The best of these sharks was Barry Reverdin. Reverdin was loathed and loved at the same time. He had enriched many of Miami's citizens with his version of "Jack-pot" justice from suing doctors of all varieties but specializing in the cosmetic surgery mishap. As with most malpractice attorneys, he didn't win a majority of his cases but his fees were high enough and the number of cases was large enough and he was able to compete successfully enough with other Miami lawyers; he took home a seven figure income regardless of what people thought of him and laughed at his enemies all the way to the bank. Tedy knew Reverdin only through his contacts at the bars he frequented. Every now and then he would see Reverdin out at one of the fancy restaurants they both frequented. Reverdin knew from past experiences that one really didn't get to know a man until you meet him in a court of law with his reputation and even his livelihood at stake. Reverdin used the seriousness with which the accused doctor took the charges against him to force the doctor, who always testified, into a misguided or arrogant statement. Any insertion of emotion into the case usually worked in the favor of the plaintiff. Reverdin was an expert in bringing out the worst attributes of a defendant; he was really quite a despicable man in the courtroom. Outside the courtroom Reverdin was the opposite, he tried to hide his true demeanor behind a bright, quick smile. He tried to be well-mannered, congenial and easy to talk to. It was this version of Reverdin that Tedy was introduced to at the Delano one weekday night. Reverdin was with his usual entourage of lackeys, sycophants, secretaries and younger associates while Tedy was, as usual, by himself seeking company.

"Bartender, send my friends over there, referring to Reverdin and his entourage, a round of drinks." Once the six of them received their libations, Reverdin nodded an acknowledgement to Tedy. He looked at Tedy for a long second and ambled over to the bar where Tedy had stationed himself.

"Don't I know you? Your face is mighty familiar and I never forget a face. Oh yes. You are the plastic surgeon who got shot several years ago at the Boat Show and made a mess of Ocean Drive. The traffic was backed up across the causeway."

"Sorry to inconvenience you but they insisted on calling an ambulance and making a big deal of all the blood coming out of me. I told them to put a Band-Aid on it and I would walk home. I did spend five days in the Intensive Care Unit trying to die."

"You became quite the story when you survived and went back to work. With that type of free publicity, your practice must be booming."

"I'm doing fine. I sincerely hope my name hasn't been mentioned in your office in terms of a patient complaint. I would only ask that you give me a heads up, if you can."

"Now, now, Dr. Merrill, I really don't think it would be helpful to my clients for me to give their adversary any information not required by law. With that said I haven't yet had a single inquiry from a patient about you. If you are busy, of course, it is inevitable that someone will take issue with something you have done."

"I suppose you are like all malpractice attorneys, in your delusions you probably are able to convince yourself that you provide a public service or some such nonsense," Tedy said.

"Dr. Merrill, your paranoia is showing. I wouldn't denigrate the service you provide to your patients so why do you insist on being a troglodyte at this fine bar serving only the finest people Miami has to offer. I really expected more from a man of your apparent education and upbringing."

"You know nothing about me you vinous asshole. If I was true to my upbringing I'd throttle you right now just on principle and because I can. "

"It appears that you and I are not destined to be the close buddies I hoped we could be. I think I will return to my friends and leave you to your bourbon. I bid you, *adieu.*"

Thinking out loud but hopefully under his breath, "What a pompous ass that guy is. I wonder if those legal eagles take an oath, like the Hippocratic Oath all doctors take, even though it is just a symbolic promise to 'do no harm.' I suspect the malpractice attorney's equivalent oath would read, 'do no harm' except if there is a significant amount of money to be made and search for justice only if it serves the benefit of a paying client."

"Bartender, another Maker's Mark on the rocks." Taking my fresh drink, I retired to a small table in a darkish corner of the expansive lobby-bar in the Delano. With several drinks on board it became easy to slip into a reflexive state-of-mind. I really knew very little about Reverdin; was he a world-class sophist or was he a true believer? Since I had probably pissed him off, I should do a little research on the man to see if I screwed up or not. As the night wore on Tedy was left alone to brood, attracting no attention at all from the mostly single female clientele which is exactly the response he was looking for. He thought of his new office manager, Marsha, who he hoped would be as loyal as previous women holding the job. There always comes a time where she would be required to have his back just as he would have hers. He thought of the new baby girl he saw in consultation at the Children's Hospital born with a horrific facial deformity which he had only seen once in his career while training in Paris as a young man. It still amazed him how wrong in utero child growth and development could go. There were so many complicated things going on at the same time in a human embryo. It is truly a wonder that things don't go wrong more often. It is by the grace of God that some of the worst defects are never seen by parents or doctors as the infants are miscarried.

As part of the "Grand Design" faces and hearts develop simultaneously causing severe brain and/or facial deformities to exist with lethal heart problems often enough to protect us from their existence. A small number of these facially deformed babies with survivable heart problems make it to plastic surgeons, many of whom have spent their lives trying to solve the Gordian knot of deformities that need to be addressed. As a young surgeon, Tedy was one of the few who worked on these children. Sometimes these children could be made whole again, only with herculean efforts, and sometimes they could not. It is the latter group that weighs so heavily on the soul of a surgeon and necessitates that only the young and idealistic ply those fields. Tedy graduated from the idealism of his youth several years ago to become a purveyor of cosmetic surgery and tried to be as diligent, engaged and creative as when he was young. After all, cosmetic surgery requires much of the surgeon as imperfection is unacceptable. It can be said of plastic surgery that it has evolved into a cult among its devotees. The "Father of 20th Century Plastic Surgery," Sir Harold Gillies, learned early on in his remarkable career that the most potent influence on the recovery of patients was their faith in him (as the leader of the cult). Gillies believed as does Tedy that the activities of the plastic surgeon are essentially creative and demand the vision and insight of an artist. These things occupy Tedy's laconic mind when the roar of the outside quiets and these are the thoughts that make him so disdainful of men like Reverdin.

The day-to-day practice of plastic surgery, while on occasion a grind, is an order of magnitude more interesting than those practices that now depend on volume in order to maintain an income. The volume practitioner works, by necessity, on roller skates unable to spend enough time with a patient to find out the ever-present nuances of psychology and state-of-mind.

The days of the family doctor as benevolent interrogator, always seeking the answer to questions not listed on the standardized patient questionnaire, is missing from doctor's offices today. The onerous government regulations and the excessive need for documentation have the effect of stripping most doctors of their time and thus their compassion. There are many plastic surgery practices where the "herd mentality" has slowly, over time, taken effect; on many occasions the evolution is so slow that it goes virtually unseen by the doctor and his staff. There are many aspects of plastic surgery that Tedy has chosen not to do including taking cases with insurance. This has the practical implication of making his office less busy and allowing him to concentrate on the aspects of plastic surgery he finds the most challenging at this point of his career. Facial rejuvenation with all of its nuances and implications, including the type surgeries Tedy performed on Anatole and Teresa Carpue, are the type of cases he chooses to concentrate on now. While the ultimate situation with the Carpue's didn't turn out as he had planned, their surgical results were exemplary. Due to this particular interest, Tedy saw numerous patients who had not necessarily had bad surgery; it was just that their specific desires had not been accomplished. Sometimes this required minor surgical adjustments and on occasion a complete redo as the surgeon had performed "his" procedure which did not exactly fit the expectations of the patient. The procedure itself may have been performed flawlessly yet an unhappy patient still exists. This is a problem of communication failure by both patient and doctor indicating that the plastic surgeon was only comfortable with the procedures he normally sells to his patients rather than doing what the patient desires. The latter encompasses the nuances of plastic surgery and is one of the primary reasons the training for board certification takes so long.

Plastic surgeons take a lot of pictures of their patients desiring cosmetic surgical procedures. Part of this compulsion stems from basic plastic surgery training. Internists may pick a stethoscope for listening to the heart and lungs as their first purchase; a neurologist may choose a tuning fork or a rubber hammer to check reflexes but a plastic surgery resident uniformly buys a camera. As one graduates and proceeds into practice the camera becomes less a learning aid and more protection against the litigious patient and a reminder to all patients how they looked before surgery, which is convenient to forget when claiming they don't look better and want further surgery for free. In such a case, good photography is a godsend, usually defusing a he said-she said scenario. It also provides a not so subtle reminder of how good the patient now looks. Accurate photographic documentation is paramount for internal practice marketing and usually gives the doctor and patient a platform to discuss the procedures available to improve their looks even further. The single circumstance where good photographs do not protect the surgeon from patient dissatisfaction is when the patient refuses to admit that the photos are not retouched and actually do not represent the patient's actual appearance. Some will actually deny that the photographic image is theirs. One of the main jobs of the plastic surgeon is to weed out patients who are mentally disturbed. A referral for a psychiatric consultation will usually cause the patient to just go away and find another plastic surgeon more willing to operate on anyone.

Tedy diligently plied his trade five days a week, hebdomadally, without missing a beat. Even though almost every patient presented a true plastic surgical challenge, Tedy and his loyal staff could not be protected from the cloying realty of private practice. Finally one day Tedy's "litigious patient" screening antennae malfunctioned and a patient decided to sue Tedy for a residual scar on her breast that was negatively impacted by her smoking cigarettes. Tedy agreed to repair the scar; the patient of course denied Tedy's offer as her attorney had advised that repairing the scar would negate the obvious damage she had sustained. It was not until sometime later that Tedy found out who was the patient's attorney- none other than Barry Reverdin.

CHAPTER SEVENTEEN

"Life is short, the art is long, opportunity fleeting, experience treacherous, judgement difficult..."

HIPPOCRATES, GREEK PHYSICIAN AND
AUTHOR OF THE HIPPOCRATIC OATH

The first substantive event after a lawsuit is filed at the courthouse is the business of interrogatives. By this point in time your malpractice insurance carrier has opened a file on your case and has appointed an attorney to defend you. You and your attorney start spending the insurance carriers' money by carefully answering the interrogatives and craft your own interrogatives for the patient, now called the plaintiff, to answer. These questions may or may not have simple answers but it is assured that now the plaintiff and defendant will proceed as adversaries and will be able to speak only through their attorneys.

After a sufficiently long interval we proceed to depositions. The only real problem with depositions is that they carry the weight of sworn testimony yet the lawyers are permitted to ask absurdly hypothetical questions. The answers to these questions can be read in open court, out of context, with the intent to catch you in a lie to impeach any credibility that the doctor may have retained. Then you become not only a greedy, insensitive, bad doctor who has purposely injured an innocent patient but a liar as well. Dueling expert witnesses are hired by each team in preparation for Tedy's day in court with twelve of his "peers" from the Miami area deciding his guilt or innocence.

Thus far, Tedy understands why Reverdin is considered one of the best in the medical malpractice arena. He was well prepared in the depositions and actually quite articulate in medical terminology, although his choice of expert witness was a bit sketchy, Reverdin overall was proving to be a worthy adversary. Now both sides play the waiting game as the judge tries to clear her docket for what she predicted to be a five day trial. Circumstances are blamed for the days Tedy clears his schedule for the five days only to be continued to a later date. Tedy is told there probably would be at least three of these continuances causing Tedy's practice many thousands of dollars in lost business. Tedy cannot divulge to his patients the reason for his absence for fear they would not return to a surgeon being sued for malpractice: regardless of the reason or the details.

During the weeks of delay when Tedy was effectively not working, he began to drink almost every night from boredom or fear that he would be found guilty. He mostly frequented out of the way places where he would not be known to the clientele. He drank bourbon, ruminated, drank more bourbon and tried not to second guess his practice and his choice of patients as he definitely operated on one he should not have. The bartender in tonight's joint was a former biker gang member, about 6 feet tall but pushing 280 pounds. He was the bar owner-operator, only investor, bouncer and bartender. He was flawless with beer (nothing on tap) and bourbon on the rocks. He wore the standard biker uniform: old jeans, a leather vest with no shirt and the mandatory key ring attached to his belt with 600, maybe 700 keys. His previous biker patches had been removed from the vest but he maintained a full complement of body ink covering his massive arms, shoulders and chest.

He said his name was Zeke. Since all of the women who frequented Zeke's Place, the name of

the establishment, had multicolored hair, numerous body and facial piercings a generous number
of tattoos memorializing former boyfriends and un-
naturally large breasts barely hidden under a denim or leather vest; Tedy thought he would be safe
in his fancy Italian suit and alligator shoes. After
a few bourbons on the rocks, even Zeke's clientele
started to look good. Tedy thought loosening his
tie would be enough to ingratiate him to the regu-
lars. Tedy stayed clear of the pool tables as the players all seemed to know each other and were not
likely to give "winners" to a stranger dressed like
some Wall Street numbnut. They were playing for
ones and fives on a table with cue sticks that would
give the home-table knowledge to the locals. Tedy
watched, as he sloshed down a couple more drinks,
how the balls rolled, where the slate irregularities
were and the intrinsic skill of the competitors. He
didn't reason that the biker boys would guess that
Tedy had a Balabushka pool cue under the seat of
his Ford F-150 pickup truck that he recently bought
and used for circumstances such as tonight when he
preferred to leave the Ferrari at home. Tedy finally
had enough to drink and decided to jump in so he
placed $20 on the table. The competitors and their
"dates" all gave Tedy that incredulous look like he
had just crawled from under a rock and they would
rather try to kick his ass than give the geek a pool

cue. Tedy maintained his insouciance while calmly placing another $20 on the table saying, "$20 just to buy into the game."

The slightly older and gnarliest player nodded in Tedy's direction non-verbally giving him winners. As he sat at the bar waiting for the current game of eight ball to end, Zeke served him another Maker's on the rocks as he whispered to Tedy, "Those old boys are pretty good pool players. They usually don't let a mark like you leave the bar if you have won their money. Just sayin…" As an aside, Tedy asked Zeke if he would mind holding on to his tie while he played. "No problem slick, just don't bleed on my floor. The shit is almost impossible to clean up." The younger of the two bikers, who they called Junior, won the game and called out "next player slick"-the nickname seemed to be sticking. The youngster then placed two $10 bills on the table, one he received from the gnarly one. "How about my friend holding the money for safe keeping?" Tedy nodded his assent while he looked at the available cues noting right away that the locals both had relatively straight cues while his choice of cues had probably been used in previous bar fights. No matter, the best of the bad only curved in one direction, a situation for which he could compensate. Gnarly racked while Junior carefully chalked his cue and successfully broke the balls sinking a solid. Junior was pretty good as he sank two more relatively straight-in shots. Tedy made a mental note that Junior hit the cue ball with too much enthusiasm negating any attempt at English. Also, his stroke didn't include a smooth follow- through making any "shape" on the next ball a result of luck. He was very good but only on short to medium range shots.

Tedy, as he walked up to the table, repressed the natural affectations that pool shooters use to intimidate opponents and began to sink the striped balls. After sinking three balls, Tedy missed a long ball leaving Junior to sink the eight ball and declare winners. Tedy placed two $20s on the table before he ambled to the bar for another Maker's. Zeke leaned in close to say, "You shouldn't hustle those people; they don't take to losing very well. " Tedy replied, "Zeke, just don't shoot me no matter what happens." Tedy returned to the table as Junior broke the balls: sinking one solid and one stripe. Junior, who was getting drunker by the minute, sank a couple more solids and then missed a straight-in medium range shot. It was at this point the fun was leaving the game for Tedy. He had no clear shots so he raised his crooked pool cue vertically and pulled off a masse, curving the cue ball around the obstructing solid ball gently hitting the corner cushion next to a striped ball which gently kissed into the pocket. Realizing that the scam was over, Tedy quickly finished off the table sinking the eight ball with a cross table carom into a side pocket. Tedy pocketed the cash, tossed his cue on the table and paid his tab leaving Zeke a sizable tip. Gnarly and Junior had already exited through the front door. After exchanging knowing glances with Zeke, Tedy left by the front door. As expected, the two biker brothers were waiting in the parking lot hoping to recoup their losses. Immediately Tedy saw the glint of the knife in Gnarly's right hand partially hidden under his sleeve. Junior was slightly behind and to Gnarly's left; he held a wine bottle in his left hand, the same way he shot pool-left handed.

It had become hotter and more humid since Tedy entered the bar earlier in the evening. He had earlier given Zeke his suit coat in addition to the tie he was now holding. Upon exiting into the parking lot and seeing the boys ready for a fight over a measly $20, Tedy wrapped his left arm with his coat as he was talking to Gnarly. "Easy does it boys I'll give you the money as well as what I have in my wallet." He could tell by Gnarly's eyes that he was not assuaged by Tedy's peace offer. As Tedy was removing his thick alligator wallet from the back right pocket of his trousers, he noticed that Gnarly for an instant lowered his eyes to the thick wallet. At the same instant Tedy tossed the wallet at Gnarly who instinctually moved his hands to catch the expensive piece of alligator. Tedy then was able to step inside whatever defense Gnarly had and covered the knife with his jacket as he flattened Gnarly's already crooked nose causing blood to explode from the injured proboscis and temporarily blinding him. Tedy knew that Junior would hesitate seeing Gnarly neutralized so quickly. A swift kick to Gnarly's groin with his now blood- covered python loafers left Tedy standing face-to-face with the much less intimidating Junior. Tedy figured if he could say something witty Junior would relent, take the money and tell his pals that he ran off the pool shark and saved Gnarly who was presently eating gravel.

"Junior, you'll spend all night in the hospital with doctors trying to remove that wine bottle from your ass if you don't take this idiot friend of yours home. Take the money. Please leave the wallet and the remainder of its contents." Junior threw the bottle away as he gathered up the cash and what was left of Gnarly and scurried home.

It didn't dawn on Tedy until he was about to get in his truck to have a quick word with Zeke who was already closing the cash register prior to locking up. "Hey Zeke, how did you know that I would be here tonight?" Zeke glanced down to the revolver Tedy knew he had for protection in his rowdy bar. Tedy had already put his jacket back on but had his silk tie just hanging, untied, around his neck. When Zeke started to reach for the revolver, Tedy had the tie wrapped twice around Zeke's tattooed neck and yanked him onto the bar before he got to his gun. Zeke was now throttled, gagging, with his head and neck draped over the edge of the bar unable to kick or wiggle free. Zeke was frantically trying to loosen the silk tie which had flattened and thinned under the tension making its removal problematic. Tedy told him to stop struggling and he would loosen the tie and allow some oxygen to his anemic brain. When Zeke relaxed so did Tedy allowing Zeke's face to turn from a hideous shade of violet back to his normal rough, scarred flushed appearance.

"Why don't you tell me how you knew I would be here?"

"Got a call from my former lawyer. He said I should expect you and to have you roughed up enough so that for your court appearance you would have to explain why you tended to get in bar fights."

"How much?"

"Five hundred for each of us."

"It's going to cost four times that amount for someone to fix Gnarly's nose. By the way, what is Gnarly's real name?"

"Bob."

"I want you to pass on to your lawyer; his name is Reverdin, right?"

"Yep."

"Tell him exactly what happened here tonight. Make sure you give him the details and let him know that this sort of shit could easily happen to him. You do believe that don't you?" Tedy retightened the tie a bit more in order to reinforce his message.

"No problem, you got anything you want. Just take that damn tie off my neck. I never would have held it for you if I knew you would try to kill me with it."

"Such are the vagaries of life. Just goes to show you Zeke, you can't trust anybody." Tedy released the tie, grabbed the revolver and told Zeke as he was walking out that he could keep the tie because Gnarly bled on it and now you managed to drool all over it.

After a second and third continuance, Tedy finally was going to have his day in court. His lawyers schooled him on his role as defendant as well as plastic surgery instructor to the jurists. He was warned that he would probably despise the plaintiff and the plaintiff's lawyer during their presentation of their case. Under no circumstances was Tedy to show even a scintilla of anger, frustration or impatience. His mien for the entirety of the trial was to be one of calm, placid confidence: a teacher for the jurists, a friend.

Tedy had determined not to acknowledge Reverdin during the trial and to stay away from him during recesses using his legal team to run interference. He wanted Reverdin to wonder what Tedy was capable of in terms of retribution for the actions at Zeke's Place. Tedy had not been out at night, even for dinner, since that night at Zeke's.

The trial inexorably crept forward, the lawyers spoke "legalese", a strange and archaic language intended for use only by lawyers when speaking to other lawyers with the intent to obfuscate the English language. The lawyers spoke to each other and to the judge in this language; Reverdin expounded his sophist arguments and the defense remained impassive during a litany of allegations with no basis in fact. The plaintiff's job is to appear injured, vulnerable, and emotional with the intent of creating sympathy among the jurors. It was Tedy's job to realize the legal issues are important but not paramount. The truth is important but subjective. Tedy learned that malpractice trials were not about uncovering medical negligence but are about assigning blame. If appearing sympathetic means a little gratuitous weeping by the plaintiff due to a loss of consortium from a husband she has not lived with for two years, then so be it.

After the plaintiff rests it is time for the defense. Tedy was called to the stand and swore to tell the truth. His goal is to appear natural and unrehearsed, trying desperately to gain the favor of the two jurors who may be sympathetic to the plaintiff. The direct examination is smooth and effective. Now it is Reverdin's chance to save his case by destroying Tedy on cross. He may have made a few points but the day went to the defense and Tedy got the impression that, toward the end of his cross examination, Reverdin was beginning to lose interest in the trial. He probably realized that he wasn't going to win the day and had started thinking about future cases where he was more likely to make money. Closing arguments were a wash. By convention the plaintiff's attorney gets the last word. The defense team felt Reverdin had already given up the fight. Of course, he had not been too defeated to ask the jury to award $800,000 for Reverdin and his client and her husband's loss of consortium.

After the judge explains the pertinent law to Tedy's twelve peers, he is told that it could take many hours for the jury to deliberate and come to a verdict. The longer the period of time, the worse for Tedy as that probably indicates a guilty verdict and the extra time is spent deciding how much money to give the plaintiff. Tedy and the defense team retired to an anteroom near the courtroom, got coffee and settled in for the wait. Tedy had just begun his own soliloquy when they were called by the bailiff back to the courtroom. Everyone on the defense team was a bit frantic as it had not been enough time for the jurors to study the eighteen exhibits, depositions and consider the testimony. Tedy begged his council for assurances that they were okay, but they didn't even know; they had never seen a malpractice case happen this fast. Back in the courtroom Tedy couldn't get a clue from the faces of the jurors. He though they caved and gave the plaintiff everything, just like Reverdin asked. The defense team stood as did the plaintiff to hear the verdict read by the judge. Tedy, with his peripheral vision, glimpsed a look at Reverdin that told him everything. The judge pronounced Tedy *"**not guilty**"* of medical malpractice. Reverdin clutched his brief case and scurried out of the courtroom rather than submit to the ritual handshakes between attorneys. But most of all he didn't want to face one pissed off Tedy Merrill.

Life soon returned to normal after the trial. Tedy slipped back into his practice, finding it interesting that no one who walked through his door knew the reason behind his recent short leave of absence. He had been through an emotional hell provided by Reverdin yet only his staff knew where he had been or what he had been through. He did admit to himself that he studied each new patient with a microscope trying to uncover any hint of litigiousness. And, if the truth be told, he would never find himself at ease with most new patients from that day forward. At night, after a few drinks and dinner, he replayed the trial in his mind; Reverdin in his Armani suits, unctuous, yet truculent in outward behavior. Time and time again he thought of what could have happened at Zeke's and what could have happened during the trial and he knew intrinsically that his business with Reverdin was not over until he decided it was over.

CHAPTER EIGHTEEN

"Revenge is a dish best served cold."

KLINGON PROVERB ATTRIBUTED TO KAHN
IN STAR TREK II

Once ensconced into the South Florida tropical lifestyle, it is hard to free oneself. Even though the weather tends to be monotonous by New England standards, those who live here find the monotony of fabulous weather to be well worth the lack of seasons that many people don't like anyway. The fall in New England is worth an airplane ticket as is the Christmas season in New York City. For ski enthusiasts, a trip to the Colorado Mountains in February is a must. From Miami International Airport there are first class accommodations to all of these destinations non-stop. For a more local getaway there is always the beautiful drive through the Florida Keys to "The Conch Republic," otherwise known as the city of Key West. As close as the Port of Miami and the Rickenbacker Causeway are daily flights on Chalk's Airline to destinations across the Bahamas. For a bucket list experience try the in water taxi next to the massive cruise ships docked at Miami harbor leading to a seaplane takeoff. First, the co-pilot turns around in his seat and hollers through the open flight deck door over the roar of the engines for everyone to buckle up, then the whine of the straining engines moves the plane forward, raising and lowering with each small disturbance in the harbor until the plane begins to level off atop the waves but still rough enough to shake your teeth. The waves splash on the windows making one acutely aware that you are taking off in the water. As you accelerate the shaking is obviously felt on the flight deck as the cockpit door is left open during take-off for all to see. The rattling in the cockpit is only a little bothersome until a random knob, usually red in color indicating that it might be important, rolls down the aisle. Feeling obliged to help in any way you can, you reach down and catch the red knob and hold onto it until we are safely airborne. Since there are no flight attendants you dutifully walk forward and offer the red knob to the co-pilot saying "I hope this is not important." To which the co-pilot answers almost screaming over the roar of the engines, "It's fine. This happens all of the time." You turn around to get to the safety of your belted seat and find what little comfort there is in the deafening, reassuring roar of the engines as you fly low enough over the Atlantic to see fish below and birds above the aircraft. The landing is not nearly as momentous as the take-off; the aircraft falls from the sky and gently touches down in the turquoise blue Caribbean, first planing above the waves then gently settling into the surf. As we taxi toward land the pilot revs the engines as we climb up the "boat" ramp to solid ground and park the aircraft at the small outbuilding that is the gate, the only gate for Chalk's airline. Once on the ground it is hard not to look back at the seaplane and wonder if it was simply luck that allows such as odd looking aircraft to both take-off in the water and fly in the air.

Tedy mostly worked these days, finding little time for anything other than going to the gym during the week after work and the gun club on the weekends. He made it back to Zeke's a couple of times calling Zeke ahead to make sure Bob and Junior weren't hanging out looking for payback and that Reverdin wasn't there. He had enough of the Reverdin drama for the time being. Between South Miami and Hollywood there were ethnic restaurants of almost every possible variety on U.S. 1. Tedy usually dined by himself, choosing a different ethnic cuisine every night that he went out. Some of it was outstanding and some just so-so. Either way he learned to enjoy the various dining experiences and the ethnicity of the ownership and wait staff who were usually uncles, aunts and cousins.

During his week of court appearances and countless hours of waiting as the wheels of justice inexorably rolled forward, Tedy took the opportunity to meet as many of the court reporters and clerks as he could. Many were female and all were in the market for plastic surgery. It didn't seem to bother them one bit that he was in the courthouse defending himself in a medical malpractice case. Most women when given the opportunity to talk plastic surgery with an expert will normally do so with enthusiasm. And so was the case with the ladies at the Dade County courthouse. There was one clerk in particular, a little older than the others, who seemed to be wired into the courthouse system a little more than the others. It didn't hurt that Deborah was attractive and looked years younger than her stated age. She had evidently had some work done by a skilled plastic surgeon as even Tedy had to study her face to detect the well camouflaged incisions. They talked during recesses and after the verdict on the phone. She and Tedy went on several informal dates as friends. During dinner conversation she mentioned one evening that she was responsible for the judge's docket and noticed Reverdin had another case to litigate, another plastic surgeon that Tedy knew peripherally. "Seems like my buddy Reverdin is up to his old tricks. Does he often file cases against plastic surgeons?"

According to Deborah, "In recent years they seem to the majority of the cases he files. I really don't recall many of the names but it seems as though most of them settle at the last moment. The judge prefers it that way so they don't mind giving Reverdin's cases priority."

"Why that wily sonofagun. That's probably why he was not quite as good in the courtroom as he was expected to be. He really doesn't litigate that many cases."

"The going rate according to the claims records for a Reverdin settlement is about two hundred fifty thousand dollars," she said.

"I guess that it's a bunch cheaper than policy limits which is usually one million per case for the doctor's malpractice. I guess he is able carry out the ruse by using his reputation, deserved or not, to leverage the insurance companies' attorneys into a settlement. It probably costs less to settle than litigate. The economics seem fairly clear then comes along someone principled and stubborn like me and the system breaks down. No wonder Reverdin dislikes me so much. I really can't blame him."

Tedy and Reverdin went their own ways but Tedy couldn't shake his contempt for the man. The part of Tedy that occasionally stepped forward creating the black aura he had come to fear was now rerouting the neural impulses that kept him reasonably sane. In his current state-of-mind he was losing the input from the areas of the brain responsible for impulse control; the wolf needed to be fed before things could get back to normal. It was in this state of mind that Tedy called Zeke to find out if Reverdin had been there. Initially reticent, Zeke offered that Reverdin tended to come in without his entourage on Thursdays to hit on the waitresses. The waitresses were usually available to him because of his generous tipping and the quality of the cocaine he typically shared with them, and Zeke. The bikers that were Zeke's main clientele had adopted a big brother type attitude toward the very generous Reverdin. Tedy sensed Zeke was trying to play both sides of the street. Zeke saw how Tedy waded through Bob and Junior so he wasn't willing to bet one way or the other and hoped just to have the remains of a bar if Reverdin and Tedy were to meet. Tedy told Zeke over the phone in a voice Zeke barely recognized, "I'll be in Thursday night. I wouldn't mention this to anyone if you want to stay out of the fray. *Capisce*? By the way, get rid of the revolver under the bar."

Tedy spent a laconic day in the office on Thursday. He took the Ford F-150 and had a small meal at the Russian and Turkish Baths on Collins. He had a relaxing sauna followed by a nice meal of borscht and smoked eel. The fact that Ivan Kasparov's men frequented the establishment was in no way a deterrent to Tedy in his current state of mind. He did notice a waitress in one of the side rooms filled with about half dozen large mafia-type men. He only saw her from behind but could not help but to notice her long shapely legs and long red hair-quite the combination. He made a mental note to come back and introduce himself at a later date.

Tedy parked on the street a block or so down from Zeke's Place as the parking lot in front of the building was almost full and he had no intention of being blocked in. He had on a comfortable pair of faded denim jeans, a Miami Hurricanes t-shirt and a light wind breaker jacket. He had a 9mm Glock 26 in an ankle holster and an expandable ASP police baton under his jacket. Tedy didn't think he would need either weapon but after talking to Mac at the gun club he decided that arming himself was the better part of valor. Mac offered to come with him but Tedy gracefully declined. He really had no intention of killing anyone and you never knew what Mac might do. Tedy didn't know what kind of car Reverdin drove but thought it a reasonable assumption that the shiny black Mercedes S-600 in a parking lot full of Harleys and pickup trucks belonged to the lawyer. The room was about half full of people, all of the pool tables were occupied and Zeke didn't enforce whatever smoking ordinance was applicable so the place was choking with cigarette smoke. Tedy sidled up to the bar taking the last stool unoccupied. "Hey Zeke, how about two shots of Maker's and a beer chaser." He pushed a $20 toward Zeke and asked, "Where's the asshole?" Zeke nodded toward a secluded table in the corner out of sight to the bar. "He's got a couple of boys with him. They don't look like the lawyer-type."

Tedy asked, "Did you talk to him?"

"Not about you. Don't do anything stupid Tedy."

"Stupid used to be my middle name but I changed it to Psycho."

Tedy thought to himself, *"Jesus Christ this is going to be a mess. I don't know how many of the boys will fall in with Reverdin. I can tell one of the guys he is with has sold coke to almost everyone in here. His table is pretty buzzed and probably drunk. At least one of them goes to the head every ten minutes; probably to pee and powder their noses."*

"I appreciate this Zeke. Don't call 911 until I'm out the door. Okay?" Tedy grabbed a cigarette from a pack on the bar and lit up hoping to add to the smoke camouflage. He pulled a Marlins cap out of his back pocket putting it on with the bill forward and down partially covering his eyes and started to walk toward Reverdin's table. The seat next to Reverdin was empty so Tedy changed course toward the head. Reverdin's man was the only one in the head. He was a large man with a bad haircut, too much hair gel, too much cologne and mismatched socks. He was fairly tall, bent in half at the waist snorting a huge line of coke off the sink counter. He snorted half the line as Tedy stood at the urinal acting like he was relieving himself. At the moment Reverdin's man finished the coke he stood up abruptly saying to anyone in the head, "Now that's some good shit." The man's eyes were widely dilated and you could see his heart racing in his chest. He saw Tedy watching and graciously offered him a line." Come on, we got tons of this shit." Tedy nodded his assent and walked behind the big man who was now bent over again tapping more coke out of an amber colored bottle. Tedy stood to the man's left, now close enough to really be disgusted by the guys combination of sweat, Old Spice and body odor. He also couldn't help to notice the man's muscles showing beneath his ill-fitting suit.

"You first," Tedy said. As the big man leaned over with $20 bill rolled up and placed in his nostril, Tedy unsheathed the baton which extended to its full length and brought the weapon hard across the man's hamstrings, dropping him immediately to his knees. Tedy then grabbed the guy by his greasy hair and slammed his face into the corner of the lavatory, breaking his nose and several other facial bones judging from the crack that ensued. The man, blinded, broken and bleeding tried to reach where he thought Tedy was only to receive another crack on the back of his head rendering him unconscious. Tedy dragged the guy into a broom closet and left him with the cleaning supplies and mop that he knew Zeke would need later. Walking out of the head, Tedy went directly to Reverdin's table and decided instantaneously that the guy across from Reverdin was the more dangerous of the remaining body guards. Unnoticed at the table due to the crowd, Tedy slid behind the next target. Tedy unsheathed the baton, held by his side now, and then swung it abruptly across the poor guy's forehead knocking him backwards in his chair. Before he regained voluntary function, Tedy removed his gun from the poorly concealed shoulder holster and bounced his head off the floor rendering him unconscious also. The younger guy sitting next to Reverdin was evidently one of the younger associates who wanted none of what was going on.

"Go to the head and help your friend by giving him some mouth-to-mouth. Give me your phone before you go." Tedy took the phone without taking his eyes off of Reverdin, asked for Reverdin's phone also and pocketed both of them. The crowd was just beginning to react to the small melee; Tedy told himself there's plenty of time. Even as Tedy was slowly walking toward Reverdin, the man had the presence of mind to feign insouciance. This pissed Tedy off even more. He locked on the lawyer's eyes now detecting some form of arrogance. Reverdin made the first mistake by standing up as if to confront Tedy who caved in Reverdin's right knee, and then kicked him in the face has he bent over to grab the injured extremity. This caused Reverdin to stumble back into the wall with some force causing a Ted Nugent framed poster to come down on his now bloody, broken face. The bar patrons now interested gathered around but gave Tedy a wide birth. Evidently they didn't care for Reverdin either. Plus he was cutting the coke making it an inferior product and way overpriced. Tedy reached into Reverdin's inside suit pocket and retrieved what was left of the white powder and tossed it to the nearest patron that looked like a coke head. As Tedy passed through the gathered crowd, everyone giving him plenty of room, he saw Zeke who was shaking his head as if secretly amused, and told him to go ahead and call 911. If asked who did this tell them his name is Batman and he has done the community a service. He doubted Reverdin would give him up while trying to explain all of the illegal narcotics found at the scene. As Tedy was walking to his truck he could hear the sirens several blocks away. He took off his windbreaker as he had worked up a little sweat at Zeke's and noticed that there was now a slight chill in the night's tropical breeze. He thought, *"Revenge is a dish best served with a slight chill in the air."*

CHAPTER NINETEEN

"Denouement"

Reverdin had to answer for all of the cocaine found at Zeke's and naturally Zeke pointed the finger at Reverdin and his friends. It took Reverdin six weeks to recover from the beating he took at the hands of Tedy. His initial response was amazement to witness a side of Tedy no one had ever seen followed by recognition that Tedy had a side to his personality that changed him physically as well as mentally. He looked at Tedy, in the eye, as he stood over the table not yet knowing what was to happen and would not have recognized Tedy if he didn't already know who he was. Tedy's evil side made him look larger than remembered from the night they were introduced at the Delano. His face had not really changed but it still looked more angular, his five day beard growth made him more sinister and unexplainably more attractive in an animal sort of way. From Tedy's perspective his new mien had been cultivated at the exact point of his life that it was needed and necessary. He had been rendered helpless after being shot by the Russians; lying in a strange hospital bed, trussed and unable to move, vision blurred by a narcotic haze with tubes and devices in every orifice. Unable to talk because of a tube stuffed down his throat and not knowing if this was his prelude to death, all he could do was search for answers with his eyes. He could hear but his "captors" refused to acknowledge him even though he heard and understood everything said. They must have had him paralyzed as he could not move his extremities. The only thing he had control of was his mind. He promised himself that if he survived he would never allow himself to be put in a place where he had no control. That was the beginning of his darker, more violent, iniquitous self; the side he was starting to prefer as it made him feel younger and more vital than his "normal "self.

The day after the night at Zeke's, Tedy was back at work, reassuring when necessary, scolding when appropriate, but most of all patient, kind and thoughtful in his deliberations. No scar too small nor wrinkle insignificant and no complaint unworthy of his most thoughtful opinion. He could continue this way without a second thought for weeks, even months at a time keeping the wolf in its cage. Several thoughts continued to intrude on his daily ministrations: He found himself enjoying his recollections of what he did to Reverdin and to Nikki Volkov; it delighted him like a good French Bordeaux and chocolate truffles.

Deciding one weekend night to reward weeks of in-office perfection with an ethnic meal and a drink or two, he recalled the Russian and Turkish baths he visited the night he went to Zeke's and the thought of the beautiful redhead he only saw from behind. It reminded him of a first encounter with a new scrub nurse; her face mostly covered with a scrub mask, with eyes visible and fully made-up, both sexy, and seductive with the rest of the face a great unknown. A scrub mask can hide great beauty or unspeakable horrors just as seeing a girl only from behind can lead to revelation or disappointment. She seemed to be working the on-site café so that is where he started. Tedy called earlier and using her description from behind was told that such a woman was working in the café tonight and, no, they wouldn't give out names on the phone. Tedy left late from work that night so he drove directly to Collins Avenue and had the valet park the Ferrari up front at the baths.

He hadn't been able to change so Tedy wore his office "uniform," a crisp white Armani shirt and a hand-made Ermenegildo Zegna suit. After inquiring about the red head he was seated in her section of the café. He had a three to five day beard growth as his normal grooming and his hair was still mostly brown and a little long as he was between haircuts. One can't live in the subtropics without a savage tan, even if you use sunscreen as Tedy recommended to all of his patients. Trying to maintain a posture of arrogant nonchalance, Tedy leaned back and studied the menu. He felt the presence of his waitress but paused for a brief moment as if there were nothing in this world more important than choosing a cocktail or an appetizer. As Tedy looked up the red head was a gorgeous woman who was smiling at him with about the biggest, happiest smile he had ever seen. His brain was in hyper-drive, he knew this person from somewhere and then with a flash he knew her. He knocked his chair over backwards getting up to through his arms around her. He was breathing a little heavy when he said, "Sophie, it's you!"

AUTHOR'S NOTE

The protagonist in this work of fiction, Tedy Merrill, is a figment of my imagination; although, after 29 years of practicing plastic surgery many who actually know me may note a degree of similarity between my actual life and the character I have created. My mind and imagination have also practiced for 29 years, so almost-true experiences may have found their way into an otherwise totally fictional tale.

The reader may have noted some degree of political commentary set in contemporary times; while some of it may ring true for physicians, it is there to add texture and a hint of reality to the plot and not to endorse a particular point-of-view. The commentary regarding The Affordable Care Act, in some cases is true, and in others may come to be true in the near future. It is mainly included to propel the story of Tedy and Jessica forward.

The stories involving the Russian mafia are mainly fictional with a smattering of investigational information gleaned from an informative book entitled ***Investigating the Russian Mafia*** by Joseph Serio. The framework of some of the tales was obtained from the archives of the ***Miami Herald*** and therefore is based on the veracity of the reported stories. All of the Russians are fictional characters and their names do not reflect any actual Russian mafia members.

The surgical procedures described actually exist and are in the armamentaria of many well trained plastic surgeons practicing today. The "Fifth Estate" and much regarding the internet is today's fiction, but according to my internet expert-wife, Pamela, may be truisms by the time this book is published.

Finally, I would like to thank a number of people who are responsible for the tales I've had the opportunity to tell because of their existence in my life. Foremost on the list is my wife, Pamela, with whom I share almost everything: including an internal organ. To my friends and family Jeff, Ruel, Clint, Isaac, Kevin and Ted (in no particular order), who have been a major part of one helluva life. And finally to the love of my life, my beautiful daughter Alex, who I hope is proud of her father, even with his many foibles.

ABOUT THE AUTHOR

Dr. Paul Howard is a Board Certified Plastic Surgeon currently practicing in Birmingham, Al. Raised in the South, Dr. Howard received his M.D. degree at The University of Alabama in Birmingham, trained in General Surgery at The University of Alabama Hospitals and in Plastic Surgery at The University of Miami and in Paris, France. As an undergraduate at Florida State University, he discovered an affinity for story-telling passed down from his grandmother and a talent for retelling historical events through the eyes of fictional characterization. Dr. Howard has contributed a number of historical pieces to medical journals and political reportage regarding medical issues affecting the practice of medicine to-day. Dr. Howard is the author of a number of blogs regarding Plastic Surgical training and procedures popular today and has taken time off from his busy practice to finish his first work of fiction, *Perception As Reality: The Life and Times of Tedy Merrill*; a tale about Tedy Merrill, a fictionalized plastic surgeon, born, raised, and trained as a surgeon in the South, and his life experiences, both good and bad, that largely transformed him as a man into the dark character he became; a Mr. Hyde to his younger Dr. Jekyll.